The Private Club

Levi Cazaly

Contents

Chapter 1

I wanted to own my own business someday. But guess what? With a life like mine, I can't have it my way. At least not yet but for now, I guess I can settle for being a receptionist and a stripper. No, I don't hate my jobs but I don't plan on keeping them either. I just need enough to pay rent, feed myself, and maybe shop a little. I can't wait to finish my business degree and start my own business in the long run and hopefully, in a couple of years, it will happen.

I look at myself in the mirror for the second time just to make sure that a strand of hair wasn't out of place as I reapply my cherry red lipstick on before I head out the door and head down the elevator into the lobby. Once the doors of the elevator open I step out and give the doorman my usual wink and flirtatious wave as I step out into the busy streets of New York and place my AirPods into my ears. It's currently six twenty-two so I should hurry if I want to make it there before Mr. Osgood gets in. I turn to the left and walk down the mile-long sidewalk to the tall building that belongs to Diamond Enterprises. I scan my ID at the front and unlock the doors.

"Good Morning Celestia." says the security guard near his post.

"Good Morning James!" I reply smiling brightly. James introduced me to my job opening years ago when he saw how much my life had hated me. I had just lost my job and my boyfriend broke up with me on that same day. James found me drunk in my sorrows and alcohol and he was nice enough to help me out. He's a bouncer at the club I work at as well. I will always thank him for showing me not one but two jobs. Who knows where I'd be if it wasn't for him. Probably in a ditch somewhere who knows. I walk behind my desk and pull out my heels from my bag. I switch my walking shoes on my feet for the heels--One of my smallest pairs by the way--as I sit down at the front desk and turn on the phone. I also open the computer in front of me to open up my emails. After looking through my emails, fishing out the important ones, and trashing the irrelevant ones I look down at the large calendar in front of me that also serves as a mat for other papers to remind myself of all the meetings Mr. Osgood was supposed to have today. Nothing much today, but that didn't mean there wasn't gonna be anything for me to do. The number of females that walk in here every day either crying, furious, or somewhere in between is quite hilarious. I get that Mr. Osgood is probably good in bed or whatever but for them to continually chase after him as if he's the one is quite annoying and stupid if you ask me. Bored out of my mind. I tap my pen against my desk and immediately stop when I notice Mr. Osgood's driver opening the side door of the car and James opening the door of the building to let him through.

"Good Morning Mr. Osgood! Your first meeting will be online with the entire Corporate of BTM at seven-thirty." I say, pressing my thick glasses back up against the bridge of my nose.

"Morning Miss Crowe, Thank you. Did you get my coffee by any chance?"

"No sir, I ordered a while ago and was just heading out to grab them now," I say as I grab my purse.

"Thank you, once you get it bring it right up."

With that, he steps into the elevator and I watch him as it closes. Shit. I totally forgot about his coffee. I let out a troubled breath and get up making my way out the door.

"You definitely forgot about his coffee didn't you?" smiles James.

"Oh shut up, like you haven't forgotten to close the doors once or twice." I smile back and swat at him playfully as I head out to the cafe across from the building. Once I get into the cafe I give a silent thanks to God that there wasn't anyone in line yet. I rush to the counter and quickly make an order to go. I get myself a frappe as well because why not, Lord knows I'll need it sooner or later. I use the Diamonde business card to pay, quickly get the drinks, and leave to cross the streets once again back into the building. I drop my frappe at my desk and walk across the lobby to the elevator and press the button to head up to the sixteenth floor. The minute I step off of the elevator I gasp as I see Mr. Osgood with a blonde female in his lap. She has her mouth all over his neck, yet he is showing no emotion whatsoever. I come a little closer and lower my head and clear my throat, hoping that they'd figure out that they weren't alone.

"He-here's your coffee, Mr. Osgood," I mumble as I place down the coffee on the edge of the large table and quickly turn back to the elevator. I jab at the down button a few times before it finally opens and I quickly get in. The second I turn around his eyes are on me. No emotion. He just stares and I feel like everything is closing in on me. Is this how he makes women feel? I say to myself as the doors of the elevator close. Once they're closed I can finally let out the breath that I didn't even know I had been holding. Definitely knew I was gonna need that frappuccino.

I avoided Mr. Osgood for the remainder of the day. There was no way in hell I was going to talk to him without that image of him with that female in my head. Yuck, honestly he should keep his private life private, and stop mingling his women with his work. The only time I saw him again was when he told me that I was done for the day. I gave him a quick nod as he left and looked at James who was waiting for me to grab my things.

"You ready to make some money Cherry Pop?" he says with a wink.

"You know it." I wink back.

Cherry Pop is my name when I'm at The Cherry Club. You wanna know why? It's because I love cherry-flavored things. And I'm always eating a cherry blow pop before I get on stage for a performance. My name even suits the club's name as well. James and I walk to his car and we head east to get to the club. He parks in the back and we enter through the backdoors that labeled performers only.

"Celestia!" squeals my best friend Lucinda as she runs up to me and wraps me with her arms.

"Hey, Lucy!"

"You're here early, did Mr bigshot let you off early?" she asks as she pulls up the flaming red corset that she's wearing.

"Why yes he did, he has somewhere to be so he closed the building early today." interrupts James as he comes around and plants a light kiss on Lucy's cheek and walks out the door to the front of the club.

"Well, that's good timing, You need to get ready as soon as possible. Kevin just informed us that the club's owner and a few of his friends will be here in a few hours, he wants you to perform your best solos tonight."

"You've gotta be kidding me. He decides to tell us this information now?"

"You know how Kevin is," she replies as she smiles at me sympathetically.

"Yeah, but he could at least be professional about it and tell me ahead of time jeez," I say as I head over to place my bag down and slip off my shoes. Lucy follows me to my little area and she slumps down in her own seat that is next to mine.

"By the way, it's masked night tonight."

"Better for me. Those people won't have to see my face." I say to her as I take off my glasses and lean towards my mirror to place in my contact lenses.

"Girl, it's more than good! I have a feeling that those friends of the owners might be a little touchy-feely tonight and I'm not for it."

"Aren't we all," I say agreeing.

I pull my hair out of the bun I had on and let it fall down to my back. I'd certainly have to brush it out later but it seemed okay for now. I quickly change into a pair of shorts I made out of fishnets, a bright red crop top, and my basic black six-inch leather boots that stopped just above my ankle. I head to the practice room full of mirrors and put my AirPods in my ears before pressing play on my phone and sliding it across the floor to the mirrors so I don't crush it. I turn around wrapping both hands around the slim pole and I close my eyes and let the music take over me.

"How was it out there?" I ask Lucy as she comes into the room and slips off her mask, just finishing a trio performance with her and the twins.

"It's packed. Word got out that the owner would be here so now the place is crawling with females trying to find the prince charming under all those masks. It's quite hilarious actually."

"Good thing I'm about to go on, I'd definitely like to see this for myself."

"Have fun girly," she says giving me a wink.

I look at the mirror one last time, fix my mask, and head out the door. I was wearing all red for this number. They called it Caio Cherry Pop as an introduction to me. I had on a red strappy thong that had multiple straps that covered my ass and made it look like stripes of red and my flesh. The top was a no-sleeved mock turtle neck crop top that showed a sliver of underboob for a teasing effect. The entire outfit was bedazzled in small white gemstones making any light out there attract to me tonight. My shoes were red lace-up heels--this time in a full eight inches--that laced up to about mid-thigh. And lastly, my cherry-flavored blow pop in my mouth. I stood in the pit and watched the commotion of voices and waited to hear my name. Once Kevin introduced me, taking long strides up the steps I make my way to the center of the stage and lean against the pole with a tempting smile.

Ramon

When the music begins I put my attention towards the front of the room. I haven't seen her before. She must be new. But then again I haven't been in my own club for years. I watch the stripper intently as she grabs the pole and makes her way to the top. Once she's there she puts her legs through her arms, dips backward to face the audience, and pushes her legs out into a spread eagle. I sat up in my chair and swallowed the rest of my bourbon. She reverses herself back to her original upright position and uses one arm to hold onto the pole as she spins back down in a spiral while moving her legs in an 'I'm walking down steps' way. I was caught off guard slightly when she swiftly changes the position of her legs to end in a middle split on the floor in front of the pole and she crooks her finger and stares directly at me with a smile as cunning as a cat's. The dom in me is begging me to claim her. Take her. Devour her. But I can't. Because I don't know her. She'll run away like everyone else. I can make up an entire list of excuses as to why I shouldn't even bother myself with her. I close my eyes and my jaw stiffens as the once small bulge in my pants now grows with hunger. I silently hiss at the movement and open my eyes. Searching for someone, anyone. Bingo. The brunette that's sitting right beside me. She's been trying to get her hands on me all night. Well now's her chance. I whisper in her ear and she gladly accepts with no hesitation. I lead her out to a private room on the second floor of the club and quickly slip out of my pants.

"Suck," I tell the brunette as I slide my hand down the length of my cock.

She simply nods and does as she is told. She would be a good sub. One who listens very well. But I've had enough of those types. I needed something new. But I don't know what.

Chapter 2

"I have no idea Lucy, I just stared at him and did this," I say as I mimic what I did as I stared at the man who was sitting in the middle of the VIP section.

"Ha! You probably made the poor man come in his pants." she laughs.

"Probably, 'cause I saw him leave with a brunette upstairs to the rooms."

"Awe the poor thing, had to satisfy his cravings." Lucy laughs again as she's changing into her next outfit.

I grin at the joke and plop myself down on my chair.

"Amazing job Cherry! They loved it tonight!" states Kevin as he wraps me in a very tight hug.

"Ha, you're welcome, I heard the owner was here tonight so I gave it my best."

"And your best paid off," he replies as he pulls out a fat wad of cash from his pocket and tips it over to me. "Courtesy of a gentleman in the VIP section, one of the owner's friends. They have a private room upstairs--number two -- and they have requested you."

"Oh." I almost shudder at the thought of all of them in that tiny room but I push the feeling down. I take the stack of money from him, stuffing it in my bag, and start to take off my shoes but Kevin stops me.

"No need to change, they want you as you are. You're doing the same routine for them."

"Ugh, fun," I say with a fake half-smile.

Kevin pats me on the back and leaves me to freshen up. I spray perfume all over me, fluff out my hair once more and place my red mask on. As I walk to the stairs in the back to the left of the VIP section, horny men are slipping bills in the straps of my underwear, and honestly, I'm not complaining. About the money I mean. Once I get to the top of the stairs I make a right turn to the series of red doors labeled with gold numbers. James was waiting in front of room two and when he sees me he wiggles his eyebrows and does a mocking pole dance as he laughs. I laugh as well, which calms my nerves down a little and he gives me a wink and mutters that I got this as he opens the door for me. I plant a kiss on his cheek and enter the room. As if there couldn't be enough red in the world. Room number two was called the red room. I was very interested in that room. There is usually some kind of bed but tonight a pole replaces it in the middle of the room with chairs and couches around it. However, the walls were still filled with many toys and all kinds of contraptions. Ropes, cuffs, whips, you name it. We had three rooms in total and each one of them was a different color, the first room was neon-ish lemon yellow, the second was cherry red, and the last was electric purple and they each had their own type of theme. The red room was BDSM. I could never figure out how many women just blatantly obeyed someone. I don't think I could ever. I never even listened to my parents as a kid, no luck trying to tame me as an adult now.

I could feel every pair of eyes that stared me down. I felt naked. And I looked like it too since my outfit was red and the lights were red, the colors mixed in with my warm beige skin. Sitting in the middle of the room near the back was the same man I crooked my finger at. This time his suit jacket is gone and his button-down shirt have all the buttons undone except for maybe the last three or four. He has a glass of bourbon in his right hand and his legs are spread out in a dominant position as if to say he can control me as he lays back in his chair. He can't control me. Tonight I owned him. I owned all of them. I take my place at the pole and I hear James at my ear on the earpiece I have in.

"You ready Cherry?" he whispers.

"Ready as I'll ever be," I whisper back and the music begins to blast through the speakers.

Ramon

The second that she hit the ground my breathing hitched. She had a hold on me and she knew it too. Her warm, dancing, lash-fringed eyes never faltered as she crawls toward me, very slowly, as if she doesn't see my already building hard-on and the quick rise and fall of my chest.

"Y'all have two seconds to leave this room," I growl at the other men in the room. Never breaking eye contact with her. They look amongst themselves then collectively leave. One whispers to me.

"Have fun. She looks yummy."

"Oh, I will," I smirk.

Once everyone is gone and it's just me and her she stands up and circles me in my chair as if I was her prey. A predator who hasn't had a meal in years. I yearn to have her closer. As I reach for her she pushes herself away just enough so that my fingers only graze her toned stomach.

"Uh, uh, uh, don't you know the rules?" she smiles and says tauntingly. "No touching."

"The rules don't apply to me."

"I'm sure that's what every man thinks." she giggles and leans over me. Her arms are on both sides of the seat and her legs are mirroring her arms so that I'm fully placed in between her, making it so I can't move. "I don't care who you are. For tonight I own you. You do not touch me unless I ask you to. You just sit there like a pretty boy and let me take care of you."

"You have a dirty mouth young lady, I can fire you for that. I'm the owner of this entire place so if we're being technical, I own you." I smile back and stare at her in the eyes. Challenging her. She comes down and squats in front of me.

"As the owner of this place, you should know the rules better than anyone, after all, you enforced them. Now I am the face of this strip club, hence the name Cherry Pop, there are a dozen other strip clubs I could be at but I'm here so either you shut your mouth and let me work or leave."

She had me dumbfounded. No one, I mean no one had ever talked to me this way.

"You may continue."

She nods gives me a wink as she spreads my legs and snakes her way in between them and moves up to meet my face. She darts out her tongue and flicks it against the tip of my nose. I'm going to lose all self-control with this woman. I want her. Right now. I grab both of her arms and twist her around in one swift motion so that she falls into my lap. I can feel her breathing quicken as she leans against me.

"Please. Let me touch you. I won't harm you I promise. I don't want to fuck. I just want to get you off. Please let me. I'll make it worth it." I breathe down her neck."

She was quiet. I'm guessing thinking of all the possibilities that I could do to make her feel good.

She sighs with a hint of moaning which awakens my erection even more. My grip tightens on her wrists and she dips her head back to look up at me.

"May I?" I whisper.

She nods again as she bites her lip and arches back. I press my lips against her neck and trail my hand down to squeeze her right breast. I continue to trail my hand down until it reached the top of her panties. I play with the elastic band of it and she then moves her right hand that was hooked around my neck and guides my hand further down. I take that as a sign and I slip a finger inside of her. She coils in satisfaction and moans into my neck. I start to stroke her clit in lazy circles and her mouth opens as she struggles to let out a full breath.

"Faster..." she finally breathes out.

I grant her wish and she continues to moan as she squirms above me. The way her ass moves against me makes me want to take her home to my room fuck her all night and then some more, and never let her leave.

"Mine," I growl as I pull my hand away and turn her around to straddle me. I smash my lips against her and her lips move with mine in sync. I stop to collect myself and I stare into her intriguing green eyes. What very pretty eyes.

"Take off your mask."

"I'd like to keep it on please," she mumbles.

"Why? I want to see your beautiful face."

"I-I just don't feel comfortable doing that. At least not now. Maybe if you stop by another time?"

I look at her and slightly cock my head to the side.

"Well can I take mine off?"

"If you'd like. You're the owner after all."

"So you finally accept it." I chuckle as I untie my mask and slip it off.

As I look up at her, her eyes seem to dilate and she stiffens up.

"Are you okay?" I ask.

"I-I'm fine. Um I'm sorry this was wonderful, but excuse me. I-I have t-to go. I understand if you want to get your money back I'll ha-"

"I don't give a fuck about the money."

"Oh-okay then. I'm so sorry," she says as she gets off of me and hurries out the door.

Celestia

Oh my God. OH MY GOD! I've never run out of a room so fast.

"Damn girl, why the rush? He didn't hurt you did he?" asks James.

"No, I'm fine. At least physically. You wanna know who's in there? See for yourself." I say as I rush down the stairs and into the nearest bathroom. I get into the furthest stall from the door and slide down against the wall until I touch the ground. I should've never let him touch me. But my sexual side just had to take over, didn't it. I wish I'd just done the routine and left. I began to slightly panic as I thought of seeing him tomorrow, the next day, and the day after that. I was going to see that man every day for the rest of my life. Know why? Cause the man that I had just let touch me was not only my boss's boss at this club but he's also none other than my boss Mr. Osgood. I should've fucking known he owned this club. He's rich, it's near his building--Damnit why haven't I placed the pieces together early on? I mentally scold myself for being so stupid until I hear a knock on the stall door.

"C are you okay? I heard what happened."

It was Lucy. I reach up to unlock the stall and she comes right in and sits on the cold floor beside me.

"I'm sorry, your life must suck right now huh."

"Yep, there's no way I can show up to work now."

"Yes you can, look at it this way, he took off his mask. Not you. So he has no idea that it was you who was all over him tonight."

"Yeah but I know, I

let

him touch me."

"You'll be fine, if anyone can get through this mess it's you," she says as she gives me a squeeze and gets up, holding out her hand. I sigh, take her hand and she pulls me up. We walk to the dressing room and I change into my second outfit of the day. This one was all black this time. I put on my long black leather boots and change my makeup style drawing a long and thick line on my eyelids. I make a fake slit on my eyebrows to change it up as well and reapply my red lipstick. Once I'm done I turn to hook my arm around Lucy's hand

and we both walk out to the pit, waiting to be announced for our duet.

As we get on stage for the last time tonight, I feel the pits of my stomach churn. I'd thought the feeling had gone down by now. There he was staring into my eyes. Even with the long distance between us, I could see the look in his eyes. Hunger, frustration, lust, and most of all, Power. I felt like my throat was closing up and my brain could no longer function. I hated this icky feeling. I will never let a man overpower me. Especially in my own territory. I quickly pull myself together and set myself in place below Lucy. I stare back at him and wink as I bite my lip. He wants to play? I'll play, and I play very dirty.

Chapter 3

She confused the hell out of me. One minute she's agreeing to let me feel her up and then the next she's running away. But what really confused me is how she acted like nothing ever happened as soon as she got on stage. And I saw her face. I saw her. She looked like she was going to have a panic attack on that stage and then it's like she puts on a mask to hide it all. I keep telling myself that she's just a stripper, I can't claim her. She most likely won't even come to terms with my lifestyle. As much as she enlarges the burning flame inside of me. I can't.

I let out a frustrated breath and rub at my temples as I'm looking over the proposal offer from a company. I shouldn't be thinking about that stripper anyway. For her own good, I really have to let her be.

Celestia

I pull at the neckline of my blouse once more, trying so hard to cover the bruise this man gave me the night before. I didn't even realize that he had given me a hickey until I took a shower this morning. I also fix my pencil skirt once more before I walk in. The lights are already on when I got to work so I'm betting that Mr. Osgood is already in his office and that he's been here during the wee hours of the morning. This is weird considering he was up all night at the club trying to talk to me. I had avoided him all night. Hiding from room to room. I even disguised myself with a wig. I shake my head at the thought of him searching for me all night, waiting for the elevator doors to open. When I stepped into his office, I found him sitting at the large glass desk he used for meeting instead of his usual desk in the corner. No random female in his lap today either.

"Here's your coffee Mr. Osgood," I say as I place it down beside him.

"Thank you," he mumbles without tearing his eyes away from the papers in front of him.

"Are you okay? You look very exhausted." I asked.

He finally looks up at me. Confusion in his eyes.

"Are you okay?" I repeat.

"Oh, yes, I'm fine. Just stayed up all night."

"Yes, I heard you stopped by at a placed you owned."

"You knew about that?"

"Y-yes, I found out from James, he works there. It's a club nearby right?"

"It is. It's a strip club if you don't know."

"Oh I know, may I ask why?"

"Why what?"

"Why own a strip club?"

"It was my father's. Not only did I take over this business of his when he died, but I also took every place he owned as well."

"Makes sense," I say as I pull at my neckline again. "Anyway, I'll head back downstairs just ring me if you need me," I add as I turn to leave.

"Wait," he says as he pulls at my sleeve. His brows furrow together as he stares at the side of my shoulder. "What happened there?" he asks as he nods toward my bruise.

I quickly pull away and cover it up with my blouse once more.

"It's nothing, just a rash. That's all."

"Your lying. You know I don't like being lied to. I'm not dumb Ms. Crowe, I can tell the difference between a rash and a hickey."

"Fine. Yes, it's a hickey but what is on my body is none of your business."

"That may be true but I'm the one who placed it on you so it does make it my business."

My entire body froze in place as he said that. He figured out who I was quick. Maybe he wasn't as stupid as I thought he'd be.

"I-I don't know what you're talking about."

He stands up and what he does next makes every hair on my body stick up. He grabs both of my wrists and swiftly turns me so that I am now sitting on his desk.

"This is the last time you will lie to me, Ms. Crowe. Or should I say Cherry Pop," he says as he gives me a deadly stare. I can see the hint of lust in his eyes as he looks at me and my insides jump. Bad. Bad reaction.

"I-"

"I'm not done. First question. And I swear if you lie to me I will not hesitate to spank that pretty ass of yours that you oh so love to show off. Why did you run last night?"

I swallow at the vulgarity of his words. The look in his eyes and his tone say that he meant what he said.

"Don't make me repeat myself."

"I-" I sigh. "I ran away because when you took off your mask I realized that you were the owner of the club and it felt weird since you are also my boss here." I breathe out.

"Is that why you didn't want to take off your mask?"

"No. I just don't like the fact that you stared me down as if I was a piece of meat. And also, I was able to hide my identity for the night and just let go. Without anyone having to know who I was. Besides, when you asked to feel me up at the time I didn't know you were who you were so I agreed thinking I agreed to a total stranger."

"So you're embarrassed that I had touched you?"

"I'm embarrassed that my

boss

touched me."

"We're both grown adults. What's wrong with that? I didn't touch you without permission."

"I know, but it still feels weird. Can I leave now?"

"No. I'm not done with you."

"Yes, you are Mr. Osgood."

"Don't test me. I will paddle your ass."

"I am

not

one of the bimbo females that you can just play with."

"Of course, you aren't. I never said or implied that you were. You wanna know what I was thinking about before you came in? You, but of course, I had no idea until I saw the hickey on your shoulder. You confuse me, Ms. Crowe. When you're at work you seem as if you're almost scared of me. But yet you seem very confident when you work at the club."

"I'm not scared of you and I never will be. I don't bow down, get one my knees, or obey for no man whatsoever."

"You don't think I can make you?"

I have no idea what came over me but I sit down on his desk, partially because I was tired of using my arms to lean against it and partially because the bold side of me wanted to see if he meant what he said.

"I know you can't" I smirk as I flick his chin up with my finger.

"Now I'm really going to paddle your ass."

He grabs a remote on the desk and with a click of a button the glass that his entire office is made up of is now foggy. He stares back at me with the same intensity and lust in his eyes as before.

"Fuck, your confusing," he says.

He smashes his lips against mine and for a second I don't know what to do. Before I can stop myself I start to kiss him back with the same hunger. I grab him by the collar of his button-down and pull him closer. After a few minutes, I'm pulling back to get a couple of breaths in and out.

"I am confusing." I breathe.

"I can't do this," he says as he begins to pull away from me.

"Now who's the confusing one?"

"No, you don't understand. I'm not like most men."

"How so?"

"I don't date, you know this. I'm always with a different woman. I-I tend to be controlling. We shouldn't be doing this."

"You're right," I say. But in my head, I'm saying the opposite as I pull him back to kiss him again. I'll admit it. I've never been this close enough to Mr. Osgood so fast. I should be downstairs. I shouldn't be with a man like him. Especially under these circumstances. But a part of me is hooked on his addicting scent of peppermint with a hint of leather.

"Celestia," he growls into my mouth.

"Yes?" I say as I move slightly back. Mostly because I realized that this was the first time he's said my first name since I've been hired.

"May I touch you?"

Red flows my cheeks as I nod. Aching for the feel of his fingers again. He smiles and starts to trail his hands on my thighs. He reaches under my skirt and I'm both physically and mentally ready for him to fill me with his fingers but that doesn't happen. He quickly hooks both of his hands under my thighs and lifts me right off the table. He sits down in his chair and places me so that I'm laying on my stomach on his lap. I look up at him in confusion and he bends down to whisper in my ear.

"I didn't forget. I meant what I said," he says as his fingers push up my skirt and draw lazy circles on each ass cheek. "I'm going to turn them red. Like that number, you wore last night. Really drove me crazy. Red's a great color on you."

He squeezes my ass and I gasp when I feel the sting of his palm as he strikes it. He rubs at the spot and repeats it all over. Every time he does it. I feel a new sense of the sensation. It almost feels as if I'm becoming deliquescent. On the seventh time instead of a strike like I was expecting, I feel him slide my underwear to the side, nearly snapping it, and shove two fingers inside of me. I moan loudly and he pushes in deeper.

"Shit. Celestia. You're so wet for me aren't you." he groans.

"I- Yes!"

"Good girl."

"What's up with you and Osgood?" asks James.

"Nothing," I say.

James looks at me with a look that says he doubts it and I sigh, plopping myself down on my chair in front of the mirror. I had a good twenty minutes before I got on stage.

"I don't know. It's, It's complicated." I reply.

"As long as your both good and know what you're doing," he warns.

"What's complicated?" questions Lucy as she hands me over a ginger ale can.

"Celestia over here got fucked by Mr. Osgood."

"What?! Her boss who's also this club's owner?"

"Yep, the same one. And for your information, Ramon and I didn't fuck." I say as I narrow my eyes at James.

"Oh, he's Ramon now, so what did happen then."

"He just felt me up really," I say as my cheeks turn red from remembering the events that happened earlier.

"Mmmhmm. As long as y'all are happy and you know what you're getting yourself into," says Lucy.

"That's exactly what I told her." seconds James.

"Yeah, yeah, don't y'all come attacking me now," I say as I get up to find my rhinestone heels for tonight. It seems that we're having more and more themes each night and honestly I kinda like the change. Tonight was disco night and I had on a bra and a pair of cheeky underwear all covered in white rhinestones. The heels I found matched them as well. I took the rest of the time gluing rhinestones and body gems to my face and certain parts of my body before we went on. As I performed, I searched the crowd for Ramon but he was nowhere in sight.

Ramon

I press the pad of my thumb against my teeth as I stare at her from the dark corners of the room. She was looking for me. I could tell. I watched as her eyes searched the crowd over and over as she moved. I thought about letting her see me. But I fought myself to stay where I was. I've never really been into strip clubs as much as my father was but she has me coming here every night that she's here. Celestia was unlike any woman I have ever been with. She'd be such a good match for the dom side of me. But she doesn't listen, she's like a flame that can't be tamed. I like more of an Anastasia Steel kind of gal. Celestia however is more like a Mimi from Bitter Moon. But that doesn't mean I don't have what it takes to claim her.

Chapter 4

The dreadful Monday finally showed up. I am on my way to the last class of my day and it is currently 3:15 pm. I'd have to drive a little faster before I'm late. I press on the gas, barely making it past a yellow light before I drive for a few minutes and turn right to the second campus of the school. Thank God that this was my last year. I don't think could handle another month of staying late at both jobs just to scrape up enough money to pay for the semester. I try and find parking closest to the building where my class would be held and grab my bag as I get out of my car. I shoot off a quick text to the girl who was supposed to meet me in front of the classroom to tell her that I'm almost there and walk up to the building. She quickly spots me and waves me over the second I'm off of the elevator on the second floor.

"Hey, Celestia!"

"Hi, Stephanie, right?"

"Yeah, you ready to head in?"

"Sure, where do you wanna sit?"

"Anywhere really," she says as she heads through the second row of desks and sits at one, patting the desk next to her. I sit at the desk she patted and silently pull out a small notebook. This was an interesting class I suppose. I had tried to get all of the major classes that I needed to graduate out of the way so that I'd have all the fun during my senior year, which worked pretty well for me. I'm not sure what convinced me to pick this class, I guess part of me just found it interesting that they even had a class such as this, and the other part of me just wanted to see what was up. Soon the professor shows up as well as the other students. Looking around I notice that the majority of the class is male. And so is the professor. He looks very young. He's quite tall and wears glasses with thick red frames.

"Good Afternoon everyone, my name is Finn Lancaster. You may address me as professor Finn or professor Lanny. The choice is yours. Choice is given. Choice can also be taken away. Choice is the opportunity or power to decide between two or more possibilities. This is where we will start our lesson for today. Trust me it'll be more light next class."

I start to take notes to what I'm guessing is a reminder on sexual consent and making good choices. Towards the end of class, professor Finn passes out a sheet of paper. I skim the list. My eyes immediately stop at the near top of the page on the second word on that list.

"On the paper, I have just given you is a list of all the topics that you can choose from for your final project which will be used as your final grade. Throughout our classes, I will be bringing in special guests that have to do with each of them so I suggest that you choose a topic to research as soon as possible. That way when your topic-related person comes, you may ask them questions later and get their contact information. Class dismissed."

I grab my notebook, regretting that I even pulled it out, and stood up, following Stephanie out of the classroom.

"Well that was very interesting," she notes as I match her walking pace.

"Ha, yeah, I've never been more confused yet so intrigued."

"I think the teacher is cute don't you?"

"He's cute I'll admit. I have a thing for glasses lol."

"No, for real like glasses have a hold on me."

"His height is kind of intimidating though."

"Really? I kinda like it."

"Yea but imagine if-"

"If what beautiful?"

Stephanie and I both look at each other and slowly turn around to see two guys staring slightly down at us.

"Sorry my friend here is a creep, I'm Ethan and this jackass here is Luke." said the one in the blue striped shirt.

"Nice to meet y'all." perks up Stephanie. Her voice, going two octaves higher.

I give her a side look and she gives me a nervous one back. I look back towards the men and I quickly and mentally assess them in my head. They were sitting in the back of the class. Ethan has wavy salt and pepper hair, and a chiseled face that somehow made me want to touch it. Luke however has more of a smoother face hidden underneath a stubble and has short straight hair. They were pretty hot if I'm being honest. Luke sent a grin my way and it snapped me out of my assessments of them.

"Yeah, nice to meet you both," I say with a smile.

"Where're you lovely ladies off to now?" says Luke.

"Uh, lunch, I guess?" Stephanie questions as she looks at me.

I nod. "Yeah, we were gonna get something to eat.

"Care if we join y'all. We have some free time to kill before our next class." perks up Ethan.

"S-sure that's fine."

I shrug, silently stating that I didn't care if they tagged along or not. We started walking to the parking lot and I looked for my car.

"We can all take mine if you guys want. There's room for the four of us."

I smile to myself because I know I'm only offering just to show my baby around. I've spent almost all of my savings on my dream car.

"Sure, does that sound good to y'all?"

"As long as you two aren't kidnapping us I'm fine," replied Ethan.

"I'd be fine even if they did kidnap me." Luke laughed.

I slightly shake my head and chuckle. I lead them to my bright red car and unlock the door. I get inside as the doors lift open and I don't need to turn to know that they're gawking.

"Are you guys coming or not?"

"There's no way. That's gotta be a rental," says Stephanie as she got into the front seat.

I shake my head. "Nah, I saved money for Lacy."

"Damn. She's a beauty."

"Thanks. Now, where are we going for lunch?"

"Ooh, I'm craving pasta. Y'all down?" declares Stephanie.

"Totally," answers Ethan.

"Pasta it is then, Olive Garden sounds good?" I ask.

"Yep, let's go. I know the one that's nearby anyway," replies Luke.

I nod and start the car. As I'm driving, he gives me directions to the restaurant and we make it there in 3 minutes. We all head out of the car and go into the restaurant. Thankfully we didn't need to wait to be seated.

"So what made you both sign up for that class?" asked Luke as we all waited for our food.

"It sounded interesting to me. I never knew schools had classes like this in the first place," said Stephanie.

"Sheer boredom and interest," I say. "What about you guys?"

"Same here for me." perks up Ethan.

"Well, not gonna lie, I'm a ladies' man and I'm here to please." Smiles Luke as he places his hands behind his head. "I just wanted to see if there was anything else to know about making a woman come."

"My God Luke, why am I, friends, with you," says Ethan as he shakes his head.

"I'm just joking. Don't get your panties up in a knot." he laughs.

Ethan just rolls his eyes but he has a large smile plastered on his face.

"Do y'all live on campus?"

"I don't," I reply.

"I don't either. I do live nearby though." seconds Stephanie.

"Oh, same here."

"Really?" brightens Stephanie. I watch as she leans a little closer across the table to him. If I didn't know better, I'd say she definitely has a thing for him.

"Yeah, I-"

The conversation was stopped by the sound of Ethan's phone. He quickly looks at it, sends off a few texts, and then places it in his pocket.

"Sorry, that was work. They've been messing with my schedule for weeks."

"Imagine. I'm still looking for one." sighs Stephanie.

"You're looking? For what kind?" I ask.

"Anything that's in a restaurant really, no one around here is needing anyone."

"Could being a waitress work for you?"

"Yeah, do you know a place that's hiring?"

"My job is, well one of them. But it isn't a restaurant though." I say quietly as I take a sip of my water.

"What is it then?"

"A club."

"Oh like a dance club?"

"Yeah kinda," I say, not wanting Anyway, I can totally get you a job there if you want.

"That would be great, thanks."

"Dance club sounds fun. We should totally party there some time," says Luke.

I practically almost spit out my water.."

"Um, I don't think that's the brightest idea."

"Awe why not," pouts Luke.

"Because I'm working tonight."

"And, we can just party by ourselves. We'll be sure to keep you company though." He winks.

My mouth forms a thin line. "Okay, okay, so it's not really a dance club per se, it's more of a cabaret-type strip club."

"What?" whispers Stephanie as she turns to face me.

"Yeah...Big surprise huh."

"That's kinda badass," says Luke. "Still wanna go though, that ain't stopping me."

"Perv," I laugh. "Do you still want the job Steph?"

"Uh, I guess so,"

"Alright then, I can swing by with you tonight if you want?"

"Sure. Um, there's no dress code, is there?"

"For you, no. You're good."

"Okay then."

"No fair, I still wanna go. I've got nothing to do tonight, let me have my fun," whines Luke.

Ethan playfully punches him in the arm just as our waiter comes by to give us our food. I dig into my shrimp alfredo and we continue to talk.

"I promise I'll be on my best behavior."

"Yeah, yeah, fine but only this once," I say giving in as I give him a look.

"Yes!"

Ethan and Stephanie both laugh and simply shake my head. Thankful for the conversation being over.

I'm waiting in my car for Steph to finish her last class of the day before we head off for The Cherry Club. A few minutes later I get a text from her saying that she is on her way out of the building. Once I spot her near I open the door for her and she slides in the passenger's seat.

"You ready?" I ask.

"Yep."

"I have to stop by my apartment first to change. Since I might be late."

"Okay, do you want me to text the boys the address?"

"Yeah," I reply as I go past a green light.

We finally make it to my apartment and I fumble with the keys as I'm trying to open the door. When we're inside, I close the door behind us and slip off my shoes on the way to my closet.

"Make yourself at home!" I yell out to Steph as I change into a dark purple number. I take off my bra and replace it with the purple nipple covers then throw the fishnet top on. I change into the sparkly purple double strap g-string and finally put on my large coat over everything. I grab my heels from the bottom of my closet and put them on halfway before I walk out.

"Aren't you going to be hot in that coat?"

"I'm not keeping it on, I had to change here so I can focus on doing my hair there."

"Ah, gotcha. By the way, the boys said that they're waiting at the front for us so we better get going."

"Yep," I say as I bend down to finish strapping up my shoes. Once I'm finished I grab my keys and Stephanie follows me out the door. We spot Ethan and Luke at the front of the club before I head to the back of the building. I park closer to the back door but we walk in the front to meet them.

"Hey, Ethan. Luke." smiles Steph, shyly I'll admit.

"Hey, wow you look nice," replies Ethan.

Luke waves at us and pulls up his jacket.

"Let's go in guys," I say as I wave them to follow me in.

James gives me a wink as he opens the doors for me

"New friends?" he asks.

I nod and smile and we enter inside.

"I have to go in the back but feel free to sit in the VIP section if y'all want. And if anyone asks just mention me. James already saw you three so if anyone gets touchy or whiny just find him."

"Yes, ma'am." laughs Luke.

I smile and give him a wink as I head towards the back room. I turn around to face forward and bump into a tall figure. I look up to see Ramon. I take a deep breath and close my eyes. Hoping they were playing tricks on me. I open them and he's still in front of me.

"What're you doing here," I say through my gritted teeth.

"This is my club remember? I see you brought friends tonight." He says as he tilts his head toward where they were.

"And?"

"Don't get so defensive I just made an observation. Why're you wearing that huge coat inside anyway?"

"Because I'm not wearing anything underneath." I smile and bat my eyes in the fakest way possible.

"Are you serious?" he whispers.

"Yes I am, now please move so I can get to the door behind you."

"Don't tempt me, Celestia."

"You should know by now that I'm not one of the women who willingly melt into a puddle of desire at the sound of your voice," I say I roll my eyes at him."

"Well, you sure as hell did last week."

I close my eyes and clench my teeth as he says those words. I nearly forgot about that day in his office.

"I-"

"I nothing, You don't know how much I-"

"C! There you are! Kevin was looking for you! I know you're not supposed to go on yet but he bumped you up to like now, Kitty sprained her ankle." rushes

"Oh, I'll be right there. I didn't even have time to do my hair or face." I say as I struggle to take the tie out of my hair and comb my fingers through it.

"This conversation isn't over, I'll be in room number 2 after you're done," whispers Ramon in my ear as he holds onto my hip.

I move away and follow Lucy to the back room. I quickly take off my coat and throw it on my chair. I look into the mirror one last time to fix my hair and apply lipstick on before I go to the other side door near the pit. I can hear Kevin calling out my name and once he's finished I climb up the few stairs and get on the stage.

Ramon

I looked at the clock on the wall opposite of me for the second time. She was only gonna be up there for two songs. It should last more than ten minutes top. Maybe she wasn't coming. I mean I didn't expect her to in the first place. But I really can't stay away from her. Her type of energy is new to me. Her boldness, her character, the way she holds herself, everything about her, everything she does just makes me want her even more than I already do. I sigh and take my jacket from the seat beside me and get up to walk out of the room. No point in staying anymore. I don't wait for anyone. It's always the other way around. Especially when it comes to women. I open the door to leave but then I see her. And she's wearing that thick coat again.

"Were you about to leave? You said you wanted to talk."

"I was. But you're here now so." I say as I step aside for her to come in.

She walks in and sits down in the seat that is left to the one I was sitting in before. She doesn't take off her coat but instead, she tightens it around her.

"Are you cold?"

"No, I just don't like walking around in my outfits here."

"Makes sense."

"I can't be here for long. What did you want to talk about?"

"Why can't you? Aren't you done anyways?"

"I am but my friends, I can't leave them out there by themselves and I have to talk to Kevin about hiring Stephanie."

"Consider her hired. I'll talk to Kevin."

"Thank you."

"Now, let me be serious with you."

She looks at me with her siren eyes which makes me lose my sense of control for a second.

"I can't seem to keep away from you Celestia, I need to but I can't."

"So you can't find the will to stay away? Well, I can. Goodbye." she replies as she starts to get up.

"Wait," I say as I grab her hand.

"What?"

"I told you I don't date but, I do want-"

"You want sex, is that what this is? You want to throw me around for a couple of nights or however long until you get bored of me or find a new girl. No thank you."

"Please, negotiate with me. I want you, Celestia."

"But I don't want you."

"You respond to my touches so well though. I think we could make this work."

"Yeah and so what, I was horny, everyone has those days."

"I know, I'm just saying I want those days with you."

"Why? Why me?"

"Because I find you very interesting."

"Sexy. Interesting and sexy are two different things. What you feel for me is pure lust."

I thought about it. Was it truly just lust?

"No. If it was I would've found some other woman to fuck and thought about you in the process."

Something seemed to ignite in her as I spoke and I could see her eyes glisten with desire. I know deep down she wants me as well. I yank her close and she stumbles onto me. Damn coat.

"I want this off. I want to see you, Celestia." I say as I start to pull off the coat.

She looks at me once I fully take it off and right then I grab her face with my hands and gently kiss her. Just like before, she doesn't respond for a few seconds then she starts to kiss me back slowly, ever so slowly it drives me insane. I drag the rest of her petite body onto my lap and toy with the band of her thong. I have an aching desire to snap it off in one move and leave no part of her untouched. Soon, I told myself. For now, I can be patient. I have to be.

Chapter 5

"Did you already pick your topic yet?" asks Steph as we walk to class along with Ethan and Luke in tow. We've all been hanging out together for a while now which has been fun since I don't really talk to too many people in the first place.

"I did, I chose BDSM," I reply.

"Really? Aren't we doing that one today?"

"Yeah, I think so, Professor Finn said that he had an old friend coming in," answers Ethan.

"Where'd you hear that from?"

"I have my sources." he laughs. as he opens the classroom door for us to enter.

"Today we'll talk about the second thing on this list which is BDSM. In order for you to get a better understanding of that, I have invited an old friend to talk about his personal life in that area. Most of you should know him anyway as he is a very known man for his business. He will be here in a few minutes so I suggest to anyone who chose this topic to write down questions you'd like to ask if you have any ahead of time."

As he says that last sentence he looks straight at me above the frames of his glasses. I don't know why he's giving me a stare but I look down at my notebook, slightly embarrassed for even picking the topic in the first place. Maybe I should've picked roleplay or something. I only chose my topic in the first place because it reminded me of the red room at the club.

"Ah, there he is, everyone meet Mr. Osgood."

No. No. Fuck no. There's no way in hell. I keep my head down and start to chew on my bottom lip. Please. Please. Please don't notice me. Thank God for the baseball cap I decided to wear today. Otherwise, I'd be a wreck.

"Thank you again for coming. I know you're a busy man."

"Anything for a friend Finn, how have you been?"

"I've been great thanks for asking, ever since I started teaching this class things have sure been interesting."

"Ha, I'm sure they have." laughs Ramon.

As they have their conversation I send the group a quick text panicking about how I wanted to just crawl inside of a whole and literally die. I finally but slowly look up to see Luke giving me a concerned look. Ethan laughs out loud by mistake and he quickly covers his mouth with his hands.

"Care to tell us what's so funny Ethan?"

"Nothing, nothing professor Finn."

"Alright settle down, I'm gonna let Ramon have the floor."

"Afternoon students. As you already know, I am a business owner and took over my father's business after he died but what most people do not know about me is that I have a very specific type of sexual life I partake in. Now, I see that most of you are confused, intimidated, or even scared for that matter now that you know this but not only am I here to inform you about this lifestyle, I'm also here for you to learn something new."

I start to drown him out as my head continues to panic. If there was a miniature version of me inside my head and you could see it, it would be rocking back and forth with its knees to its chest. I tip my hat down and lift my head up so I could see him. Just to make sure he wasn't looking my way. He wasn't wearing a suit. And that surprised me somehow. Mostly because I've never seen him without one. He has on a very fitted white shirt and casual black jeans. Before he could turn his head all the way to me, I tilted my head down once more.

"That's all I have for today. If anyone is interested in learning more I'll leave my number and email with Professor Finn. Thank you for having me."

Finally.

"Okay, now class you're dismissed. Except for you Celestia, I need to have a talk with you."

I grimace and deeply sigh as everyone gets up to leave. Stephanie whispers to me as she walks by saying that she'll text me later. I grab my bag and haul it over my shoulder as I go up to him.

"You've had your head down all class. Is everything okay?"

"Yes, I'm fine. I was just a little surprised that's all."

"May I ask why? You did choose this topic beforehand."

"It's just that Mr. Osgood, well he's kind of my boss where I work and-"

"You didn't expect him to be into things like BDSM?"

"No."

"Well, there's no need to give you his info since you pretty much know him already but I suggest that you do talk to him. He's a reliable source."

"I know, but-"

"Look you don't have to do this topic if you don't want to. I can allow you to change it if you want but you'll have to give me a new one by tomorrow."

"No, I can do the topic."

"Are you sure? I don't like seeing students fail my class."

"Yes, I'm sure,"

"Okay then, you may go."

"Thank you," I mumble as I leave out the door.

"I knew it was you under that hat."

I freeze mid-step because I knew it was him. He must've stayed behind.

"You just love to follow me everywhere don't you?" I fume as I whirl around to face him.

"No, I don't. How was I supposed to know if you were in this specific class?"

"I don't know, you have your ways, you could've gotten the entire school's roster for all I know."

"I'm not a stalker Celestia."

"Well, you sure act like one."

"Just because I end up in the same places as you from time to time doesn't make me a stalker."

He had me there, He was right in a way. I just sigh. "This conversation is over. I have somewhere to be."

"Where, the club?"

"Yes, and don't follow me there either."

"You can't tell me where I can or cannot go."

"Yeah, but I sure as hell can avoid you. I'm leaving."

I don't wait for him to say anything I just leave and go straight for my car. Once I lock myself inside I hit my head against the steering wheel. Fuck my life honestly. I lay there for a few minutes before I turn on the car and drive off. The second I get to the club I go straight behind the bar and grab a large bottle of booze. I didn't care what it was I just grabbed whatever I saw. I went to the back and changed into a red outfit so I wouldn't have to change later. I also grab a robe and slip it on all while trying to twist open the bottle in my hand. I grab my phone and head upstairs to the red room. I put on a playlist, turn the volume up to max and proceed to sprawl out on the couch with my legs dangling from the side of it. The day wasn't even over yet and I'm fed up and pissed off, and not to mention drunk soon.

Ramon

I call her cell again and it rings until it goes to voice messaging. I speed past yet another light. I quickly get to the club and don't even take my time to park well. No one ever walks away from me. Ever. I barge inside and look around. She's not on stage and she's not in the crowd either. Maybe she knew I wouldn't listen and follow her here anyway. Smart girl. I make my way over to the back room and knock. A young woman opens it and she straightens up when she notices me.

"Has Celestia been here?" I ask.

"Um, no sir."

"Thank you," I quickly say as I head for the stairs. I open the first door. Nothing. Then I come up to the second door. I hear music coming from the inside. I swing the door open and there she was, drowning down the last of the bottle she had in her hand. Legs wide open. My head wanted it as a silent invitation.

"Hello, my pretty little stalker." she smiles as she throws the empty bottle to the other seat.

"You're drunk."

"Am I now?"

"Celestia," I say as I move closer to her.

"No, don't come any closer. Every time I'm near you something bad always happens so stay away."

"I just wanna talk."

"You always want to talk, it's the same excuse. You just want to get near me and peel every layer of my sanity away until I'm all vulnerable so you can toy with me."

"That's not true. You just can't handle the truth."

"What truth? There is no truth to whatever this is. It's just a bunch of shitty lies. All you've been doing here is trying to get laid."

"Celestia, you're not thinking straight. Don't move I'll get you some water."

I leave the room and quickly grab a water bottle from the mini-fridge at the bar downstairs. Once I'm back in the room I close the door behind me. As I turn around I witness the robe falling down her shoulders to the floor. She was wearing one of her getups which made me swallow the lump in my throat. She sits back down and looks at my rigid face.

"What? I was getting hot."

"I didn't say anything," I reply as I hand her over the water. She looks up at me but takes the bottle and chugs it down.

"Feel better?"

"No, what do you want from me, Ramon."

"I already told you what I want. It's just a matter of getting you to admit that you and I both want the same thing."

"No, we don't"

"Stop lying to yourself Celestia, it's not good for you."

"Let's say I am lying, so what, that still doesn't mean that I'm gonna let you touch me again."

"Are you sure about that? Let me tell you a few things. One. I'm not even near you and I can smell your arousal." I take a step closer. "Two. Every time we happen to talk about sex I see the way your eyes glow brighter as if you love hanging onto my every word." A couple of steps more. "And three. I always get what I want and what I want right now is you." I finally say as I am now towering over her with each hand on the armchairs.

That finally shut her up. She looked like sin. A beautiful sin just begging me.

"May I ask you a question?" I ask.

"You just did."

"Don't get smart with me Celestia or you will regret it."

"Fine. What?"

"Why did you choose BDSM as your topic from that list?"

"Because it seemed interesting I guess." she shrugs.

"Is it? Or is it because there's a part of you that wants to know more. How it feels like. To be dominated by someone."

"I'm not like that."

"How do you know if you haven't even tried it yet?"

"I-I don't know," she says as she looks down.

"Celestia look at me when I'm talking to you."

She still looks down but she begins to bite her lips. I take my hand and pick her chin up to force her to look at me.

"Don't bite your lip like that. I'm already losing my self-control with you."

She visibly swallows and all I can do is imagine her swallowing me whole with that pretty little mouth of hers.

"Give me a week," I whisper to her as I lean in and use my thumb to pull her now nearly swollen bottom lip free.

"A week for what?"

"A week to show you how good BDSM can be."

"Why, I'm doing research on it. I don't need to have sex with you to know about it."

"I promise it's worth it. I can give you a better understanding of it."

"I'll think about it."

"You will?"

"Yes, I will if it'll make you get off my back for a while."

"That's the problem, I can't stay away from you. Ever since I saw you enter my office for that first interview I've had my eyes on you."

"I thought this was a recent thing."

"No, this has been from the beginning. You have this sort of drive and way you hold yourself that makes you look so bold and beautiful. Fuck, I can't take it anymore let me touch you. Please."

Her gasp at my words only made me want her more. I take my hand and start to trail it all over her legs until it reaches her hips. My fingers play with the strap of her thong and I look up at her. She surprises me when she pushes my hands away, but not from her body. She pushes them so she can get through and she starts to kiss me roughly.

"A week. That's it." she moans into my mouth.

"I'll make sure that it's the best week you've ever had."

I grab her and pull her up. She locks her legs around my waist and I tilt my head back at the contact. She continues to kiss me for a few minutes before we're both out of breath and panting. I lay her back down on the couch and pull off my shirt. She drags her fingers across my abdomen and I groan.

"I want to feel you around me, Celestia."

She bites her lip again and I bend down until I'm close to her again.

"I want this off," I state as I flick her right breast.

"You're gonna have to say please."

I take her hands and cross them above her head while keeping a tight grip on them.

"Rule number one. I am now your dom and you are my sub. You reply to me only when I say so. You can only call me two names. Master and Sir. I do not have to say please to you."

"But-"

"But nothing. Welcome to the life of BDSM sweetheart," I smile. "I will not repeat myself again. Take. It. Off."

She nods slowly as I let go of her arms. She brings them behind her, unclasps her bra, and lets it fall off. I take it and throw it to the other couch. I glide my hand down to her waist again.

"This is coming off too," I whisper.

She starts to squirm and I stop.

"Are you scared? Do you want to stop?"

"No," she breathes out.

I continue to pull her panties down until they're all the way off and I toss them to the couch where her bra was. I look down at her and she timidly covers up with her hands.

"Don't do that. You're beautiful Celestia."

"I don't like being stared at."

"You have people stare at you all the time when you're dancing. This isn't any different."

"Well can you do something and stop gawking?"

"Oh, I will don't worry. But you're mine. I can look at you all I want."

I bend down and pull a nipple to my mouth. She gasps as I swirl my tongue around it and gently bite. I move on to the next and do the same. She arches her back which pushes her closer to me. I dip my hand in between her legs and glide a finger through her slit.

"You're really wet for me aren't you."

"Y-yes."

I remove my hands off of her and look her in the eye. She whimpers at the loss of contact and starts to reach for my hand.

"Yes, what?"

"Yes, sir. I am wet."

"Good girl. Don't move." I say as I go over to the small stand behind her. I open the top drawer and pull out three red lace ribbons from the pile of handcuffs. When I'm back in front of her I grab her hands and tie them behind her with one ribbon. I used the next two to tie her ankles to the end of the other two seats next to her so that she was now spread out in front of me. I bend down and bury myself in between her legs and as she moans they grow louder. She starts to quiver as I can feel her orgasm rising and I stop and let go.

"S-sir, please. I- I need, I need to come. I'm so close." she breaths out rigidly as she tries desperately to reach for me.

"Rule number two. I decided when you come." I say as I slowly slip a set of fingers inside of her. She moans, falls back down onto the couch, and starts to move her hips in a circular motion. I speed up my pace as I pump my fingers in and out of her. She starts to shake again and I move faster.

"Don't you dare come or I will punish you. I want you to come around me and only me but you're nowhere near that right now." I whisper in her ear, moving even faster with every word.

"P-please sir, I can't-"

"Yes, you can. And you will."

I slip my fingers out of her and stand up to remove the rest of my clothes. She watches intensely as my cock springs out. I watch her as she licks her lips and I move closer to her.

"You think you're ready for this? I'll have you screaming the walls down."

She says nothing but she leans forward until her lips are near the head of my cock. She looks up at me, gives me a mischievous smile, and darts her tongue across the tip of it.

"You really want it bad don't you."

"Yes sir," she replies.

I untie her ankles and her arms and grab her legs to place them on my shoulders.

"Are you on birth control?"

"Yes, I am."

"Good because I want to feel you raw. And I want you to know how it feels to be filled to the brim."

I bend down to kiss her once more before I plunge myself inside of her fully.

"Fuck yes!" she screams as her fingers dig into my back.

"You're so tight around me." I groan.

I begin pounding into her and I lift her up so that my hands are holding her by her thighs to do so. The sounds of skin smashing down into one another echoes the walls. She starts to shake again for the third time and I gently place her down on the couch as I slowly go in and out.

"You can come for me now Celestia. And I wanna hear you scream my name."

Chapter 6

Ramon is the type of man that I tend to avoid. Look at me now, playing along with his little games. But it's only a week. I'm only spending seven days in this penthouse alone with him and I make sure to remind myself of that every damn day.

"Celestia."

I snap out of my thoughts and look up at Ramon.

"Sorry, lost in thought," I mumble.

"What's wrong?"

"What? Nothings wrong." I smile.

"I might not have talked to you as much as I do now but I know you, something is definitely on your mind," he says as he drags my suitcase across the floor.

"It's nothing," I repeat.

He stops and turns around, letting go of my suitcase.

"Celestia, how many times do I have to tell you not to lie to me. When I ask you a question I expect you to answer it and to answer it truthfully."

"I don't-"

Before I could finish my sentence, he abruptly kisses me.

"No more talking. I want you in my bed. I still haven't had enough of you yet." he says after his lips retreat from mine.

I feel a blush creep up my cheeks and I duck my head. He takes my face in his hands and brings my head back up to look up at him.

"Why do you always do that? You're quite cute when you blush."

"Because I'm embarrassed why else?" I mutter.

"Why?"

"The things you say are so vulgar Ramon, I don't understand how you can just say things without thinking of how it'll affect others."

"Am I not allowed to say the things that I feel?"

"You ask way too many questions for a person who wants to get me to bed."

"Now look who's vulgar." he chuckles. "I only ask questions because you confuse me, Celestia. I'm only trying to get to know you better, that's all."

"Now, it's my turn to ask the questions. Why?"

"Because I find you very interesting. Now let's go."

He takes my hand and I follow him down the hall until he stops at a room on the left.

"You seemed like the type to want privacy so you can stay in this room if you'd like. I won't ever come in here unless you want me to. Just worry about getting comfortable for today."

"Okay, thank you," I say as I peer inside.

"I'll let you get settled. Did you eat yet?"

"Um-"

"I'll take that as a no. When you're finished, the kitchen is right around the corner, you'll find me there."

I nod and thank him as he leaves and I close the door. I start to unpack my things and place them in the drawers of the dressing table. Once I was done I head to the kitchen. I spot Ramon by the counter putting some fruits in a bowl beside another bowl with salad in it, topped with bits of chicken. When he sees me he pushes both bowls near the other side of the counter across from a chair.

"Here, eat."

"Why do you always do that?" I ask as I sit down.

"Do what?"

"Tell people what to do as if they won't question it and they'll blindly listen."

"I don't know. I'm just used to it I guess."

"Mm," I reply

"You're thinking again."

"So what if I am?"

"There's nothing wrong with that but you know how curious I am."

"So you wanna know what I'm thinking all the time?"

"Pretty much, yeah," he replies as he leans closer across the counter.

"And you're just gonna watch me eat?"

"Pretty much, yeah," he repeated with a smile as he picked a strawberry from the bowl in front of me.

He lifts the strawberry to my lips. Figuring that he wants me to eat it I obey and bite half of it. He pulls back and uses his thumb to wipe away the escaping juice from the side of my lip. He then takes his thumb and sucks on it all while staring deep into my eyes.

"Is this how women fall for you? If so it's not working." I laugh.

"Who said this is how I get my women?"

"I am curious to know how you do it since you seem to have an effect on most women. Except me."

"I'm curious to know how far you can bend."

"Ha, funny. I'm not bending for anyone."

"Oh for me, you will."

I lift a brow at him and he just continues to look at me with no emotion. Not going to lie it suddenly made me feel hot and bothered.

"It's your eyes," I say as I leave the kitchen.

"What about my eyes?" he asks as he follows me out.

"That makes every female swoon. Except for me of course." I giggle.

"Why do you keep saying that?"

I laugh. He sounds slightly annoyed. Like a little kid almost. I ignore his question and enter my room.

"Ah, ah, ah, you said that you will never come in here without my permission remember?"

"That's not fair, you always run away when we're having a conversation."

"Doesn't it occur to you that it might be for other reasons?"

"No."

"Well, for your information, I have to change. I've been wearing these work clothes for too long." I say as I start to unbutton the corset blouse.

"There's no need, I'm going to rip them off of you anyway so if you want to keep your clothes in one piece I suggest you wear nothing."

"I thought you said we weren't doing anything today," I reply.

"You're right, I'm getting ahead of myself. I'll let you be now, my room is right across from you and the bathroom is the next door to it."

"Thank you," I say as I close the door.

———————

Ramon

All I could currently think about was taking her out of that room and fucking her senseless. She was teasing me with that red lacy bra of hers that did a great show of perking her breasts up. And she knew it too. Suddenly I hear her door open and close. These walls were very thin and you could hear everything. I lean against my door, ready to open it in case she's coming here. But I don't get a thing. I hear her footsteps as they go past my door to the bathroom. I start to hear the water running. The water continues to run for about six minutes. When she turns it off I hear her step inside. I shouldn't be doing this. I sigh as I push myself off the wall and sit on the edge of my bed. I close my eyes and try to distract myself but I couldn't. Especially since I suddenly hear moaning coming from the bathroom. I immediately jerk up and squeeze the foot of the bed. It's either she knew I was able to hear her and she's doing this on purpose, or she has no idea and she's horny as hell. Either way, I knew she wasn't able to resist me.

———————.

Celestia

I wrap the fluffy red towel around my body and look at myself in the mirror.

"You're fine. It's only a week, you feel better now after that bath." I mumble to myself. I sigh and open the door to stare at Ramon.

"Oh! You scared me."

"I changed my mind. Let's go."

"Huh? Changed your mind about what?" I say as he takes my hand and drags me down the hall. I use my other hand to try to keep my towel up as he continues to pull me. We reach a room with a different style of door than the other ones and he takes us both inside. It was very dark and there was only a small amount of light that was behind me from the sides of the doors. I could see him walk forward until there is a good amount of space in between us and then he turns to look at me.

"What's wrong with you?" I ask as I try to reach out for him.

"No touching, drop the towel."

"What? No, why? Why did you bring me here Ramon? I need to put clothes on."

"I heard you in the bathroom." he sighs

"You heard-"

"Everything."

My eyes widen and I squeeze at the towel even more.

"What I do in there is none of your concern."

"Oh it definitely is my concern. Now let me ask you a question. Tell me why you needed that orgasm."

"What I do with my own body is my own choice Ramon, I don't need a man to tell me what I can or can't do."

"You're avoiding the question. Rule number three. When I ask you a question you answer it not go around it."

"I'm not fighting on this with you tonight Ramon, I'm fucking cold and I just want to get some damn clothes on."

"Answer the question first. Then i'll decide if I wanna let you go or not."

I sigh and close my eyes, turning around so that I can't look at him in the eye.

"I was kind of sexually frustrated okay? And I just wanted to relax." I say as I place my hand on the doorknob. Before I can even slightly open the door I feel his hands slip around my waist and I stiffen.

"Why did you turn around? Was that so hard to tell me?"

"Yes. It was. You can be very intimidating sometimes which is why I avoid you."

"Are you relaxed now?"

"Not in the slightest bit after you dragged me in here."

"Then let me help you. Drop the towel."

"I don't think-"

"You think too much with your brain. What does your heart want, and most importantly what does your body want?"

I close my eyes again and swallow the down the lump in my throat.

"Your body is betraying you. I can smell your arousal."

He takes a hand and flicks at my left breast.

"Your nipples are hard as diamonds."

He takes the same hand and trails it down to my leg, slipping it under the towel just near my pussy.

"And I bet if I slipped a finger in right now, you'd be extremely wet for me. Am I wrong?"

I stay quiet.

"Drop the towel Celestia, I'm dying to slip my cock into that sweet and tight pussy of yours again." he whispers ever so softly into my ear.

Without warning a moan escapes my mouth and I quickly muffle it with my hand.

"See what I mean, you know you're just yearning for it. Last time I'm gonna say it. Drop the towel."

Everything inside of me is screaming for him to touch me but my head is the only part that's being logical. Sure Ramon was a good fuck, and yeah I was getting some inside info for my project, and I was definitely horny- who am I kidding. He is right. I do lie to myself. I let go of the towel and let it fall to the ground.

Chapter 7

"Face me and give me your arms."

I obey him and hold out my arms to him. He takes them, wraps a red silk tie around my wrists, and pulls me closer until our chests touch. He brings his lip to my ears, his hands around my waist.

"Don't worry, this is the only bound you'll be getting. Tonight, I just want to see how many times you're able to come."

I let out a small gasp. I could feel his lips curl into a smile. Without letting go of me he pulls me to the bed and lays me on it. He puts my hands above my head and climbs above me. He starts to lick up starting from my thighs. Trailing up to my breast and nipping at them. With every bite he has me arching my back closer to him. He continues back down and stops just above my pussy.

"R-Ramon, please. D-don't tease me." I struggle out of my mouth in one breath.

"I'm not done yet," he replies as he plays with my clit. I can barely feel it and I push myself forward with the hope of feeling more. He moves his hand completely and grips my thighs.

"Tsk, so needy."

"I need to come. Like n-"

Before I finish that sentence his lips are on mine in seconds. And it isn't the one on my face. I moan loudly as he pushes two fingers inside, giving me even more. He moves faster after each and every shove and I feel a sense of euphoria. I feel like I'm at bliss right now and I never want to leave from it. Just as quickly as the moment came, it was quickly gone as well. I open my eyes to find Ramon chucking away his clothes. God, was he a very fine man. I watch as he moves back onto me and it's quite a sight that just made me hunger for him even more. He then moves up to kiss me again. His cock brushed against me.

"I'm gonna make you cum at least seven times before the night is over."

"Seven?!" I gasp.

"Yes, seven. You have no idea what I'm capable of and I'm ready to test the limits of your entire body," he says as he smiles down on me.

He places his hand in between us and begins to push his tip against my entrance.

"You ready?" he whispers.

I nod and he fills me in one move.

"O-oh, God!"

"Not God, Ramon," he says as he pushes inside of me again.

My eyes begin to roll back and I already feel the bubbly orgasm that might rush out any time soon. As he continuously pounds into me my breathing gets heavier. I've never had a man make me feel this wonderful. Ever. It's as if Ramon knew my weak spots, exactly where to hit and when to hit it. His mouth is on my breasts again and I feel alive. The orgasm hits me hard and fast.

Ramon

She looked extremely tired and even then she wanted more. I've never had a woman beg for more even as they're on the brink of passing out. She mumbles something under her breath and I shake my head as I kiss her forehead.

"You're tired Celestia, let's get you to bed." I whisper.

"But I want-"

"Shh, close your eyes, sleep."

She easily obeys, at least when she isn't thinking as much, and her eyes flutter closed. I hear her relaxed breathing as she falls asleep. I smile to myself and pick her up into my arms.

I take her to my room and I place her naked body on the bed and sigh, I might have worn her out too much. I climb into bed with her, something that I never do with any woman after we fuck. But Celestia, she was different. It's like she was Godsent for me. She's exactly what I need and I don't plan on letting her go.

Chapter 8

I wake up to find myself not in the room that I was given. I look around in confusion and when I turn to my left I see a peacefully sleeping Ramon. I look down at him and then down at myself, realizing we were both still naked. I can feel my cheeks turning red again and I press the palms of my hands on them to cool them down. As I grab the covers to pull it over me, I sigh and lay back down, facing Ramon. To think that I'd be in the same bed as him, let alone nude. I find myself faintly moving my fingers across his bare chest, careful not to wake him up. I felt oddly at ease which is quite funny if you ask me since I've managed to avoid this man for years.

I sigh and get up from the bed. I decided to take a bath again this morning. It's not like I had anything to do today either. I pad across the floor to the open-spaced bathroom. I silently giggle to myself at the large and weirdly shaped bathtub. After I turn on the water, I let it run for a few minutes until it reached halfway. I place a clean towel to the side of the tub and dip myself in the warm water. I look to the sides of the tub and find a button near my arm. Beside the button, there are a few candles. I'd never peg Ramon as a candle person.

I laughed to myself again. There sure is a lot of things that I don't know about him. Maybe he isn't the emotionless person he's always shown to others. Maybe that's just his way of protecting who he really is. I fiddle with the button, then finally press it out of curiosity.

"Oh!" I exclaim as the jets suddenly turn on.

I close my eyes and let the jet beat against my back and my legs. Once my back had enough I turn around to face the jets. It gently presses against my breasts and all I could think of was Ramon and the way he nipped at them. I shake my head to take away the thoughts of him and I feel the water move behind me. I dart open my eyes when I feel hands on me.

"Good Morning," says Ramon as he pulls me to him on the other side of the tub.

"Morning." I sigh as I rest my head against the side of his neck. Now, this was a great start to my morning.

He pulls me closer as if there was no more space between us. I can feel his hard-on and my stomach jitters.

"You're hard," I whisper.

"And you're wet."

"No shit, I'm in a bathtub," I say as I roll my eyes, trying to fight the smile that wants to escape.

"I meant here," he says as he dipped his hands in between my legs and slipped a finger in.

I gasp and without thinking my body squeezes and does a jerk-like motion.

"You can't tell."

"Yes, I definitely can," he responds as he curls his finger deeper inside.

"R-Ramon, don't s-start something you can't finish." I moan.

"Oh, I do plan on finishing what I started. God Celestia, you gripping my finger makes me want to fuck you again. Are you sore from yesterday?"

"N-no." I breathe out in a rush.

"Good," he says and he takes his finger out of me and moves me around to face him.

I look into his eyes filled with lust and he positions me right on top of his cock. He moves me down his length and I moan again as I tilt my head back. The water moves as I move like a boat moving against waves. I continuously ride him until I reach orgasm. My nails dig into his back and he groans as he releases soon after me. We're both panting as we stare at each other, neither knowing what to do or how to react.

"That makes seven," he says as he pulls me down to kiss me.

"That doesn't count."

"We get a pass, you were too tired. Even as you were begging for more."

My cheeks turn red for the second time this morning and I tip my head down.

"There's no need for that."

"I've just never had anyone make me come as much and as hard as you Ramon. It just feels different." I mumble.

"Mm, well that's only part of what I can do, you haven't seen half."

"I know you still have to show me your way around ropes and ties and whatnot."

"There's so much more than just ropes and ties Celestia. And I plan on showing everything to you."

"There's simply no way you can show me everything in the next five days."

"I could. But if you'd like to stay for more than a week, I wouldn't stop you." he smiles.

I search his face for any sign of a joke. Anything that would tell me that he wasn't serious.

"Can I ask you a question?" I say as I fold my arms around his neck.

"Shoot."

"This, thing. Between us, how are we gonna handle it when the week is over or even if I decide to stay a little longer. When it's over, and we go back to our normal lives, how's that gonna be? Won't it be super awkward?"

"If you'd let me, I'd never stop doing this with you. You're different from the other women I've had. I told you before that I've had my eyes on you since the moment you walked into my office with that tight black and white patterned dress for that interview."

"You remember what I wore?"

"Yes, I did, I pay attention to detail. Anyway, it won't be weird for me. I'll treat you just as I do now. But I won't touch you without your permission if you know what I mean."

"Yeah, I get it."

"Are you worried that I'll ignore you?"

"No, I'm worried that I'll try and avoid you as I did before."

"Why?"

"You've always intimidated me. I told myself that I never needed to be near you unless it was for work. And I've been damn good at it too."

"Indeed you have," he replies as he slips himself out of me. I move off of him, immediately feeling empty once more. I lay my head on his shoulder beside him and mindlessly trace images on his chest.

This was very calming and I cannot believe I'm saying this but I think I like this.

Chapter 9

"I would prefer if you'd ride with me." I plead.

"But I don't want anyone making assumptions Ramon."

"What are they gonna say?"

"They're gonna ask why I'm with you and one thought will lead to another. What I'm saying is that they'll know that we had sex."

"And? What's wrong with that?"

"If they start thinking that I'm sleeping with you for raise, promotion, or anything, I will personally attack you. With my stripper heels."

"Anyone even so much as looks at you a different way, come to me and I'll deal with them."

"That's just going to make it worse Ramon."

"I don't care, you are mine. I will not have anyone messing with you in any way, shape, or form."

"I'm not yours Ramon. I'm not an object."

Shit. I shouldn't have said that. I rub my face in frustration and sigh.

"I'm sorry, I don't know what came over me. Just, please let me. I swear it'll be fine. If anyone says anything to you just text me. Please."

"Okay! Okay, fine since you're never gonna give this up," she replies as she rolls her eyes.

"Don't roll your eyes at me."

"I'll roll them all I want Ramon."

I grab her arm pull her closer to me and whisper in her ear.

"I'll deal with you later, then your eyes will really be rolling back."

She gasps and bites her lip. I smile, feeling satisfied, and pull her to the car that was waiting for us outside. She gets in without complaining again and I follow behind her.

"I wanna take you somewhere tonight, is that okay with you?"

"Yeah, that's fine."

"Okay good, you don't need to worry about what to wear. I'm bringing you something."

"Okay, wait. You don't know my sizes."

"Yes, I do. I checked."

"And you claim you aren't a stalker."

"I'm not don't worry." I laugh as I pull her closer to me. "You're too far away."

"You can't keep your hands off of me?"

"No, I cannot."

Her laugh echoes throughout the car and I smile at her widely. When we get to the building, I get out and offer my hand for her to take. She simply gives me a look and slightly shakes her head. Well, it was worth a try.

Celestia

I didn't expect Ramon to understand the situation I was in. He wouldn't get it. Of course, he wouldn't, he never gets the short end of the stick when it comes to consequences or anything else negative for that matter. We have our annual team meeting today in the large conference room and he kept darting his eyes at me whenever he had the chance to. And of course, I tried to avoid his gaze. Anyone who was looking could obviously see a silent staring competition if I looked back, or they'll see it as silent flirting. Either way, someone would notice. I couldn't handle any questions relating to him and me today. As he speaks to us, I can see his sense of power, and it looks good. He looks at me again. I stare at him back and bite my lip. He stutters on his words and I silently giggle under my breath.

"Alright, you all may leave now, except for you Celestia, I need you."

My heels stop echoing across the floor as he says my name. I look around and let out a silent breath after seeing the last person leave the room without looking back. Thankfully everyone fit in the elevator at once so there was no one else waiting to leave. As soon as the elevator closes, I turn around and walk back to him, stopping with just enough space in between us.

"Yes, sir?"

"Hm, I like the way you call me sir." he rasps as he gestures for me to come closer.

"Well, we are in the office, and that is what I called you before, nothing has changed," I reply.

"Ah, let me have my fun."

"We can have fun later." I wink.

"Why can't we have fun now?"

"There's no way-"

"Oh yes there is," he says as he picks up the remote from his desk. I already knew what the remote was meant for and my head began to come up with all types of things we could do in this very room. Right now. It's as if we both knew, how much we were craving for one another. We lunge at each other and I drop my pad and pen to the floor. I never knew that this side of me existed. When I'm with Ramon, I feel powerful, sexy, seductive. He brings out the confidence in me. As we continue to kiss, he lifts me and I wrap my legs around his waist. We're traveling from the desk to the wall. And God I can't get enough! He unbuttons my top, with a few flying across the room in his rushed-like manner. He uses one hand to keep me up and the other to pull out his cock. He pushes my panties to the side and I softly moan as the tip of his cock plays with my clit.

"Shit! Ramon. I need it in. Now."

"As you wish," he says as he brings his lips to mine and slips into me.

I moan into his mouth and pushes into me harder.

"I love how you're so tight for me."

"I love how you feel inside me," I reply.

He continues to pound into me until we're both finished and heavily panting. He pulls himself out and gently places me down. Before he attends to himself he takes his time to snap my panties back and place and fix my skirt.

"Damn, your shirt. I didn't think."

"It's okay, I have another top in my bag. It might not be appropriate for work though." I mumble.

"It's fine, hold on", give me your shirt," he says as he pulls out his phone. He takes a picture of it on the desk and proceeds to dial a number.

"Hey, I sent you a picture, I need you to go to a store and grab me a black button-down in size medium for women. I need it asap. Thank you."

He finishes his call and turns to me.

"Stay here, I'm getting you a new shirt."

"You didn't have to Ramon, I have another top and I can cover it up with something."

"It's my fault, I ripped the buttons off in my quickness. I'm getting you another shirt and that's final."

I stayed quiet, not wanting to speak of it, I also did not want to wear what I had either if I'm being quite honest. I wrap my arms around my chest and Ramon notices. He takes off his jacket and wraps it around me.

"Thank you," I mutter.

He nods and takes my hand, bringing me over to his desk.

"I have a virtual meeting to be in, in about three minutes and another one right after. You're staying here. On my lap," he says as he puts me there.

"What? No, isn't your camera going to be on?"

"Yes."

"Are you trying to ruin your reputation or something?"

I shuffle in his lap, trying to get up but I can't. He's holding onto me like there's no tomorrow.

"It'll be fine it isn't like a business meeting per se. If I didn't have you here, they'd question things."

"So what kind of meeting is it then if it isn't business?"

"A sexual one you can say."

"I knew it, I knew it! I'm just another bitch to you. Fuck you."

"You already did, wanna do it again?" he grins.

"It's not funny! I don't wanna be here while you get off on some stranger touching themselves." I whine as I hit his chest.

"No, it's not like that, I'm joking." he laughs.

"Then what?"

"Your so innocent, I love it."

"Now, you're just making fun of me."

"I'm not, I do love it. And I love how I'm the one to teach you new things."

"Yea, yea."

"The place I'm taking you to tonight is another place that I own. It's a BDSM club. I'm just having a meeting with a few people who I put in charge."

"Those places exist?"

"Yes, don't worry, it's not that bad."

"I'm not worried."

"Your voice just went an octave higher. Lie to me again and I'll spank that ass of yours."

I swallow, debating whether or not to lie again. Anything to get him to touch me again. He lifts a brow at me and I look away, biting my bottom lip. He takes another remote from his desk and presses a button. A projector screen slides down in front of the foggy glass and he turns the projector on. After a few minutes, he enters the meeting.

"Ramon!" squeaked a woman with really bright red hair. She was very pretty. And I immediately wondered how she and Ramon met. Bad. That's none of my business.

"Hey, Rose, how's everything?"

"Great, great! Oh my God is this her?"

"Yes, this is her. Rose meet Celestia, Celestia meet Rose."

"Omg I can't wait to meet you!" she screams as she quickly waves at me. I wave back and smile.

"I'll be bringing her today."

"That's good, I could use a new girlfriend."

"What's been happening since I was last at the club?" Ramon asks.

"Well, you did miss a huge fight over the new girl between Theo and Apollo. But it's been settled, she likes both of them and they made a compromise that they'd share her. It's quite interesting actually."

"Okay, good to know, anything else?"

"That's pretty much all, by the way, should I tell everyone you're coming? Should I tell them you're bringing her too?"

"Do whatever you want. Announcing me isn't going to change anything."

"Yeah, but haven't you claimed her already? You don't want anyone to take her from you."

Ramon kept his mouth closed shut.

"Ramon? Did you?"

"No, enough about it. I'll be there around nine or so. I'll see you later Rose."

"We're not done with this convo mister. Bye Celestia!"

Ramon ended the meeting and signed onto another one.

"Okay, now this one is business, if you want to stay on my lap, that's fine by me."

"I don't want people saying things behind your back."

"I don't care."

"Okay, how about I just stay right here, away from the camera's view."

"Or, how about I just close the camera, and you can stay on my lap."

"That's very unprofessional Ramon."

"Again, I don't care. I own every one of these people anyway. What I say goes."

"Fine, but only because I'm already comfortable."

"See, I always win."

"Not for long you won't-"

"Sir, there's a bag waiting for you downstairs," says James through the intercom on the wall.

"Damn, you have James doing my job, I should get back downstairs Ramon."

"Nope, you're staying here with me. You have notes to take." he winks.

I roll my eyes as I smile and wiggle off of him.

"Fine, I'll be back, just let me get my shirt."

"Come right back, if I have to get up from this chair to bring you back, you won't be able to sit for weeks."

"Do it, you won't," I say as I head to the elevator. I slip my arms through his jacket and tighten it around me as I step out to the first floor. James catches me and grins widely.

"Shut up,"

"I didn't say anything." he smiles.

"Yea, but you did think it," I say as I grab the bag from my desk.

"What's in the bag?"

"A shirt."

"And what happened to the one you came in with?"

"I dropped some coffee on it."

"You know you're a bad liar right."

"Ugh, not you too."

"Well, well, well, this is definitely a tale to tell Lucy. I sat down here and played secretary by day, security by night, while you were upstairs playing house with Ramon." he mocks as he wiggles his brows towards me.

"God, you're such a child." I laugh as I get back on the elevator.

"Ah, you do listen," says Ramon the second I step out.

I tilt my head to the side and blink once as I walk over to him. Instead of going back to him, I stand in front of the screen and smile as I let his jacket fall to the ground. I kick off my heels, drop the bag on the floor and start to unzip the back of my skirt. It drops with a faint thud. I step out of it and walk up to Ramon, stopping right in front of the desk. He gestures for me to come and I shake my head as I kneel to the ground, disappearing from his sight. I crawl under the table towards him and spread his legs apart. I feel him beginning to tense up as he speaks. Good. I stick my head in between him and once he finishes speaking he takes a quick look down and gives me a surprised look. I put my pointer finger to my lips in a hush sign and unbuckle his belt. Just being near him makes me want to do things I would never do with anyone else. It's as if he was the key to unlocking this part of me. I take out his cock and it twitches in my hands. I knew it was big but as I look at it I noticed that its length and thickness make my hands look smaller than they already are.

Ramon

God, she knew how to play dirty. I clench my teeth, desperately trying not to show the workers that anything else was happening besides the fact that they think I'm listening to them. I can't fucking focus while she's down there sucking me whole. The power she holds over me. I made the mistake of darting my eyes downward and our eyes meet as she continues to move her wet, luscious, pink lips over the tip and downward. I can feel her tongue pressing against my skin as she tries to swallow and I silently hiss as I cover my mouth with my hand. She has me mentally drunk as she giggles, uses her hands to part my legs wider, and laps up the spilling cum, starting from the bottom of my balls to the tip of my cock.

"Alright, we can resume this soon, I must attend to something gentlemen. Have a great day." I say as I quickly listen to their good-byes and slam the button on the remote to turn off the projector. I bend down and grab her chin as I pull her up from the floor.

"Now, what do I do with you?"

"Kiss me, take these off of me, and fuck me," she says as she loops her hand around my necktie and pulls at it.

"That, I can do,"

I pull her down to me and begin to move my mouth all over her as I take off the rest of her clothes. I pick her up and practically slam her down on my cock and she immediately moans in delight.

"Yes, Ramon! Fuck!"

"Yes, princess, scream for me all you want. These windows are soundproof." I smile.

The way she tightens around me gets me every time she goes down makes me lose all control.

"Mm, I like the sound of that." she rasps before she gasps as I hold her up and thrust into her fully and fast. I stand up and lay her on the desk, kissing her all over her chest. She moans again as I bite at her nipples every time I push inside of her with long and slow strokes. I use my hand to trail down and make circles on her clit.

"Ramon, f-faster p-please!"

"No, not yet. I don't think you're ready to come yet."

"I am! Just please Ramon."

"You can take it babygirl, for me."

She moans my name and I get a sense of shiver.

Celestia was made for me. I just know it. And I cannot wait to claim her and permanently call her mine.

Chapter 10

I watch Ramon as he buttons my shirt. Even after he took my breath away, he still takes his time to make sure that I'm fine. It might've been the heat of the moment but I felt like the only woman in the world when he called me princess.

"When are we heading out?" I ask.

"It's about an hour away from here so we'll need to go home at around seven."

"Alright then. I'll head back downstairs, and no do not ask me to stay, I've been here all day up here with you."

"What's wrong with staying up here with me?"

"Nothing, you're just keeping me away from my job. Now, what if some person walks in here unannounced."

"That's why James is here for."

"You're going to see me later anyway. Bye." I say as I kiss his cheek. He tries to kiss my lips but I shake my head at him.

"Uh, uh, If I let you, you'll never let me leave."

"You know me so well," he replies smiling.

I get downstairs to find James pushing out a man who seems vaguely familiar. I shrug to myself as it wasn't my problem to deal with and go to sit at my desk.

"Who was that?" I ask.

"I have no idea, he said he knew you and wanted to speak to you."

"He looked familiar, but I don't remember where from."

"Ah, well I'll keep an eye out for him, he looked pretty sketchy."

"Okay, did anyone come by besides him?"

"Nope, you were lucky today." he winks.

I smile and shake my head at him. Until six-thirty, I checked through my emails multiple times and played a few card games with James. He won the last game just as Ramon steps out of the elevator and comes up to my desk.

"You ready?"

"Yes," I say as I pick up my bag from the side of my chair. "I'll see you later James."

"Yep, bye CC." he winks. He then nods to Ramon and he nods back as he places his hand on the small of my back. We leave the building and Ramon's driver is already waiting outside for us. We get in after he opens the door and he drives us home. I meant Ramon's home.

"Here, your clothes are in these bags, wear everything," Ramon says as he hands me the red bags.

I take it from him and go to change in my room. I take out everything in the bags and my eyes nearly leave their sockets. He gave me everything from undergarments to accessories and shoes. Everything was an ombre of red and black. I undress and start with the underwear. It was a matching pair of open-crotch panties that was sinfully filling my mind with all sorts of things and a lace demi bra. After putting those on I put on the garters, attached the fishnet tights, and slipped on the black five-inch Louboutin heels. Lastly, I place in my earrings, add some red lipstick to my lips, and fluff out my hair. I leave my room and go to knock on Ramon's door. A few seconds pass before he opens the door. When he stares down, I start to feel very subconscious and move my hand to hide my sex.

"Don't do that." He says as he gently swats away my hand. He pulls me close to him and takes my chin in his hand.

"You're too beautiful, don't hide anything from me, princess."

I would've melted into a puddle if he wasn't holding me up. I look into his eyes and see that it's filled with not lust but pure affection and my heart skips a beat.

"We should go now, I have a coat for you to wear by the door," he says as he takes me down the hall. When we're outside, I see no sign of his driver and I see a different car than the one he usually drives in. He opens the passenger side for me and I thank him as I get inside. He moves around to get to his seat and he drives south.

Ramon

I tighten my arm around her waist as we enter the club. I give our coats to the front and I can sense the eyes on her. She has no collar on her, therefore if I left her alone for even a second she'd have a line of people wanting her. But they can't have her, because she's mine. Collar or no collar, she belongs to me. I look down at Celestia, looking for her reactions. She looks around in awe like a child coming to a theme park for the first time. I spot Rose heading towards us with the brightest smile on her face.

"Ahh! You're here! God, you're so pretty! Care to share Ramon?"

"No, where's your pet anyway?"

"He'll be here soon. In the meantime, I'm having my fun with Yasmin."

"Ahh, I see," I reply as I look back toward Celestia who was now looking at two men with a naked woman in between them.

"You interested?" I whisper in her ear.

"N-no, I was just looking," she mumbles and darts her eyes away from the scene.

"I'll let you two be, Yasmin is probably pouting right about now, Welcome back master." winks Rose as she walks away.

I take Celestia's hand and take her upstairs to a room. As we pass the other rooms with doors open, I see the look on her face as she sees the submissives being whipped and spanked. She isn't reacting as much as I thought she would which makes me confirm that she must have had fantasies about being dominated. I find an empty room and I lead her inside and close the door behind us. I turn to face her with my hands crossed across my chest.

"Celestia."

"Yes?"

"Yes, what?"

"Oh, yes sir?"

"I want you to walk to the bed, turn around, and kneel in front of it with your arms out."

She nods and does as I say without complaint.

"Good girl," I say as I move her hair from her face and kiss her forehead.

I go to the drawers in the corner of the room, opening the top one, and taking out a red rope. I come over to her and tie the rope around her wrists, binding her hands together securely.

"Is it too tight?"

"No sir."

"Good, now stand up."

She hasn't said anything snarky at all ever since we got home. This isn't the Celestia I knew. She stands up and looks at me with the same facial expression she had when she entered the place. I get closer and take her chin in my hand.

"You haven't said much lately, are you okay? Do you want me to stop?"

"No sir, I'm just thinking," she mumbles.

"About what Celestia?"

"Someone who showed up asking for me today,"

"Who?"

"I don't know, but they looked very familiar," she says in a flat tone.

"Why didn't you tell me earlier?"

"I don't know, I guess there was no need to."

"As long as you're with me, I want to hear everything. Even if it seems insignificant. Got it?"

"Yes sir."

"I love this obedient side of you," I whisper as I bend down to kiss her lips. I pull at her nipple and she shivers under me as she moans into my mouth. I let go of her and she looks at me, needy, desperate, waiting for me to touch her again.

"Get on the bed, face me, and spread your legs."

Her eyes glow with a lustful imagination as she gets on the mattress. She spreads her legs wide but moves her bonded hands to cover herself.

"What did I tell you about doing that Celestia, if you do it again, I will punish you."

"Y-yes sir, sorry sir," she says while she moves her hands. I see how tempted she is to put her knees together or to hide under the covers entirely.

"Touch yourself."

"Um, sorry?"

"I said touch yourself, don't make me repeat it a third time."

"I-"

"Celestia, you don't question, you just do."

"Yes, sir," she mumbles as she slowly brings her hand down to her center. She takes a finger and begins to move it around her clit. She turns her head away and bites her lip as she does.

"Celestia, look at me while you do it," I say as I walk closer. "Touch yourself like you did when you desperately wanted that orgasm in the bathroom."

She nods and moves her fingers faster in a circular motion. She moans as she looks into my eyes, I can feel her build up from where I stand. Her wetness starts to coat her fingers and her legs start to shake as she enters a finger inside of her.

"That's enough."

She doesn't stop.

"Celestia, that's enough," I say as I pull her hands away.

"I- I need to-"

"No, you're not ready to come yet," I reply as I take her fingers and suck them into my mouth.

"Sweet, just like you," I whisper.

Her cheeks turn a light shade of red and I move beside her onto the bed. I pick her up and place her in between my legs in front of me. Entwining our legs so she can't close hers, I trail my hand across her breast and down her abdomen until I reach her pussy. I place two fingers inside and she arches her back with pleasure.

"Rub your clit while my fingers fuck you. And don't you dare come." I say.

"Y-Yes sir!" she moans as she immediately does what I ask.

"Such a good princess."

I push in and out faster than before and she moans one after the other. When I feel her shake above me I withdraw myself from her.

"Sir, please."

"Not yet, princess," I say, shaking my head. I move her off of me and set her back down on the bed. I take off my own clothes and open the other drawers filled with toys, more ropes, and whips. I grab a few things before I get back on the bed in front of her.

"Turn around for me."

"Yes, sir," she says as she obeys.

"This might feel cold," I warn as I slowly push in the buttplug. She gasps as the foreign object enters her ass."

"Oh! Sir, I haven't done this before."

"You're fine, you're taking it very well."

"It feels good."

"Wait till you get the real thing. Face me," I whisper in her ear as I pull her hair.

She moans and I let go, continuing with the ropes.

I take her ankles and tie them both to the edges of the bed. Then I use another rope to loop it around the one wrapping her hands and tie it to the headboard. I love how she's all spread out for me, ready for anything I give her. I kiss her neck and move down until I reach her sex. I haven't fucked her yet and her cream is nearly spilling out of her. She squirms as I lap up her juices and I use my hands to pin her legs down as she tries to squeeze. Her moans echo the room as I suck on her clit. I can't get enough of her. Before she can come I quickly unbind her legs, flip her around, and remove the plug with a slight pop. I replace it with the tip of my cock and she pushes down on me. Halfway in, she groans.

"Does it hurt?" I ask

"No sir, I want, need more," she says breathlessly.

I push the rest of my length inside of her and she screams with great pleasure.

"Harder sir, please." she moans.

I pull out and push myself right back in with full force. As I pound into her tightness, I grab a fistful of her hair and tilt her head back. I use my other hand to finger her deeply.

"Come for me, princess."

"Yes!" she screams as her orgasm comes crashing down.

"Get the fuck off of her!"

We both turn to see a very livid man at the door. I look back at Celestia and her eyes got big. She tries to pull her hands from the rope and I grab her hands to untie her.

"Really, Celestia? You're such a slut. My sex wasn't enough for you was it. You just had to turn into a whore, didn't you? Your-"

I get up and put my pants on before I face this scrawny man. He looks at me with anger in his eyes.

"I don't what you did, what drugs you gave her, she doesn't belong here. You're corrupting my wife."

"I don't see a ring on her finger. I'm giving you two seconds to leave. Before I slam your small ass head against every surface in this room. Celestia isn't yours she's mine. Now leave." I spit out through my clenched jaw. I wanted to fucking bash his head in through the door her came from, but I had no idea who he was and what he meant to Celestia.

"Celestia! Your gonna let him talk to me like this? Figures. You've changed a lot. I told you I'd come back for you and this is how you welcome me? By sneaking around and letting all types of men fuck you? And don't think I haven't seen that little job you have as well. You are such a nasty whore. I can't even look at you anymore. In all honesty, you weren't even a decent lay bi-"

I threw a punch at his face and his head came in contact with the door frame.

"Don't ever fucking talk to her that way you fucking lowlife."

I press a small button on the wall which alarms security. Within minutes they show up and I simply point at the passed-out man on the floor. I turn to Celestia and my heart shatters. I swiftly run to her and scoop her in my arms. I take off the ropes from her hands and rub them gently with my thumbs. Her tears are spilling on my chest as she sobs and it makes me want to personally make the man's life a living hell.

"Princess, don't cry, let's get you home."

She nods against my chest and I put my shirt back on, and take her hand, leading her out of the room. I pull her close to me and she buries her face in my side. I take her downstairs, a few people giving us respectful nods with a hint of lust in their eyes. I grab her coat and wrap it around her as we walk out. Once we reach the car, I pick her up, place her in the passenger seat, and get into the driver's seat. I speed out onto the road and drive at an unreasonable speed. Celestia never deserves to cry. That man made her feel like shit and he'd pay for it.

Chapter 11

I barely ate my food as I sat across the counter from Ramon. He tried to get me to look at him but I avoid his eyes. I can't believe he came back, just when I had forgotten about him.

"Alright, let's go." sighs Ramon.

He gently takes my hand and brings me to his room.

"Sit," he says as he gestures to the bed.

I obey and sit on the edge of the bed, fidgeting with my hands. He crouches down in front of me and takes my hands in his.

"Celestia, look at me."

"I don't want to."

"Please? I don't like that you won't talk to me. Talk to me, princess."

"If I look at you, I'm going to cry, Ramon. I don't want you to see that."

"See what? You being human? Celestia, you're a strong, independent woman, just because you cry doesn't mean that you're less than who you are. Now please tell me what's wrong. You can cry all you want. I'm here."

I sigh and close my eyes, fighting back the tears before I speak.

"T-that man yesterday, his name is Mike. He's my ex. He broke up with me years ago, and it ended badly so I have no idea why he's back now. I'm not his wife, never was, and never will be."

"If he followed us out to the club who knows what he'll do."

"He's all bark and no bite. I know him. He was probably drunk and I was the first person on his mind."

"That may be true, but we don't know what he's capable of, we don't know what he's thinking."

"I'll be careful."

"That's not right, you shouldn't have to live your life, terrified shitless of this man."

I just shrug and say nothing. I didn't have time to think about Mike, nor did I want to.

"I don't like seeing you upset."

"I'm not upset, I'm-"

"You are-"

"I wasn't finished. I'm stressed, not upset."

"I can help you release that stress," he says smiling as he squeezes my thigh.

He gets up from his crouched position and picks me up, wrapping my legs around his waist. I roll my eyes at him but play along.

"Then shut up and kiss me already."

"Yes ma'am," he responds as he puts his lips over mine.

He moves us onto the bed and lays me down.

"I'm going to make you come for me and then we're gonna have a nice bath together where I'll give you a nice massage and we can take a nap after, does that sound nice."

"Mm, yes that sounds nice, I haven't had a nap in ages."

"All the more reason you should take one with me." he smiles as he bends down to kiss my forehead.

He takes off his shirt and his shorts, and I do the same. Before I can take off my underwear he does it for me and his mouth immediately goes to my center. I arch forward and he pins me back down, spreading my legs with his hands even wider. He's sucking my entire soul and I love it. I want to give him everything, all, and more. He buries his face deeper and I can feel his tongue rolling inside of me. As I'm on the verge of releasing he moves up to my breasts again. He takes his cock and slips it in as if it was a perfect match. He begins to slowly go in and out without missing a beat and speeds up as each second goes by. I claw at his back with my nails as I release an orgasm. He doesn't stop and I feel bliss as my body builds up yet another release after the other.

"Come for me again princess." he groans as he begins to slow down and tighten his grip on my waist.

"Yes!"

"Come with me. Now." as he pushes in one more time.

We both release at the same time and I feel a sense of warmth as he fills me. He takes himself out of me and spreads my legs once again, watching his own doing spill out of my pussy. He then slips into me again, slowly smiling.

"I like the way my cum drips out of you. Come on let's get you cleaned up," he says as he picks me up with him still inside me. He moves us to his bathroom and sits on the edge, turning the water on.

"Are you not gonna take yourself out?" I ask as we wait for the water to fill the tub.

"No, he lives there now," he smirks as he gives me a slight push inside.

"Well then, I guess he's in for a ride." I moan softly.

I begin to move my hips in slow, lazy circles as I stare deep into Ramon's eyes.

"You're playing with fire, Princess," he says.

He holds me up and starts to pound into me again and again. Another orgasm quickly comes and my legs quiver as it leaves my body.

"Ramon the water!" I laugh, looking behind him.

He turns around and quickly moves to turn it off. After that, he places me in the tub and comes in behind me. He starts to rub my shoulders and my neck and moves down to my waist. I close my eyes and I lay back against Ramon as I exhale a long breath. He continued to rub at my skin and I was extremely at ease.

"Ramon?"

"Yes, Princess?" he says smoothly and I smile.

"Why is it that you never told me, that you were interested in me, and how come whenever I walked into your office, you were with another woman?"

"Well, I never wanted to scare you away with my sexual lifestyle, when I first heard your voice, you sounded very alluring, and even as I saw you for the first time, If I'm being honest, I was desperate to know how you would feel under me. So, I used other women as a distraction. They were never enough. Most of them didn't even last the whole day. When I realized that you were a stripper, I saw the confidence and the openness inside of you. You seemed like the type to never be afraid of anything, someone who's willing to try new things."

"And what if I said no to this week with you?"

"I would've most likely annoyed you until you did," he laughs as he rubs at the spot between my neck and shoulders.

"Really?" I giggle.

"Truly."

Ramon

Celestia finally drifted off to sleep. We were naked under the thick covers and she was nestled in between my arms with her back against my chest. Holding onto her feels very pleasant. I would stay like this an entire day if I could. Am I slightly taking a liking to her? Possibly. Is that a good thing? Most likely not. I fill my head with all of these questions that are left unanswered and it begins to tire me out as well. I pull her closer to me and kiss her head. I don't want her to leave me. Ever. For her sake, maybe I will give dating a try.

Chapter 12

"Hey, wake up."

As I flutter my eyes open, I wake up and feel very wet and icky. Ramon has a calm yet concerned look on his face as he has his hand on my shoulder.

"Mm, good morning. What's wrong?"

"Nothing, let's just get you out of these dirty sheets first," he replies.

I furrow my brows together and look down at the sheets. I see the dried-up blood underneath me, and I scramble off the bed, nearly falling off.

"Shit!"

"Hey, hey! It's okay, you're fine. It's fine."

"It's not fine I just bled all over your bed," I complain as I look down at myself. My period must've started in the middle of the night. I curse at myself for not even thinking of it before I came here.

"It's just blood, Celestia."

"God, that's so embarrassing."

"It happens, it shouldn't be. Sit and stay put, I'm gonna run you a bath and you can stay in there until I get back from the store alright?" he says as he places me back on the bed and wraps the blankets around my body.

He goes into the bathroom and turns on the water. After a few minutes, he comes out swoops me into his hands, carrying me to the tub. He places me in it and then crouches in front of me.

"Do you wear pads or tampons?"

"Both," I mumble.

"I'll bring you your phone, I want you to text me the ones you buy so I can get them. If you need anything else just call me. I'll be back." he says and he gets up, brings me my phone, and walks into his closet to put clothes on.

As I sat there in the warm water, I look at Ramon with a feeling of appreciation. Mike would've never gone out of his way to do such a thing. He always avoided this kinda thing. But Ramon, powerful but gentle Ramon, is taking care of me. I feel like he's slowly peeling away his defensive layers and showing me his true self. Before he leaves, he kisses me on the forehead and splashes a few droplets of water onto my face. I grin and splash him back playfully, grateful for the distraction. I watch him leave and I put myself deeper into the water. After a few relaxing minutes, I clean myself off and step out, wrapping a towel around myself. I take my phone and text, Ramon, what I need then sat on the toilet, afraid of getting my blood on anything else.

"How long have you been sitting there?"

"Awhile, I didn't want to get anything else" I replied, looking up from my phone as he walks in the bathroom with bags. Way too many for just a box of pads and a box of tampons I might add.

"Which of these do you want?" he laughs as he pulls out two boxes.

"Give me the pad, my first days are heavy, God I hate being a woman sometimes," I whine.

He opens up the box himself and hands me one. He then goes into another box and pulls out a matching set of sweats and a sweater in the color red.

"You probably don't have anything comfortable to wear so I got you this. I also got you some Advil, snacks, and other junk food as well,"

"You didn't have to do all that Ramon, I-"

"I know I didn't. I just wanted to."

"Thank you," I say. What I really wanted to say was that he was amazing and so caring and that I really didn't want to leave after the next two days were over. But I wasn't going to tell him that. At least not now I won't.

My stomach pain was unbearable. Nothing I ate would stay down. I heave once more and Ramon continues to hold my hair back.

"Are you sure you're fine princess? I can take you to the emergency room."

"No, no. I'm fine, this always happens on the first day. I'll be fine by tonight." I mumble as I get up to wash my mouth in the sink.

"Pregnancy's gonna be a breeze for you." he laughs as he follows me back onto the bed.

"Shut up Ramon," I reply as I bury myself under the covers. He follows suit and pulls me closer to him. His warm hand rests against my lower stomach which calms my pain.

"Ramon, will you hold me till I fall asleep?"

"Yes, princess. I can do that."

"You know what I just thought of?"

"What?"

"You won't be able to fuck me the rest of this week."

"You're in pain and you're worried about sex?" he laughs.

"Don't laugh, you're the one losing here." I smile.

"I could care less, you wanna know something?"

"Yeah?"

"The reason I kiss you on your forehead all the time? It's because I don't see you as just a good lay or a sex object Celestia. I like your spunk and your personality."

I say nothing but I place my hands over his and squeeze. He wraps the rest of his hands around me and twists me over to face him. He takes my chin in his hands and stares at me. We stare at each other, unmoving, just listening to the beating of our hearts, and our breath going in and out. I move closer to him until our lips are millimeters away.

"Ramon."

"Yes, princess?"

"I-I don't want to leave."

"You're here,"

"I mean you, I don't want to leave you."

"Then don't."

"But you don't do the dating thing."

"I will, for you ," he replies and his lips finally move over mine.

To think that'd he'd do such a thing for me. All I know is that I've changed, he's changed, we've changed. And we did it together.

Chapter 13

I have never been happier when she said that she wanted to stay. I never wanted her to leave. As she sleeps peacefully in my arms, I comb my fingers through her hair and close my eyes, wishing we could stay like this forever. She moved in with me almost a week ago and it still feels like the first week she was here. Celestia, God, there are so many words and ways to describe her. She's like my magic rose in a bell jar that no one can touch.

"Hey princess, how was work?" I say as I hear the door opening.

"It was fine," she replies as her lips form a straight line.

"That means it was not, what happened?" I respond and tilt her head up to look at me.

"I got touched again," she mumbles as she slightly shivers at the word touch.

"Who was it? Why don't you quit? I don't like people touching what's mine."

"I know it was a regular, but I don't care enough to know their names. And no I'm not quitting I need to pay my last year of college."

"I can pay for you."

"I don't want your money, Casanova. I'll be fine," she says as she pats my cheek.

"It's no trouble real-did you just call me Casanova?" I laugh.

"You are my full-time lover are you not?" she smiles as she walks away.

"Now wait a minute,"

She continues to walk away, peeling off her coat and hanging it up in the hall. My heart skips a beat as she exposes her getup. Her fishnets were tempting me to run to her and rip them off, burying myself into her sweetness.

"Yes?" she taunts.

"Now, you're just teasing me. And you know what happens when you do that." I mumble as I nibble at her shoulder.

"Do I? she replies as she moves away. She turns around and gives me a small peck and goes into our room. I walk back into the kitchen, avoiding the urge to turn around and go back to her. To hell with it, I thought as I turn off the stove. I turn around to see her opening a pack of strawberries from the fridge. I grin and walk up to her, my hands sliding around her waist.

"Why are you naked Celestia," I mumble as I slide the back of my hand down her arm and nibble on her neck.

"Nothing you haven't seen, and last time I checked, you did say I didn't need clothes," she says as she grabs the yogurt and whipped cream and closes the fridge.

"I never expected you to take that seriously but maybe I should keep you like this," I mumble again as I pick her up and place her on the counter. I stare down at her with a smile and she swipes a strawberry into the yogurt, adds a dip of whipped cream on it, and throws it into her mouth.

"Oh, I take your words very seriously. I do obey you after all," she says and bites another strawberry clean in half.

"Mm, yes you do, because if not, I'd punish you in any way I want. But it wouldn't be punishment would it since you love the pain, you naughty woman." I laugh.

"Your naughty woman."

"Yes, mine," I say and bend down to kiss her. She kisses me back with force as if she's been missing my lips all day.

I pick her up and carry my beautiful fiery goddess into the room at the end of the hall.

"You shouldn't have teased me," I say as I lay her on the bed.

"And why not sir?"

"Because now I'm gonna tie you up. Tonight you're going to be my sexy Andromeda, and I, your Perseus."

"But if you're tying me up doesn't that make you Cepheus?"

"I see you know your greek myths princess. But let's not be bratty now, or I'll fuck you so good, and just as you're about to come, I'll give you one last deep, hard, stroke, just to put you even more on edge, and then slip out of you. You'll be begging me to let you come."

"You wouldn't dare." she whimpers under me.

"Oh I would, so I wouldn't test me if I were you, princess," I say as I get up.

I grab two very long red ropes and move back to face her.

"Sit up on your knees and put your arms behind your back."

"Yes sir."

"Good girl," I reply and reward her with snagging teeth on her nipple. She moans and squirms against me.

I move to the bed and sit behind her, wrapping one of the ropes into a box tie around her breasts, her neck, and tying her arms back.

"Is this too tight princess?"

"No sir, it feels good."

I reward her again as I move her knees apart to expose her sex and slip a finger inside. She coils and slightly shivers.

"Princess, look at the ceiling mirror, look at me in it while I touch you," I whisper in her ear.

She nods and looks up, her mouth slightly ajar as I go in deeper. She starts to move her hips and I can feel her wet juices sliding down my finger. I pull out to put it in front of her.

"Suck," I say and she opens her mouth wider. Her mouth feels hot and sexy and I can just imagine how it would feel on my cock. I slip my finger out of her mouth and move from behind her.

"Lay back," I say as I go back into the drawers to grab another item.

When I turn around her eyes begin to glow with both curiosity and arousal as she sees the pole in my hand.

"Do you know what this is princess?"

"Kind of sir. I think I saw it in a movie once?"

"Interesting." I grin. "I'm going to attach this pole in between your legs, if you move, it'll spread your legs wider, got it?"

"Yes sir," she replies as I attach each end to her ankles. Once I'm finished she looks down and tugs. "Oh!" she then exclaims as the pole moves out a few inches on each side.

"I had a feeling you would do that." I chuckle as I get on the bed and tower over her. She looks at me with challenging eyes as if she has the power. I take the bar in my hands and pull at it just as she did. Her legs spread wider and I can see her juices dripping from her sex and onto the bed. I push it up so that her legs are now in the air.

I push it back until her feet touch the pillows and while keeping it up, I lick up her juices and she tries to squeeze her legs together but it was no use. I begin to drive her crazy as I suck on her nonstop. Her moans move across the room like music notes and I like a composer I want to hear more and more. I finally stop and release her from the restraining pole and grab the other rope.

"Bend your legs, princess."

"Yes, sir."

I take the second rope in my hand and tie her legs in a leg tie. She looks so beautiful as she sits here in front of me, silently begging me with her playful eyes.

"I would keep you like this all day," I whisper to her as I bite her soft skin. I then take off my clothes, giving her a full view, and she visibly swallows. "What do you wanna do princess?" I ask her.

"Suck you."

"You want what now?" I say as I get closer.

"I want to suck you, sir."

"Where, here?" I respond and touch my neck.

"No sir, right there."

"Where princess, say it."

"Your cock sir, let me suck your cock."

"As you wish princess."

I bring myself closer to her until her face meets my erection. She looks up at me as if asking for permission and I nod once. Her mouth immediately covers the tip of my cock and moves down. I tilt my head back and groan at the pleasure her hot mouth is giving me.

"God, princess, that feels so good."

Her head bobs up and down as she continues to swallow the rest of my length down to the back of her throat. She gags once it reaches and then moves her lips backward. She slides back down and I just love the way her tongue feels against my skin. I swear she makes me go crazy and lose my sanity. She moves faster as each second goes by and I can no longer keep it in. As I come, she swallows down on me.

"I have to bury myself in that sweet cunt of yours."|

I pull myself away, lay her down, and immediately push myself inside of her warm entrance.

"Fuck!" she screams.

"Yeah, princess,"

Her orgasm comes crashing down and I come again right behind her. I push myself in deeper, filling her with all I have. She feels so good wrapped around me.

Once she stops shaking, I turn her around and untie all the ropes from her legs and arms.

"Feel better?"

"Much." she smiles. "Now I'm tired."

"You should go to sleep princess. You have work tomorrow."

"And so do you, sleep with me."

"Of course princess, why would I not?"

"No, sleep inside me."

"As in-"

"I said what I said," she replies as she spreads her legs to me once more.

I think I just finally met my match.

Chapter 14

I wake up naked on top of Ramon and smile. He was still inside of me and I can feel my pussy throbbing around his cock as I remember last night. He was still asleep as I kissed his lips. I prop myself up, placing both of my hands on his chest. I start to roll my hips against him and he begins to stir inside of me. I slightly pick up the pace and his cock is now fully erect inside of me. Ramon is now awake and greets me with a smile.

"Good morning princess."

"Good morning handsome. How'd you sleep?"

"Like a child. But this, is a great way to wake up," he says as he flips us over and slowly pounds into me while his teeth snag at my breasts.

"Fuck, Ramon, you always seem to know exactly where to hit." I moan as my head tilts back onto the pillow and my back folds closer to him.

"Yes, princess, I could do this all day. I wanna know your body inside and out. I'm gonna invade each and every one of your holes, find each and every sensitive spot, and every time I fuck you, you won't know what'll be next to come. You're mine. And I don't plan on sharing you with anyone else." As he says these words, he moves inside of me faster, going harder with each long stroke and it drives me insane. I wrap my legs around his waist as he begins to slow back down and made sure he wasn't able to move.

"Come inside of me Ramon. Look at me while you do, fill me up until it spills out, and then do it all over again. Just. Don't. Stop. Don't ever stop."

"I fucking love that dirty little mouth of yours princess," he replies as he speeds up once more for a few seconds before it all comes down. And as he gives me one deep push, so deep, I can feel it in my stomach, he comes inside of me in quick thrusts. I can feel his warm liquid dripping out from me and he bends down to kiss me.

"Princess."

"Yes?"

"Be my girlfriend."

I laugh. "What happened to 'I don't do dating'?"

"I'm serious Celestia. I meant it when I said that I don't plan on sharing you with anyone else. I want you all to myself."

"Are you sure you're ready for the whole label thing?"

"Yeah, I'm fine with that, just as long as the world knows you're mine."

"You've just upset every female and male that has a crush on you."

"They'll live." he laughs and kisses me.

"Speaking of living, we both have a job to get to," I say.

"Right, let's go shower so we can leave princess."

"What're you up to right now, have you had your lunch yet babe?" Ramon asks me as he comes up to my desk.

"Shh school work, and no not yet, kinda busy."

"Come have lunch with me. You can finish it when we get home."

"This is due tomorrow, If I leave this, when I get home you're going to distract me," I say not daring to look up as I fight the smile on my face.

"Me? Distract you? Never." he smiles.

"Ugh, fine. I'm coming, but only because I'm hungry."

"Great, let's go," he says then turns to James. "James take care of here for me."

"I will, sir," he replies quickly.

I save all of my work, exit out of the window, and turn off my laptop. From the side of my eye, I can see James practically jumping in his seat with the urge to ask me so many questions. I never filled him or my other friends of my relationship status as of today and I already know he's going to tell Lucy.

"I'll see you later James, don't wait for me tonight."

"Oh, I won't. See ya later." he grins.

Ramon and I leave out of the building where his driver awaits.

"Drive us to the restaurant please."

His driver goes down the road and drives for about ten minutes or so. Once we get to the restaurant I look at the outside of it and gasp. It was breathtaking. Ramon takes my hand as we enter the building.

"Reservation for two, Osgood."

"Welcome Mr. Osgood, follow me please."

We follow the woman to a private table where the section was nearly empty. She took us to the furthest table in the back by the window and sat our menus down on the table and left.

"Babe, I am so underdressed." I say, placing my hand on his arm as I look at the other women with long slim dresses.

"That's the first time you've ever called me that. It sounds go good when you say it. But you look fine princess." he replies as he pulls me closer.

"Ha, you'll be hearing that a lot." I smile.

"Hi, my name is Sofia and I will be your server today, can I get you guys anything to drink?"

"May I get some ginger ale please?" I ask.

"Sure, and for you Mr.Osgood?"

"Just water for me is fine, thanks."

I watch as the woman stares him down and an awful feeling of jealousy arises in me. She finally leaves after taking the rest of our orders as well.

"What's wrong?"

"Nothing, why?"

"You were digging into my side."

"I was? Sorry."

"You're fine. But you didn't answer my question. What's wrong."

"Nothing baby, I'm fine, I just got a little jealous."

"Why?"

"She kept looking at you."

"Who, the waitress?"

"Yes, and it wasn't only her. I don't think you remember the effect you have on people."

"I'm aware. But I choose to ignore it. And you should too."

"It's kinda hard to when they're watching you like hawks," I say quietly under my breath as Sofia comes back with our drinks. I watch her intensely as she leans toward Ramon as she places them on the table a little too slow for me. What I notice is that her top two buttons from her shirt are now unbuttoned, letting her double D breasts spill out. I look to Ramon and find him not even looking her way, instead, his eyes are on me and his fingers are playing with the waist of my slacks. The feeling of jealousy goes away and I'm calm once again.

"I can hear that pretty head of yours comparing yourself to her. Don't do that princess, you're far more beautiful," he whispers in my ear. He was right, deep down I wish that I had even just half of her cup size to add onto my B cups. He then bites on my earlobe which sends a warm and electric feeling down my spine.

"Ramon." I quietly moan.

"Spread your legs for me," he whispers.

"We can't do this here baby, later."

"Oh yes, we can, open for me, baby."

The need gives in and I spread my legs apart under the table.

"Good girl," he says and moves his hands to slip it inside of my pants. I try not to squirm as he finds my clit and begins to rub at it slowly with his pointer finger while his middle fingers slide up and down in between my folds.

"I'm gonna make you come for me right here."

"Yes, yes, please make me come," I whisper breathlessly.

He pushes a finger inside and I press my lips together, my eyes rolling back.

"Does that feel good princess?"

"Yes,"

"Yes, what?"

"Yes, s-sir."

"Good girl," he whispers back. I whimper and moan as he moves his fingers faster and I squeeze my shaky legs together as I orgasm. He withdraws his hand and sucks on his middle and pointer finger as he looks me in the eye. I blush and turn my head away and he laughs, turning me to face him and giving me a small peck on the lips.

"If we were home I'd lick you clean but we don't want people wondering why I'm suddenly under the table and why you're moaning nonstop."

"If only." I smile at him.

Sofia finally shows up with our food and I can see two other waitresses that tailed along. They were taking plates off of tables but every second or so they dart their eyes towards us. I fight the urge to roll my eyes and shake my head.

"You ready to leave princess?" asks Ramon as I take the last sip of my ginger ale.

"Yeah, thank you for this."

"Anything for you," he replies.

We get up to leave and the second we step outside, something flashes right at me. Then more flashing with shouts being added along to it.

"Shit."

"Oh my God, Ramon, what is going on," I whisper.

"Mr. Osgood! Is this your girlfriend?"

"How old is she?"

"What is your name, young lady?"

"Aren't you his secretary?"

All these questions are being thrown at us and I start to feel dizzy.

"No comment." Ramon simply says and takes my hand. He pulls me along to where his driver was parking, waiting for us with the back door open. I go in first and Ramon goes in after me. His driver closes the door and goes gets in. Before he can drive away, one more flash gets directed towards us through the window and I flinch.

"Are you okay princess? I'm so sorry this happened. Someone must've called them."

"I'm fine, just a little shaken, but are you okay?"

"I'm fine, this is normal, the paparazzi are nothing but annoying and revolting."

"It's so weird, I've never seen them so up close. How do you deal with this?"

"I don't even know honestly. Take us home please Wyatt. And call the decoy."

"Home? I thought we were going back to work?"

"That's the last place we should be right now. They're probably traveling there as we speak. And

I bet you half of them are at my house right now. But it's fine I have another way in beside the front door."

"Okay."

When we get there, sure enough, there are people with cameras glued to their hands running towards the car. But not the one we were in. It was a car similar to it. We pass the house and turn onto a small road, then turn onto an even smaller roadway that led to the back of the house. Ramon takes my hand and pulls me out of the car. We walk to a door in the back and get in through there.

"Thank you, Wyatt."

"You're welcome, sir."

"Yes, Thank you so much."

"Anytime miss," he says as he drives away.

Ramon goes to the front and peeks through the window.

"Sometimes, they can be so stupid."

I laugh as I take off my heels. "True," I respond.

He turns around and picks me up, swinging me around.

"You're such a child." I smile.

"That's because you make me feel like one again." he grins and proceeds to bury his face into the split of my breasts.

"Ramon, come on, I have to change. You made me all wet remember?"

"I can make you wet again," he whispers.

I bite my lip and he gives me ass a slap that echoes the halls.

"I'll take that as a yes."

He carries me to our room and begins to pull everything off of me. I lay there bare for him and I can't help but feel a sense of confidence and sexiness. I love the way his eyes roam over me just as his hands and mouth do. He leaves no part of me untouched. And I love it. He stops and goes into a drawer and brings back some sort of rope with two velcro-like cuffs on each end. He fits them both around my ankles and then pulls the middle behind my neck. Now my legs are bent and spread out for him and I can't move them.

"Time to lick you clean like I said I'd do," he says then sucks on my clit hungrily.

"Fuck, Ramon, yes!" I scream.

I love the way he touches me. I feel so alive when he does. Imagine what this could be if only we'd talked sooner. When I'm with him, I feel like there is no one else and no worries of any kind.

Chapter 15

"C, you have to see this!" screams Stephanie as she runs over to me with a newspaper. She surprised me yesterday when I showed up at the club, Ramon kept his word and hired her as a waitress here.

I stare at the front page and nearly faint. There was a picture of Ramon and me on the front page, with us kissing at the restaurant we went to yesterday, and a smaller one on the side of us holding hands as we tried to avoid the paparazzi.

"Oh my God. This can't be happening."

"Why did you tell me!"

"I planned on telling you guys, it just slipped my mind."

"Come, Lucy and James are definitely waiting for this hot tea," she says as she grabs my hand and pulls me to the back room.

"Well, well, well."

"Don't look at me like that Lu," I whine. "I forgot to tell you yesterday."

"I saw it first here people! He took her out to lunch and they didn't even come back."

"Hush James. Let her tell her story."

"He's right, we did go out. We were going to go back to work and as soon as we left the restaurant they swarmed us so we went home instead but he knew they'd be there as well so he sent a decoy car to wait in the front while we went to the back and went in that way."

"Interesting."

"Notice how she says home and not his home." giggles Lucy.

"Omg! You're living together?" asks Stephanie.

"Y-yeah..."

"How's that like, How's he like? Let me leech on your romance please!" squeals Lucy with excitement.

"Alright!" I laugh. "I'll tell you while I change."

They hung onto my every word as I told them about the relationship between Ramon and me. What surprised me was when Lucy and Stephanie both agreed that I had the curiosity of BDSM in me. I guess I just denied it and told myself otherwise.

"You're on in two Cherry," says Kevin.

"Gotcha, I'll be out in a sec," I reply as I lace up my heel.

I walk out and get on stage to do my first number. The music starts and I spin around the pole with one hand, moving my legs slowly. When I stop spinning I get on the floor in front with my back facing the crowd. I slowly slide down with my legs spread and land in a middle split on the floor. The men in the front holler and slip bills into the sides of my panties.

BANG!

There was a loud gunshot that rang over the loud music followed by screaming. I quickly turn around and look towards the chaotic scene in front of me. Men and women ran out of side doors and seeing it made me panic. I quickly get up and run down the small stairs. Before I can make it through the back door, someone grabs me from behind.

"Why are you running away from your husband baby?"

I know that voice from anywhere.

"Let go of me you asshole!" I scream and slam the heel of my shoe against his knee.

"Argh! Fuck! You bitch!" he yells as his hands retreat from me to attend to his knee.

I run to the back and slam open the door to find the others still there.

"Go! Get out, there's a fucking shooter."

Their eyes go wide and they all panic and leave out of the back door as quickly as possible. I follow them out after I check the bathroom, making sure no one else was left behind.

"Sweetie! Where'd you run off too? I just wanna bring you home!" yells out Mike. Shit. I get back inside of the bathroom since he managed to come inside the back room. I back up into a stall and look up. There was a small window and I quickly take off my heels and step onto the toilet seat and push the window open. I push myself up and prop half of my body outside the window. I spot James with the girls and yell out his name.

"James!"

"C? Shit, hold on!" he says as he runs to me. "Just jump I'll catch you."

"Okay, hold o-"

"You're not going anywhere."

I scream as Mike grabs my waist and pulls me towards him from the inside.

"No!"

"Yes," he says as he pulls me out of the window and drags me out of the bathroom.

I fight him until I'm tired and can't fight anymore. My nails are broken and bloody from scratching at him and I give him one last hit before I feel myself passing out.

Chapter 16

"Dammit, where did he take her!" I yell as I knock over a large standing vase.

"Calm down, we'll find her. We have a picture of him, the police are searching, and everyone is helping," says Rose as she tries to calm me down.

"I know, but I can't leave her with that fucker for another second. You know that." I grit through my teeth, trying not to break anything else.

"We're going to find her Ramon, I know you won't leave any stone untouched in order to find her."

Hell, she is right. I won't be able to rest until my princess is back in my arms safe and sound. I take a deep breath in and rub at my restless eyes. Thinking of where he could've taken her. If this man wanted money, he could have it all. Suddenly my phone rings on the table, interrupting my thoughts. I answer it in one quick move.

"Ramon."

"Ah, great! She wasn't lying." says the voice on the other side.

"Dammit, where is she?"

"Somewhere safe, with me, her husband. She should've been with me all along. But instead, she met you and became corrupted. Now, I'm gonna get my Celestia back, my old, sweet, innocent, Celestia."

"Is it him? Keep him talking." mouths Rose as she uses her phone to record the conversation after I put it on speaker, and begins to rapidly type on her computer, just far away enough for him not to hear the keys.

"Mike, we can work this out. There's no need to forcefully take her to get your way-"

"It was the only way! She's been so hypnotized by you and your perverted ways, she isn't the same Celestia anymore! I'm gonna fix her, you'll see!"

I couldn't get another word in before he hung up the phone.

"Piece of shit!" I yell slamming the palm of my hand against the desk.

"I'm sending the recording to the police right now," says Rose.

"I need to find her. Like now. That sicko is most likely going to torture or even worse rape her."

I struggled to get those last words out of my mouth. It left a bad taste in my mouth and a very bad feeling in me that I did not want to surface.

"I'm leaving. Please tell me if you find anything new." I told Rose as I stood up.

"Of course! Go home, get some rest. You haven't slept."

"I can't every time I close my eyes all I can see is her and when I open them she isn't fucking there."

"I know," she replies and pulls me in for a hug. She kisses my cheek and pats the same area with her hand and smiles. "I promise you, they will find her. The ones who are in love will always find each other. No matter how far."

"S-she said sh-"

"I'm not talking about her Ramon. I'm talking about you."

"I'm not-"

"Shh, don't worry about it, go home." she smiles.

I sigh, take my phone off the desk, and leave out the door. I drive home, speeding through lights and stop signs, not being able to care any less. Once I get home I scowl as I enter the kitchen. I drop my keys on the counter and head into the bedroom. I frown even more. Everything here reminds me of her. I go and take a cold shower and don't leave out of it until I'm near damn freezing. I get into my bed and lay there facing the ceiling. There is no way I can go to sleep now.

My phone rings from my nightstand and I quickly snatch it.

"R-Ramon."

"Shit! Baby are you okay? Where are you?"

"I don't have much t-time. H-he might be here any minute but he ha-has me in his old home. S-somewhere far, F-find L-Lucy and ask her about Mike she can-"

"Oh, you're a very naughty wife, Celestia. I didn't give you phone privileges hon, put the phone down and come here. Daddy wants to play now."

"Don't touch me! DON'T TOUCH ME!"

The phone cuts off and I can hear my heavy breathing. I scramble out of bed and grab the nearest pants and shirt I can find, throwing them on while slipping on boots. I grab my pistol in the safe in my closet and check the number of bullets it had. As I place it against my back, under my shirt, I dial Kevin's number and thankfully he answers on the first ring.

"Ramon? Are you okay? Did you find her?"

"Not yet, do me a favor. I need to talk to Lucinda. Is she at the club?"

"No she's at home right now, I closed the club for a couple of days."

"Okay, send me her address, please. She might know something of Celestia's whereabouts."

"Got it. Sending as we speak."

"Thank you, Kevin."

I hang up, grab my keys that I dropped on the kitchen counter, and leave. Once I get the address I speed over to her apartment which was close by. I climb up the stairs to the fourth floor, skipping steps. When I get to her door I bang against it hard. She opens the door and stares at me in shock.

"Oh my god! Did you find her?"

"No, but she found a phone and called me but that bastard found her with it. She said to talk to you. Something about Mike's old home."

When I said that, her eyes grew wide, and gestured for me to come inside. I couldn't sit down, I was too shaky so I paced around as she talked.

"We need to get you on a plane fast. She's all the way in Tennessee."

"Tennessee? How the fuck?"

"Yeah, he owns a home there but doesn't use it much. I have the address but the sooner you get on a plane, the better. Take James with you just knock on the next door to the right, Mike is a dangerous man. He has counts of abuse under his belt."

"Gotcha, I'll take my jet then, I might get there faster. Anything else I need to know?"

"I'll tell you more when you're on your way there. I know how to get in and out of his house without being seen. That man needs help Ramon, he's a two-faced lying bastard who takes advantage of women. Celestia fell for his charm and that's what made them date in the first place. He broke up with her and they were always on and off. When he broke up with her for good, she was a mess. That's when I met her at the club when James brought her in. Please, Ramon, find her and bring her back. I can't lose my best friend over him."

"Don't worry, I will. Thank you." I say and leave. I then knock at the door next to hers and it immediately opens.

"The walls are thin. I heard everything. Let's go." says James.

We run down the stairs and leave the building, running to my car. Once we're inside, I speed again through the nearly empty streets. When we get to the airport, we find my jet ready and waiting for us.

"Are we just gonna barge in there?"

"No, Lucinda said she knew how to get in and out without him knowing."

"Ah, gotcha. I hope to God she's safe, that's my best friend right there."

"Lucinda also mentioned something about you meeting her and bringing her to the club, is that how she ended up working there?"

"Yeah, I was on my way there one night and I saw her with a practically finished bottle of alcohol, walking in the empty streets. That was the day Mike broke up with her as well. I asked her to come with me so she could sober up and be safe for the night, so I took her to the club, Lucy took care of her and convinced her not to give a fucking crap about him anymore. Celestia changed that night, she never talked to men, she saw them simply as toys in a chess game that she could bend to her will, and she used stripping as a method of luring them in. Although it gave the club a great boost, I could tell that she wasn't herself behind the whole confidence charade. She wanted more money to go to school so I also gave her the application to be your secretary when you needed one."

"I see. Thank you for that. Otherwise, I would've never met her. She's an amazing woman."

"That she is."

"How much do you like her?" says James through the thick silence.

"A lot."

"I can tell, I've seen you with many women, and none of them have managed to last as long as her. What's so special about her to you?"

"She just makes me feel, me, I know it sounds cheesy or whatever but it's true."

"No, I get it. You like her. You got it bad."

"Ha, I guess I do." I chuckle.

I think losing Celestia made me become sensitive and wear my heart on my sleeve. First Rose and now James have called out my feelings out for her. I didn't want to think about it right now, all I was currently worried about bringing my princess home safe.

Chapter 17

Celestia

I'm cold, hungry, tired, and more importantly fed up. I rock back and forth in a corner and look at the clock on the wall in front of me. I'm still wearing the same sheer outfit from when he took me. He refused to give me any clothing because he likes to come home and see me like this. I think I've been here for a day now? Two? I'm not sure. I really hope Ramon heard me and he's on his way here.

"Wifey! I'm home! Have you been a good girl for me?"

I put my head down to my knees, refusing to look at his face. He comes into the room and yanks my hair, forcefully making me look at him.

"Look at me when I talk to you bitch! Now, aren't you happy to see your husband?"

"I'm being treated like an animal by you as I'm in chains, I haven't changed in days, and you want me to be happy to see you? Are you out of your fucking mind?"

Anger flashes in his eyes and his palm connects with my cheek, making a sound that echoed the walls. My eyes begin to water and his anger turns to concern. He rubs my cheek gently.

"I'm sorry, baby, you just made daddy very upset. Come here. Let me make you feel good." he says as he takes off my chain and picks me up from the ground. I put all my weight down and stay loose to make myself heavy.

"Come on baby. get up!"

He managed to pick me up and throw me over his shoulder. I scream and kick against him but nothing works. He throws me onto the bed and climbs over me as he licks his lips. I squirm under his hold as he pulls my panties down and touches me. I start to cry and thankfully he stops.

"Awe, my love, what's wrong? Why're you crying?"

"Get off of me!"

"I'll do whatever I want with you." he spits out.

"No, the fuck you will not."

"Talk back to me one more time and I'll make you regret it. Let's go." He snarks as he throws me over his shoulder once more and takes me out of the room. I try to look for the door that led outside, mentally planning on how to escape but from my dim memories, I think we were near the back of the house. He takes me out the back door and I push against him, trying to break free from his hold. I scream out for someone to help me until my throat is dry and I feel like I can no longer breathe.

"Shut up! You're so goddamn annoying, no one can hear you."

It was worth a try.

He takes me into the large barn at the side of his house and throws me to the ground. My shoulder rubs against the old wooden floor and I get a few splinters. I wince and struggle to pick myself up. With the strength I manage to gain, I grab an old pipe next to me and swing as hard as I can. I miss and he grabs me, pulling away from the pipe from my hand.

"Don't do that, that wasn't nice," he growls as he grabs a rope and slams me down in a chair. He wraps the rope around me tight and makes sure that I had no inch left to move.

"Look at these," he says and removes the large sheet that covered the other half of the barn.

"LOOK AT THEM!" He repeats loudly and goes behind me, jerking my head up to force me to look at the pictures in front of me.

Pictures were hanging everywhere on strings, taped to the walls, laying on desks. They all were pictures of me, Ramon, and the both of us together. All the way back to that day when Ramon first met Cherry at the club. There were pictures of us in our homes. I gasp when I look at a specific one and realize that it was the day when the paparazzi were surrounding the house. Mike had been following me for a long time. And these pictures proved it.

"What the fuck is wrong with you."

"Why won't you love me the way you love him? Huh? Why can he touch you, yet I can't. You're my wife, not his. He doesn't want you. He's just using you. Rich guys like him only want girls like you for sex. And look at that shit you call a job. Showing off your body for money? It's disgusting. But don't worry, I'll fix you."

"Keep his name out of your dirty fucking mouth psycho. You know nothing about him. And what I do with my life is none of your business, I can do whatever the hell I want."

He kicks the chair and I fall flat on my face. Then he puts his foot on the back of the chair and presses down.

"Shut your mouth."

I grunt under him and my head begins to hurt.

"I will not tolerate this disrespect from my wife like this."

"Stop saying I'm your wife! You're delusional and crazy.

You broke up with me, remember that? It wasn't the other way around. We never even talked about marriage in the first place. I don't know if you fell down a couple flights of stairs or something but you need to get it through your thick head that I don't belong to you!"

"SHUT UP! SHUT UP! SHUT UP! DAMMIT!"

My eyes widen as he pulls out a knife from his pocket and bends down towards me.

"I love you, Celestia! I'm sorry, that was wrong of me to break up with you. It was a mistake. I-I needed help. So I left and got it. But now I'm back, and I wanna make things right again. But you won't let me! You're making this hard for the both of us. I don't wanna hurt you, baby, you know that! Now, come on baby. let's go back in the house, I'll make you feel good."

I calm down slightly when he puts the knife away. He picks up the chair and unties me, but still keeps the rough rope around me so I couldn't move. He drags me back into the house, back to the room, and throws me on the bed. He rips off my bra and starts to fondle with my breasts as he leans in to kiss me.

"Stop! Please Mike stop it!"

"But I thought you liked this sort of thing, especially with ropes."

"P-please, just s-stop." I cry.

BANG!

A loud gunshot goes off and I look towards the door, and I have never been so happy. Both Ramon and James were in front of the door with guns in hand.

"How the hell did you get here!" yells Mike.

"That's none of your business, give us Celestia. No one has to get hurt," replies James.

"No! She's mine!"

"I don't think you understand what's going on here. we didn't give you a choice in this matter. Now, I'm fed up, tired, and pissed off and I'm this close to blowing your fucking brain out. Celestia isn't your fucking wife, never was, and never will be. She doesn't belong to you." says Ramon through his tightened jaw.

This was my chance to get him off me while he was distracted. I slowly move my leg up then harshly kick at his stomach. I can hear something crack as he falls off of the bed and to the floor. He screams out in pain and I scurry out of the awful bed, right into Ramon's arms. The tears begin to fall out of extreme happiness. I don't think I could ever handle this trauma ever again.

Chapter 18

Ramon and I were laying on the bed for what seemed like hours. After he pretty much gave me the best sex I've ever had, he coddled me like a baby and whispered sweet nothings in my ears until I fell asleep. When I woke up, his arms were wrapped around me and when I looked at him our eyes met and he softly smiled.

"Good morning princess,"

"Good morning my Casanova," I reply as I pull him close to kiss him.

"Are you sore?"

I shrug and lift myself up, letting the sheet fall off of me, my legs begin to twitch and in between my legs throbbed.

"Yep, looks like it. Is it bad that I wanna do that again?" I say as I place myself on top of him.

"Yes, and no." he laughs. "But that's enough for you today, if you had any more, I'd have to carry you out."

"Maybe, but it'd be worth it." I smile. "What time is it anyway?"

"Last time I checked it was around nine-thirty AM."

"We've been here for fourteen hours?! Ramon!"

"What? It's not like we fucked during all of them." he grins.

I shake my head and him, smiling as well.

"What do you wanna do today princess?"

"No work today then?"

"Fuck work, it can wait."

"Hmm, I don't really know what I wanna do, honestly I'm fine with going anywhere, as long as I'm with you," I say as I lay on his chest then quickly get up.

"Damn even my boobs are sore," I whine as I rub them with my palm.

"You chose the clamps, not me." he laughs.

"Yeah, yeah. I should put them on you, see how it feels."

He bursts out in laughter even more and I swat his chest.

"Alright, we should go now," he says.

I nod in agreement and move off of him, gently standing up. I look around for my undergarments but they're nowhere in sight.

"Babe, where did my things go?"

"Right here," he says as he lifts them up. He tosses them over to me and I frown at the little pieces in my hand.

"They're shredded to pieces."

"I know." he smiles. "That's why while you were asleep I went out and got you another pair."

"You're proud of yourself aren't you?"

"Yes, I am," he says as he gives me the pair he bought and a light pink dress.

"What's the dress for?" I state as I put the undergarments on the bed and pick up the dress.

"We're going to the beach for brunch."

"The beach? There's no beach here."

"I know, we're going to Virginia."

"As in now?"

"Yep," he replies as he grabs two towels from the dresser and hands one over to me.

"Come take a shower with me," he says.

"There are showers here?" I question.

"Yep, for the ones with shower fantasies." he winks.

"Oh," I blush.

He takes me by the hand and I follow him out of the room and down the hall to the left. As a woman walks by with a man. I can't help but look at the cuffs on her hands and the clamps on he breasts. As the male drags her along, I notice the look in her eyes, how she looks at him in awe. It reminds me of myself. Then I quickly realize that I was naked. Ramon has made me so comfortable with my own body that I haven't thought about others. When we get to the bathroom, he turns on the showerhead and we wait for the water to get warm. When it is, we both get inside him behind me. He massages my shoulders, my breasts, my waist. I lean against him and sigh. He kisses my collar bone, pulls me closer, and drags his hands down my chest. His hands roam my body, very gentle as if he's trying to memorize every part of me. His fingers trace all of my curves and they glide ever so faintly on my palms, slightly tickling them which sends a calming feeling down my arm to my spine and down to my legs. I felt at ease.

Ramon finishes putting on his matching white short-sleeved button-down and shorts. He left the shirt open to show off his very toned stomach which I loved dragging my hands all over. The dress he got me was in a bohemian style and it was long and very flowy.

After I put on the dress, he brings up a pair of white block heel shoes. I try to take it from him but he shakes his head and takes my hand in his, guiding me to the bed and gesturing for me to sit down. When I do, he takes my leg and slips on the shoes for me, and buckles the straps as well.

"Thank you."

"Of course, my princess deserves the best," he whispers as he takes my hand again and he grabs my phone from the dresser and hands it over to me. He takes his and puts it in his pocket.

"You ready?"

"Ready as I'll ever be." I smile as he opens the door and we leave the room.

When we get downstairs, we spot Rose sitting on the bar counter in the corner, chatting up a storm with the person behind it.

"Ahh, I see you two finally decided to emerge into the real world."

"Well hello to you too Rose." I laugh.

"He did a number on you didn't he." she giggles. "You look like you're having trouble getting down here."

I blush as I smile and hook my arm around Ramon's.

"Don't you have somewhere to be Rose? Why're you still here?"

"You weren't the only one fucking like rabbits last night," she smirks. "Where are y'all headed?"

"The beach," Ramon replies to her.

"That's sweet, have fun!" says Rose as she hops off the counter and saunters away.

"Bye Rose," I say as Ramon and I leave the building.

He drives us to the airport and I see his driver waiting for us near it.

"Hello, Wyatt." greets Ramon as he steps onto the jet.

"Good morning sir,"

"Hi Wyatt, are you taking us to Virginia?"

"Yes, I am ma'am."

"Oh please, call me Celestia, I hate being called ma'am, makes me feel old." I smile.

Ramon pulls me up and I look around once I'm inside.

"So this is what the inside of a jet looks like."

"Yeah. I haven't used it much," he says as he holds onto me.

Wyatt goes to the front and soon the jet starts.

"What else do you do Wyatt?" I ask him as he sits in the chair across from Ramon and me.

"Besides, being Ramon's driver and pilot, I'm actually a stay-at-home dad."

"Oh really?"

"Yeah, I have two daughters and a son."

"How cute! May you tell me about them?"

"Sure, I have pictures of them as well, if you'd like to see them."

"Omg, yes!" I exclaim as I move over to sit in the seat next to him.

"Here is little Mateo, he's three."

"He's so adorable, he looks exactly like you."

"Yeah, that's what everyone says. I think he has his mother's eyes though. This is is Luna, she's six and a very artistic girl, she's the one who looks exactly like her mother."

"Your wife must be gorgeous then, because she is so beautiful, what's that in her hair?"

"That's paint." laughs Wyatt. "There's not one day where I don't take my time taking it out of her hair. And lastly, this is Evelyn

Veazey, our new addition to the family. She was born a week ago. Ramon got her the onesie she's wearing right now."

"Awe, congrats! She is so precious, He does have good taste in clothing." I laugh. "Ramon, look at her tiny hands. May I?" I say as I ask Wyatt for his phone. He nods and hands it over to me and I show the picture to Ramon.

"She's very adorable Wyatt, congrats," smiles Ramon as he hands over the phone.

"God, I can't wait to have a daughter of my own, I'm gonna spoil her crazy." I sigh as I wonder what it would be like to be a mother.

"I'm sure you'll have beautiful children someday."

"I hope so," I smile and get up, making my way to my seat again. Ramon pats his lap and I go to him.

"Sir, we're here," states Wyatt as he checks his phone and gets up to go back to the front of the jet.

"Great, thank you," says Ramon as he buries his face in my neck.

When we land he takes my hand and we get out of the jet after Wyatt. A bright red open-top Ferrari Portofino waits for us at the bottom and Ramon opens the passenger side for me.

"Wyatt."

"Yes sir?"

"Come and join us, I have something for you at the beach."

"Okay,"

Ramon gets in the driver's seat as Wyatt hops in the back and then we're off.

Chapter 19

I love you? I didn't mean for it to slip out like that. My heart beats faster as I look towards her. She falls asleep fast, she might've not heard me. I sigh and close my eyes in relief, as I see her sleeping. I wanted to find the right time to tell her. But now is not the time. I don't wanna scare her away.

"You're gonna do amazing," I tell her for the hundredth time as I drive her to the university.

"I know, I practiced my presentation over and over so I'll be fine. I'm just worried about what my professor will think."

"Professor Finn is a kind man, and I think he'll give you a good grade."

"Let's hope so," she mumbles as I park.

She kisses me before she gets out of the car and I watch her walk up to the building. Once she makes it safely inside, I feel calm and turn up the music on the radio as I back out of the parking.

I keep thinking about how to tell her how I feel, but knowing me I might mess things up. I am so damn afraid to lose her, it always feels as if she has one foot out in this relationship, and any little thing I do that might upset her could end it all. And I don't want that to happen.

"Babe! Are you okay?"

I zone back in and I'm met with a concerned look on her face.

"Sorry, zoned out for a bit, just thinking."

"About?" she says as she buckles her seatbelt.

"Nothing really, how was your presentation?"

"It was weird talking about it and all but I think it went great, that's a relief." she smiles.

"See I told you that you'd be fine princess," I reply as I pull her in and kiss her forehead.

"Yeah, yeah, you did." she mocks.

I laugh lightly and back out of the parking.

"Do you want to go out to eat?" I ask.

"No, I think I'll just eat at home later, I'm not really hungry anyway." she shrugs.

"Alright then," I reply smiling to myself.

"You went shopping?" she asks as she looks at the bags in front of her feet.

"Yes, those are for you."

"Ooh, really?" and she starts to lunge for them.

"Not so fast, you can open them when you get home princess."

"No fair, you should've placed them in the back where I couldn't have seen them."

"Too late now," I laugh.

Before she could get out of the car when I parked in the driveway, I swoop her up into my arms and toss her over my shoulder before I go to unlock the front door.

"Ramon! Put me down!" she gasps.

"No can do, I'm hungry."

"What does that have to do with me?" she questions as I take her to the kitchen and place her on the counter along with the bags.

"Everything," I grin.

She gets the hint and smiles at me, biting her bottom lip.

"Well, I'm all yours."

"Not yet though. You can open your bags now."

"Is it a puppy?"

"Now why would a puppy be in a bag?"

"You never know," she laughs as she takes the first bag and pulls out a box.

She carefully unties the bow on the box and sets it aside. When she opens the cover she gasps at the pair of shoes.

"These are gorgeous! You shouldn't have."

"I know but I saw them and thought of you so I bought them for you."

"Thank you," she says as she plants a large kiss on me.

"You're welcome, but you're not done yet," I say as I hand her the other bag.

She takes it from my hand and pulls out another large box similar to the one before.

"More shoes?"

"Nope, something else, maybe it is the puppy." I grin.

"Ha, ha, very funny." she smiles, shaking her head at me.

She opens the box, looks down at the sheer garments and looks back at me.

"What's this for?"

"Something for tonight." I wink as I take the box from her and put it to the side.

"What's tonight?"

"I want to take you back to the club, I still haven't shown you everything yet."

"There's more?"

"So much more," I whisper and kiss her neck.

"When are we going?"

"Later, right now I'm still hungry."

"I can make you something, what would you like?"

"You," I say and spread her legs apart.

She looks at me with gleaming eyes and slips off her top, bearing her bra-held breasts that are ready to burst out.

"Did your boobs get bigger?"

"I don't think so," she says looking down at them. "Do they look bigger? It might be the bra, why are you complaining?" she grins.

"Not complaining sweetheart, I think this might be my favorite bra," I say as I crook my finger in the middle and pull it down, freeing both of them. I put my mouth over one and she gasps.

"Don't stop Ramon." she moans.

"I would take you right here, right now, on this counter. But it might be a little uncomfortable." I smile.

"Then what are you waiting for? You don't need an invitation to throw me over your shoulder and bring me to that room of yours," she replies as she wraps her legs around me and uses it to pull me closer.

"I think we should just head over to the club now then, there are plenty more things to play with."

"Well, let's go then," she says as she flicks up my chin with her finger.

As we enter the club, Rose spots her and runs toward us.

"Oh my goodness Celestia you're back!" she shouts as she brings her in for a tight hug.

"Hi Rose," she replies to her.

"Are you okay? When did you get back?"

"About three days ago."

"And you didn't bring her earlier?" says Rose as she whirls around to face me.

I put my hands up in defeat and shrug.

"It's all good Rose, all that matters is that I'm back."

"Well, I'm glad to see you safe and sound. This man right here went to hell and back trying to find you." Rose replied as she gave me a wink.

"Alright, unhand my girl, I want her back now,"

"You're never any fun." Rose pouts as she lets go of Celestia. "See you later lovebirds." she then says smiling and walks away to the back room where she came from.

I take Celestia upstairs but into a different room, one that was much larger than the other rooms down the hall where you could hear loud moans and the sound of whips.

"This room is different," she noted.

"Yeah, this is my personal room. No one comes up here but me."

"It's bigger than the others. What's that for?"

"That means more space for me to toss you around, and that right there, is a sex swing," I say as I move behind her.

"Will we be using that tonight?"

"I'm not sure, that depends on how far you're willing to go. I just got you back, I'm sure you're still a little uncomfortable with all this."

"With you, never," she whispers as she turns around to face me.

I smile at her, thinking to myself, how on God's green earth did I get so lucky to meet a woman like her. I take both of her hands in mine, entwining our fingers together, and pull her closer to my chest. I kiss her softly then gently bite on the bottom of her lip and she melts into me. I pick her up and move her onto the bed. As she's under me, I look at her and the rise and fall of her chest.

"No smart remarks or backtalks today?" I ask her.

"None at all." she shakes her head as she chews against her bottom lip.

"Good. Cause tonight, I'm going to taste every single part of your body, I'm going to push your limits as much as I can, and I'm going to make you feel every beautiful sensation there is.

"Then what are you waiting for?" she whispers.

"I just need to ask you one question first."

"What is it?"

"Did you hear me say anything last night?"

"Um, not that I recall, no, why?"

"No reason," I say and kiss her forehead.

Chapter 20

Ramon and I were laying on the bed for what seemed like hours. After he pretty much gave me the best sex I've ever had, he coddled me like a baby and whispered sweet nothings in my ears until I fell asleep. When I woke up, his arms were wrapped around me and when I looked at him our eyes met and he softly smiled.

"Good morning princess,"

"Good morning my Casanova," I reply as I pull him close to kiss him.

"Are you sore?"

I shrug and lift myself up, letting the sheet fall off of me, my legs begin to twitch and in between my legs throbbed.

"Yep, looks like it. Is it bad that I wanna do that again?" I say as I place myself on top of him.

"Yes, and no." he laughs. "But that's enough for you today, if you had any more, I'd have to carry you out."

"Maybe, but it'd be worth it." I smile. "What time is it anyway?"

"Last time I checked it was around nine-thirty AM."

"We've been here for fourteen hours?! Ramon!"

"What? It's not like we fucked during all of them." he grins.

I shake my head and him, smiling as well.

"What do you wanna do today princess?"

"No work today then?"

"Fuck work, it can wait."

"Hmm, I don't really know what I wanna do, honestly I'm fine with going anywhere, as long as I'm with you," I say as I lay on his chest then quickly get up.

"Damn even my boobs are sore," I whine as I rub them with my palm.

"You chose the clamps, not me." he laughs.

"Yeah, yeah. I should put them on you, see how it feels."

He bursts out in laughter even more and I swat his chest.

"Alright, we should go now," he says.

I nod in agreement and move off of him, gently standing up. I look around for my undergarments but they're nowhere in sight.

"Babe, where did my things go?"

"Right here," he says as he lifts them up. He tosses them over to me and I frown at the little pieces in my hand.

"They're shredded to pieces."

"I know." he smiles. "That's why while you were asleep I went out and got you another pair."

"You're proud of yourself aren't you?"

"Yes, I am," he says as he gives me the pair he bought and a light pink dress.

"What's the dress for?" I state as I put the undergarments on the bed and pick up the dress.

"We're going to the beach for brunch."

"The beach? There's no beach here."

"I know, we're going to Virginia."

"As in now?"

"Yep," he replies as he grabs two towels from the dresser and hands one over to me.

"Come take a shower with me," he says.

"There are showers here?" I question.

"Yep, for the ones with shower fantasies." he winks.

"Oh," I blush.

He takes me by the hand and I follow him out of the room and down the hall to the left. As a woman walks by with a man. I can't help but look at the cuffs on her hands and the clamps on he breasts. As the male drags her along, I notice the look in her eyes, how she looks at him in awe. It reminds me of myself. Then I quickly realize that I was naked. Ramon has made me so comfortable with my own body that I haven't thought about others. When we get to the bathroom, he turns on the showerhead and we wait for the water to get warm. When it is, we both get inside him behind me. He massages my shoulders, my breasts, my waist. I lean against him and sigh. He kisses my collar bone, pulls me closer, and drags his hands down my chest. His hands roam my body, very gentle as if he's trying to memorize every part of me. His fingers trace all of my curves and they glide ever so faintly on my palms, slightly tickling them which sends a calming feeling down my arm to my spine and down to my legs. I felt at ease.

Ramon finishes putting on his matching white short-sleeved button-down and shorts. He left the shirt open to show off his very toned stomach which I loved dragging my hands all over. The dress he got me was in a bohemian style and it was long and very flowy.

After I put on the dress, he brings up a pair of white block heel shoes. I try to take it from him but he shakes his head and takes my hand in his, guiding me to the bed and gesturing for me to sit down. When I do, he takes my leg and slips on the shoes for me, and buckles the straps as well.

"Thank you."

"Of course, my princess deserves the best," he whispers as he takes my hand again and he grabs my phone from the dresser and hands it over to me. He takes his and puts it in his pocket.

"You ready?"

"Ready as I'll ever be." I smile as he opens the door and we leave the room.

When we get downstairs, we spot Rose sitting on the bar counter in the corner, chatting up a storm with the person behind it.

"Ahh, I see you two finally decided to emerge into the real world."

"Well hello to you too Rose." I laugh.

"He did a number on you didn't he." she giggles. "You look like you're having trouble getting down here."

I blush as I smile and hook my arm around Ramon's.

"Don't you have somewhere to be Rose? Why're you still here?"

"You weren't the only one fucking like rabbits last night," she smirks. "Where are y'all headed?"

"The beach," Ramon replies to her.

"That's sweet, have fun!" says Rose as she hops off the counter and saunters away.

"Bye Rose," I say as Ramon and I leave the building.

He drives us to the airport and I see his driver waiting for us near it.

"Hello, Wyatt." greets Ramon as he steps onto the jet.

"Good morning sir,"

"Hi Wyatt, are you taking us to Virginia?"

"Yes, I am ma'am."

"Oh please, call me Celestia, I hate being called ma'am, makes me feel old." I smile.

Ramon pulls me up and I look around once I'm inside.

"So this is what the inside of a jet looks like."

"Yeah. I haven't used it much," he says as he holds onto me.

Wyatt goes to the front and soon the jet starts.

"What else do you do Wyatt?" I ask him as he sits in the chair across from Ramon and me.

"Besides, being Ramon's driver and pilot, I'm actually a stay-at-home dad."

"Oh really?"

"Yeah, I have two daughters and a son."

"How cute! May you tell me about them?"

"Sure, I have pictures of them as well, if you'd like to see them."

"Omg, yes!" I exclaim as I move over to sit in the seat next to him.

"Here is little Mateo, he's three."

"He's so adorable, he looks exactly like you."

"Yeah, that's what everyone says. I think he has his mother's eyes though. This is is Luna, she's six and a very artistic girl, she's the one who looks exactly like her mother."

"Your wife must be gorgeous then, because she is so beautiful, what's that in her hair?"

"That's paint." laughs Wyatt. "There's not one day where I don't take my time taking it out of her hair. And lastly, this is Evelyn

Veazey, our new addition to the family. She's ten months old. Ramon got her the onesie she's wearing right now."

"Awe, congrats! She is so precious, He does have good taste in clothing." I laugh. "Ramon, look at her tiny hands. May I?" I say as I ask Wyatt for his phone. He nods and hands it over to me and I show the picture to Ramon.

"She's very adorable Wyatt, congrats," smiles Ramon as he hands over the phone.

"God, I can't wait to have a daughter of my own, I'm gonna spoil her crazy." I sigh as I wonder what it would be like to be a mother.

"I'm sure you'll have beautiful children someday."

"I hope so," I smile and get up, making my way to my seat again. Ramon pats his lap and I go to him.

"Sir, we're here," states Wyatt as he checks his phone and gets up to go back to the front of the jet.

"Great, thank you," says Ramon as he buries his face in my neck.

When we land he takes my hand and we get out of the jet after Wyatt. A bright red open-top Ferrari Portofino waits for us at the bottom and Ramon opens the passenger side for me.

"Wyatt."

"Yes sir?"

"Come and join us, I have something for you at the beach."

"Okay,"

Ramon gets in the driver's seat as Wyatt hops in the back and then we're off.

Chapter 21

"This beach is so beautiful Ramon!" exclaims Celestia as we walk up to the house on the sand. If only she knew that the real beauty here was her. Only her. As she looks around, I gesture for Wyatt to come to the door. He looks at me confused but walks to me anyway. I hand him over the key and tilt my head towards the door.

"Open it. There's something for you inside."

"Sir, you've given me everything and more, there's no need."

"It's not an item, well the first part isn't. Just go inside." I smile.

He takes a breath and unlocks the door.

"Surprise!"

"Hi, daddy!" screams Luna as she runs to her father's feet.

Wyatt looks at me shocked.

"How did you-"

"You thought this wonderful man would forget about your birthday?"

"Aurora, my love is that you?"

"Yeah, baby, I'm here too," she says as she emerges from the kitchen with Evelyn in hand.

He rushes over to her and kisses her tenderly. Aurora looks at me as Wyatt takes the baby out of her hands and she mouths a thank you. I nod at her and before I turn to find Celestia, her arms wrap around me.

"That was very sweet of you," she whispers behind me.

"His wife told me that he hadn't celebrated his birthday in years and she wanted to do something special for him this year, so I brought them here."

"He'll remember this birthday forever." she smiles as she waves at Aurora who is now coming towards us.

"Thank you, Ramon, he's so happy. I can never thank you enough."

"It's no problem Aurora, where's Mateo by the way?"

"Oh!" shouts Celestia.

We all turn to see Mateo holding a small crab in his hands. He was smiling, showing his missing tooth.

"There you are, Matty. Look at you, you're all dirty with sand."

Aurora moves around us and picks up Mateo.

"Hi, Mr.Osy!

"Hi, buddy." I smile as I give him a high five.

"So this is the amazing Mateo, I've heard about." smiles Celestia as she waves at him.

"I am amazing, I am!" he squeals and laughs. He holds his hands out to her and Aurora hands him over.

"What's your name?"

"I'm Celestia,"

"Are you princess Celestia from My Little Pony?" he says as his eyes go wide.

"No, she's way better than me. I don't have any wings, see?"

As we all go inside and Aurora taps my arm.

"Is she it?"

"What do you mean?" I question her as I watch Celestia play with Mateo.

"Is she the one, I mean. Let's not forget you had a reputation with women, everyone saw you both on the front page. And I haven't seen you with anyone new. She's your secretary right?"

"Yeah, she is."

"And does she live with you now?"

"Yes,"

"And she knows about your sexual lifestyle,"

"I-"

"I'm not dumb Ramon, I have eyes. I can see the faint cuff marks on her wrists."

"Yeah, she's into it."

"Then what are you waiting for? When you asked me to set up the back of the house for you, I knew that you were head over heels."

"What do you mean by that?"

"You're clearly in love with the girl."

I take a deep breath and look at her.

"I am. But I don't know how to bring it up to her."

"Just tell her. There's never a perfect time Ramon. But all I'm going to say is that when you say it, make sure you mean it."

"I will," I reply just as Celestia comes up to us.

"You ready to leave princess?"

"You're a princess?!" brightens Luna as she comes in with Wyatt. "Mom I wanna be a princess too!"

"You are a princess sweetie, you're my princess."

"Where are we going?" asks Celestia.

"Next door."

"Next door?"

"Yep," I say as I take her hand.

"Bye-bye CC!" shouts Mateo.

"Bye, sweetie!"

"You must be hungry," I say once we get outside.

"A little yeah."

"Sorry, I just wanted to give Wyatt his gift first.

"It's all good. I enjoyed my time with the kids."

I take her into the other beach house next door and bring her out to the back. Aurora had placed lanterns everywhere and the small table was adorned with flowers.

"Wow, this is so pretty."

I pull out her chair and she sits down.

"Thank you."

"You're welcome," I reply. "Don't move I'll be right back,"

She nods and I go back inside to find aurora bringing in the food just in time.

"Thank you again for this."

"Anytime Ramon, remember what I said earlier."

"I know, I'm thinking about it."

"Good, I'll talk to you later," she says as she walks out.

I grab the food tray from the counter and go back outside with it.

"Ooh, what are we having?"

"Omelets, french toast, Belgian waffles, and sandwiches," I reply as I set the long tray on the table and sit down.

"You're going to spoil me rotten Ramon,"

"That's my plan." I chuckle, picking up a waffle with my fork as we continue to talk about anything and everything. Life and death, past and future.

"Thank you again for this Ramon, I loved everything."

"Oh, we aren't done yet," I say as I smile and loop my arms around her. "We're going dancing."

"Dancing?" she laughs. "Since when do you dance?"

"Since I've started dating you, princess."

"Well then, I guess we're going dancing." she smiles.

We walk hand in hand in silence on the edge of the beach to the lights that were now bright and reflecting on the ocean waves. We spot Wyatt and Aurora swinging gently side to side, and the kids were playing in the sand.

"Their family is so lovely," whispers Celestia.

"I know,"

"Celestia! How was your lunch?" says Aurora as she looks at us.

"It was wonderful, I just loved your decorations!"

"Why thank you," she smiles as she lays her head on her husband's chest.

"Oh! May I hold her?" asks Celestia as she points to Evelyn sitting on the sand.

"Sure, If she'll let you." Aurora laughs. "She's so clingy to me and doesn't like anyone."

"She's so cute, I'm gonna try anyway."

Celestia walks over to the kids and sits down on the sand with them, fanning out her dress. Evelyn pats her tiny hands on the sand in front of her sister as they build a small lopsided sandcastle. I continue to watch as Celestia picks up a smooth seashell and holds out her hand to Evelyn. She looks at the seashell and moves into a standing position. Evelyn looks at the shell, then back at Celestia. To our surprise, she takes a few wobbly steps closer to her. When she's in reach, Celestia picks her up gently and places her in her lap, dangling the shell and smiling at Evelyn who was now laughing.

"She must be good with kids," says Aurora as she and Wyatt come up to me.

"I think I just fell in love all over again," I whispered.

"I know," she says. "You look absolutely whipped."

"We're gonna head in you two, we have to get these kids to bed. Have a great rest of your night" Aurora says.

"Alright, goodnight Aurora, night Wyatt!"

"Night."

Luna and Mateo run to Celestia once more and hug her. She gives them a squeeze and runs her hands through their hair as she smiles at them.

"Night night, Princess CC," mutters Mateo.

"Goodnight cuties," Celestia replies as she lets go of them.

They run back to their parents and as she watches them leave I take her hand and spin her around to face me. She collides with my chest and I smile at her.

"It seems that I haven't been getting much attention, but now I have you all to myself."

"Sorry, I can't help it. Children are so precious," she replies.

"It was fine, I loved watching you play with them. It suits you."

"Whatever do you mean by that?" she questions as I spin her around again as we dance on the sand.

"I mean that you're just good with children, you'd be a great mother too."

She softly smiles. "Thank you, I don't know though, I do love playing with them, and I have imagined having my own someday but-"

"But?"

"I don't think I could handle carrying one for nine months. I can't even handle my period cramps."

"I think you'll be fine. You're a strong woman, and very determined with a drive like none other."

"You're too sweet Ramon," she blushes as she ducks her head to the side.

"I have something for you."

"Another gift? Babe quit spoiling me, you're not gonna like the outcome of it." she laughs.

"This gift is a special gift."

"What is it?"

"Now, it wouldn't be a gift if I told you, would it?"

"I suppose not,"

I take her hand and we walk to the porch of the beach house. I take the box from the table next to the door and sit next to her on the stairs.

"Before I give this to you, I just wanted you to know that over the past few weeks I've grown to like you even more than I did before. If you say no to the question I'm going to ask you once you open this, I will be fine." I say as I hand her the box.

Lies. All lies. There is no way in hell I'd be fine if she said no. I'd be so damn heartbroken. I don't even know what I'd do. My heart beats faster as she slowly opens the box. Her mouth becomes slightly ajar as she looks at the item in front of her. She looks up at me and I sigh.

"It's a collar. Not just any collar. Celestia, I want to claim you as mine. You don't know how much I adore you. I can't stand the thought of anyone taking you away from me. You're precious to me. When that dreadful fucker of a man took you away from me, I was ready to go to hell and back to make sure you were back in my arms again. I-." I take a deep breath and close my eyes. "I love you, Celestia, I'm in love with you. I love the way you tease me, I love the way you look at me every day, I love our late-night conversations, I love every. Single. Thing. About you."

I swallow the lump in my throat and open my eyes. Celestia looked at me fondly with tears in the corner of her eyes.

"It's fine if you don't love me back I don't know what I was thinking-"

"But I do." she smiles as she pulls me close and kisses me. "I do love you, Ramon."

"Really?"

"Yes really, I didn't want to admit it to myself, but you make me whole. You're the reason why I want to wake up every day smiling. I love you."

"God, you don't know how long I've been wanting to hear that from you."

"This isn't a promise ring," I say as I take the collar out of the box and put it around her neck. "But think of it as one, because I promise you that I will never let anyone break us apart. Ever."

I pull her closer and kiss her passionately. As we kiss underneath the stars and the bright lights of the lanterns, I can't help but smile.

Celestia was mine and no one else's. Mine to hold, mine to comfort, mine to love, mine to fuck. All mine.

Chapter 22

I look at myself in the mirror across from the bed and smile. My hand goes up to feel the velvet collar and I sigh happily. There was a time when I thought that I would never end up in a wonderful situation like this. Especially after Mike ended things with me for the last time. But here I am, with a man who showed me nothing but love. Not only does he love me and I love him, but he also made me love myself in a way I never thought I could.

"Good morning my princess," says Ramon as he plants kisses all over my shoulders and neck.

"Good morning, my love."

"Did you sleep well?"

"I did, I always do when you're by my side," I say, turning around to face him.

He takes my right leg and moves it so that I straddle him. I lay on his chest, letting his breathing move me as he combs his hands through my hair. Out peaceful moment gets interrupted when my phone rings from the nightstand. Ramon grabs it and hands it over to me.

"It's my mom."

"Are you not going to answer it?"

"I am, but, I'm just confused, we haven't talked in a year," I say as I answer the phone.

"Hello?"

"Celestia, thank God. Are you okay?"

"Yeah, why wouldn't I be?"

"I just heard that Mike kidnapped you and I panicked. It's all over the news honey."

"Wait. What?"

"Yes honey, there are pictures he took of you and some billionaire, Ramon Osgood right? I must say, some of those pictures concern me. Are you sure you're okay?"

"Yes, I am mom," I say as I move to grab the remote for the TV. I turn it on and shuffle through the channels until I see the news. There was a picture of Ramon and me in bed, a picture of me dancing at the club, and another picture of me sitting at my desk.

"Oh my God, Mom how much do you know, what did the news say?"

"They said that Mike took you back to this home in Tennessee and held you there for days. Then they said that Ramon went to Tennessee to find you and when he did he killed him. After seeing those pictures as well, C, I'm worried about you, how could you not tell your mother about this?"

"I-I don't know, I'm sorry, we haven't talked in a while and I didn't think it'd be this big of an issue. Who released the photos anyway? We didn't permit that. And Ramon didn't kill anyone-"

"Well, they found him dead a few yards away from his house in the woods."

"Well, I'm telling you it wasn't Ramon, when he found me he took me straight home, my friend James was there as well. What the fuck is wrong with people, butting into people's personal lives like this?"

"I don't know but, I'm coming to see you. And I don't want to hear anything. I'm coming whether you like it or not."

"I'm not gonna be at the apartment."

"Then where are you now?"

"I'm living with Ramon."

"That's fine, I'll be there by the afternoon. Send me the address."

"Mom you can't just-"

"Don't test me, young lady, I want to make sure my baby is safe."

"Fine." I sigh. "I'll see you later."

"I love you. I'll be there soon."

"I love you too mom," I reply and hang up.

"What happened sweetheart?"

"My mom is coming to see me."

"What's wrong with that?"

"She can be a handful at times,"

"Aren't all mothers?"

"I guess so, but we need to head back to New York. I think-"

Ramon's phone rings. We both look at it and he picks it up, answering it.

"Slow down. No, I haven't said anything to anyone. Alright, I'll be there soon."

"Who was that?"

"My lawyer, rumors are spreading around that I killed Mike."

"That's what my mom told me,"

"Yeah, it's fine though, Thank God I brought James with me, otherwise, I wouldn't have anything to back me up. Alright, let's go see Wyatt and then we gotta go."

We get up from the bed and we rush to put on our clothes. When we finish, we walk to Wyatt's and knock on the door. Aurora opens it and looks at us questionably.

"Y'all okay? You looked pissed more than terrified."

"We are," Ramon responds.

"Celestia, just keep your head up, it'll be over soon before you know it."

"You already know what's happening?"

"Gosh, it's on every TV station. They really have it out for the both of you."

"Both of us?" I question. "What did I do?"

"Nothing, it's just a bunch of women trying to get under your skin as well as get their fifteen minutes of fame."

"I just want to go back to yesterday," I sigh and squeeze my eyes shut.

"We're gonna be fine princess," whispers Ramon as he pulls me close and kisses the top of my head. "Thank you Aurora, tell Wyatt he can have the rest of the week off as well."

"You're welcome, get there safe you two," she says as we walk away.

When we step out of the car, reporters, journalists, and random females engulf us. Ramon tightens his grip on me as they attack us with questions and claims.

"Did you kill Mike?"

"What is Celestia to you?"

"What's your relationship with Mike Celestia?"

"Are you a stripper?"

I close my eyes and try desperately to close them out as we walk to the front of the house.

"I'm giving everyone five seconds to get off my property, or I'm fining all of you for trespassing," says Ramon boldly.

He unlocks the door and we step inside, locking it behind us. I move the blinds, I see them retreating and getting into vans, driving away. I sigh and rub my temple.

"I'm sorry, my love," says Ramon as he pulls me in for a tight hug.

"Sorry for what? This isn't your fault. People are just ignorant."

"I know, but you're clearly upset, and you know I don't like seeing you upset baby."

"I'll be fine, let's just clear everything up and get this situation out of everyone's heads."

"Alright, first let's get some food in you, then we'll go to my lawyer and figure everything out."

"Don't forget we have to be back before my mother gets here."

"I didn't forget, I have a car waiting for her at the airport that will bring her here.

"Okay, thank you."

"Anything for you princess."

Chapter 23

"Why can't I just say something to the press?"

"Even if you do, you're still going to have to go to court. Not only are you being accused of killing Mike, there are multiple women, claiming that you have abused them, and there's one in particular who claims that their unborn child is yours."

"That's bullshit. Where were all of these allegations before? Why are they bringing this up now?"

"You know how it is, everyone is looking for fame nowadays. All I'm saying is that you should go. It's not like you're lying on anything since you both did nothing wrong."

"Alright then, did a court date get released yet?"

"No, I have a few dates for you to choose from right here," he says as he pulls out a post-it note with three dates on it.

"You have tomorrow, the day after, or Tuesday next week."

"I'll go tomorrow, I want this done and over with as soon as possible,"

"Got it, I'll do all the work from here, I'll text you the time later and I'll call all the witnesses."

"Thank you, Ben."

"No problem. It was nice meeting you, Celestia,"

"Likewise, thank you for your help."

"Of course."

I take her hand and we leave the building. She was quiet as I drove us home. When we got inside, I pull her close to me.

"How are you feeling?"

"Sick."

I sigh. "If only I could've prevented this."

"It's fine, I just want to get through this day honestly."

"It's almost over. And tomorrow will go just as quick, then we can get back to our normal lives, I promise."

As I held her tightly, I could feel her shivering under me. She didn't want to show it, but she was truly scared.

"Princess, look at me," I said as I tilt her chin up. Her eyes were glassy and she looked like she was ready to cry.

"What if they take you away from me?"

"They won't. I will stay by your side. Always."

She presses her head against my chest and I rub her back gently. Suddenly the doorbell rang.

"God, she's here." Celestia sighs as she wipes her eyes and composes herself.

"Sit, I'll bring her up," I say as I curve my hand under the chin and give her a quick kiss. She smiles at me and goes off to sit on the loveseat by the TV.

I go downstairs and answer the door, opening it to a woman who might as well be Celestia herself.

"Welcome, Mrs. Crowe,"

"Ramon. Hmm, you look even more handsome than the pictures on TV and in magazines. Where's my dear daughter?"

"She's upstairs, may I take your bags?"

"What a gentleman, thank you. I wonder why she had to hide you from me." she smiles as she hands over the suitcase.

I take it from her hands and gestured for her to follow me. When she spots Celestia on the couch she rushes over to her, engulfing her with a hug.

"My precious sweetheart,"

"Hi, mom,"

"You look pale." She then turns to me. "Is she eating? How many meals a day does she eat? Cause I know she'll-"

"Mom, I'm still right here. And yes I eat, I'm just tired."

"Look at you, still can't seem to take care of your wellbeing."

"Mom," she whines as she tilts her head back on the couch.

"Alright, alright, I'll stop fussing. But, why didn't you bother to tell me about this fine young man?"

"I don't know as I said on the phone, we haven't talked to each other in a while, and it's not like you've ever found my love life interesting." She mumbles.

"Well, now I am. After what I've seen from the past few weeks you've been through hell with Mike. I had no idea that boy was that evil and heartless. I'm staying with you for the rest of this week."

"Mom, no."

"Oh please, I have nothing better to do sitting in that house alone. We can have a girl's night, It'll be fun! You're going to send your own mother away so soon? You don't mind me staying do you, Ramon?" She says as he turns to me again.

"No ma'am."

"See? Ramon doesn't mind. I like him more already."

Celestia glares at me and groans.

"Okay, I'll let you be for now. Ramon, lead the way to a room please." she smiles as she gets up from the couch.

I take her suitcase and she follows me upstairs. She loops her arm through my arm and pats my shoulder.

"Now, how long has this thing been going on between you two?"

"Well, we only started dating a month ago."

"Only a month? Are you sure y'all aren't moving too fast?"

"Not if you love the person, no."

"Ohh, so you're already that deep."

"Yes ma'am."

"Call me Madeline, ma'am makes me feel old." she laughs, which sounds just the same as Celestia's.

"She looks a lot like you by the way,"

"Yes, she does, doesn't she. The only thing that she has that reminds me of her father are her eyes. But everything else is from me. Except for her stubbornness. That's from her dad as well. That's how he died. Saving a mother and her baby. Don't let her stubbornness scare you away though."

"She was exceedingly stubborn with me but she's been nothing but loving as we got closer."

"That's good."

"Oh, this is your room,"

"Thank you, Ramon,"

"Of course Mrs. Madeline," I nod.

I go back downstairs to find Celestia still on the couch. I walk over to her and kiss her head as I rub my hands down her arms.

"You look, tired baby."

"I feel tired, but at the same time I'm not."

"I get it. Do you wanna go to bed then?"

"Nah, I think I'll just stay here and curl up with a book or watch a show or something."

"Alright my love, if you need anything I'll be in the kitchen."

"Okay," she says as she rests her hand on mine before she lays her head down on the couch, taking the remote and flipping through Netflix.

I go into the kitchen, but the house phone rings before I can even do anything. I answer it and hear deep breathing on the other side.

"Hello?"

"I-is this Ramon?"

"This is he,"

"I-I love you, Ramon. Just give me another chance. I know we've only spent three days together but those were the best days of my life. I-I can't live without you."

"Who is this?"

"T-this is Beverly, remember me?"

"No."

"Don't be so cold Ramon, just because you have a new bitch doesn't mean you can forget about me. You're the father of my baby Ramon. You have to come back to me. I can't take care of this child alone. And if you refuse, I'll make sure your life turns to hell."

"Listen here, Bethany-"

"Beverly."

"I don't care. I don't know who you think you are, but just because you make false claims on a child being mine many times doesn't make it true. Now, there are so many ways to find out whether that child is mine or not. We can easily get you tested. Not only will you be seen as a liar, but you'll also be seen as a crazy stalker because I know for a fact that I've probably only had sex with you once-with a condom-so don't ever try that bullshit. As for my girlfriend, she's not going anywhere. I'm going to say this one thing, and I mean it in the most disrespectful way possible. Don't ever call this place again, don't ever call my girl a bitch, and don't ever mess with me, or I'll make sure your life turns to hell."

I end the call, block the number, and slam the phone back into its place. Then I pull out my phone from my pocket and call Ben.

"What's up?"

"The woman who claimed that her child was mine just called my house."

"Oh shit."

"Yeah, her name is Bethany. I know for a fact that the child isn't mine, will she be at the court tomorrow?"

"Yes, most likely they're going to do a test."

"Great, I'm ready to get this shit done and over with. It's starting to really piss me off and it's taking a toll on Celestia."

"Don't worry, everything is ready for tomorrow,"

"Thank you again, Ben."

"No problem."

I hang up and sit at the counter, pressing my face against the palms of my hands. I then feel small hands moving along my back, waist, and shoulders.

"Baby, are you okay?"

"Yes, I'm fine princess," I say as I turn to face her. "You want something?"

"No, I just wanted to cuddle with you. It's okay if you're busy."

"No, no, I'm not busy. Just stressed." I reply as I get up and hook my arm around her.

"Okay,"

"Come on," I say as I take her hand and bring us to our room.

I get on the bed and pat the space next to me which she fills. She moves closer to me under the thick blanket and looks at me with innocent eyes.

"Yes, princess?"

She doesn't say anything, she simply moves on top of me and lays on my chest. She starts to plant kisses all over my neck and chest, gliding her fingers up under my shirt.

"Baby, your mom is-"

"Shhh," she says. "Just let me touch you, my love."

She snags at my skin with her teeth as she swiftly pulls off my shirt. She then moves down and tugs roughly at my shorts, pulling them down to free my cock.

"You're hard."

"I'm always hard around you." I smile.

"Good. As you should be."

She folds her hands around it and her tongue slowly glides against it from the bottom up. She looks at me dead in the eye as she does so.

"Fuck, baby."

She reaches the tip and starts to suck on it. Driving me to the edge.

"That's right, baby, suck on my cock." I groan.

She opens her mouth wider and slides it down my length. Her warm mouth feels so good that I take her head and push it down till she reaches the end. She moves back up and releases me with a pop.

Her mouth glistens with saliva and she teases me as she lips them clean. She pulls off her dress and I immediately pull her down to me. As one hand is around her chin, I slip my other hand in between us and cup her pussy.

"That's all you're gonna do?" she smiles.

"Hell no," I state as I slip two fingers inside of her deeply.

She squirms and immediately tightens up around me.

"Look at you, all wet for me. I'm going to make you scream, but you can't can you, you're mother is right down the hall, you wouldn't want her to hear you now."

"Do your worst."

"With pleasure."

I slip my fingers out of her and pin her to the bed in my place. I suck on her neck, inhaling her scent of cherries blossoms. I move down to put all my attention on her breasts. I move down again, spread her legs apart, and bury my head in between her legs. I take two fingers and spread her wet pussy open.

"Ramon, you're going to slow." she moans.

"I know, I want you to feel every single lap of my tongue when I eat you out," I slowly move my tongue in between her inner folds.

"Every sensation as my sinful fingers touch you," I glide my fingers up and around her inner thighs.

"And every stroke of my cock drilling inside of you." I slip a finger deep inside of her.

She moans, arches her back, and bites her lips at my words and I flick my tongue against her clit.

"Faster, Ramon, please faster!"

"Shh, my love," I whisper as I suck on the twitching bud.

I take my free hand and shove two fingers into her, thrusting back and forth, moving faster until she shakes. Her wetness shoots out and hits my arm. I stop and look at her with my brows raised.

"That's new."

She clasps her mouth with her hand and looks down.

"I-I didn't even know I could do that."

"I'm definitely going to love pounding into that." I smile as I take my fingers out of her and put them into my mouth. I take my cock in my hand and move it up and down her now throbbing cunt. Suddenly she grabs it herself and shoves it in. Moaning as she does so.

"Damn woman." I hiss.

"You were taking too long," she smirks.

I press on her lower abdomen and thrust into her deep enough to feel myself under my palm.

"Oh, fuck!" she rushes out as she covers her mouth with her hands, trying to muffle her moans.

"Covering that mouth won't do anything princess," I say as I continue to apply pressure as I push through her tightness.

I lean down to kiss her and her moans invade my mouth. Just to play around with her sanity I pull out, place her legs by her head and suck on her clit while pumping two fingers inside of her. She gasps and nearly lifts her entire body off of the bed as she squirms.

"I'm gonna cum, Ramon!"

"Not, yet my love," I say as I push my cock inside of her again. Slowly I move in and out so that she feels every part of me slide against her walls. As I was getting close, I go faster and push harder.

"Cum with me princess, now."

She didn't wait for me to repeat myself and our orgasms erupted from our bodies.

"Mm, I love seeing my cum drip from your pussy. Just knowing that I did that makes me want to fuck you all over again."

"I love you, Ramon," she whispers as I move us and hold her in my arms.

"I love you too princess."

Chapter 24

She wore a bright yellow dress and her pregnancy showed. I grit my teeth and swallow the nasty feeling, threatening to jump out of me. I don't know who this woman thinks she is but I don't think she realizes how badly this could be for her and her reputation. But I'm convinced that she doesn't give a shit as to whether people hate her or not. Any type of attention is still attention, and as long as all eyes are on her she's content. I have never seen someone so dumb.

"Your honor, we have evidence that this child, isn't Mr. Osgood's," states Ben.

"Continue."

"Mr. Osgood claims that he uses a condom with every intercourse he's ever had, and there are witnesses to agree with him as well."

Ugh, I wanted to slap the smirk off the bitches face as she sat there.

"We found out that Ms. Harrison has a husband, but they filed for divorce a few months ago. The husband refuses to sign the papers, believing that the unborn child she bears is his. We have talked to said husband and he agreed to have a NIPP test done. He obtained a blood sample from Ms. Harrison-"

"What?!" screamed the lady.

"Quiet down!" said the judge in a harsh tone. "Continue, sir."

"Thank you, your honor, as I was saying, Mr. Harrison then got the results of the test which I have right here on paper."

"Approach the bench, sir."

"Yes, your honor," Ben replies as he does so. The judge looks over the paper and then hands it back to Ben who takes it and goes back to his seat.

"As you can see clearly, that child is not my client's."

"Thank you, Ms. Harrison, you may now speak." says the judge. "Mr. Osgood, you may go back to your seat."

My eyes are on Ramon now as he nods and walks back to his seat beside Ben. He turns around and our eyes meet. I find every ounce of courage inside of me not to cry as he takes my hand and gently kisses the top of it before he turns back around.

Ms. Harrison makes a show of waddling up to the stand and I roll my eyes. God, maybe if this doesn't end badly for her she should be an actress. Fake ass bitch.

"Ramon and I's relationship was different than those other women he has been with. I became with child the day before he ended our relationship. Those papers that his lawyer has are fake. I filed a divorce with my husband, yes, so I haven't been with any other man than Ramon. This is all I have to say." she says as she waddles back to her seat. As I watch her, I had a hint of sympathy in me. Not for her, but for the poor kid. Suddenly the doors in the back open and everyone turns to see a man with a sheet of paper in one hand as he drags a kid by the arm with his other. The police from the corners of the room stop them from getting any closer but stop when the man yells out.

"Your honor! I have proof that the child isn't Mr. Osgood's!" he states.

"Let him through." says the judge.

They release him and the boy and he takes the boy and sits him next to me on the edge of the bench. The boy didn't look a day over 17. He was visibly shaking.

"Are you okay?" I whisper to him as I place a hand on his shaky ones.

"I'm scared. I don't wanna get in trouble," he whispers back.

"Get in trouble for what? You didn't-"

"Swear to tell the whole truth and nothing but the truth."

"I do." says the man on the stand.

I look up at him, waiting for him to speak.

"I am Mr. Harrison. Mr. Osgood's lawyer is correct when he says that the child isn't his client's. I have another copy of the paper in my hand. The child is not mine either. I have found out that it is this boy's child. He came to me after finding out on the news and came clean. He stated to me that my wife raped him and paid him off to not say a word. The poor boy is only 17. I have contacted his family as well and they want to press charges against her which I fully agree to. I have finally signed the divorce papers without any hesitation. Thank you your honor." he finished and left the stand.

The entire room was quiet. Many hands were covering mouths at the shock of events. I look at the kid who was now crying beside me with his head in his hands and I pull him close and wrap my arms around him. Then I look at the woman with a sneer on my face.

How could she do such a thing? She looked so dumbfounded and embarrassed. As she should be.

"The trial of Ramon Osgood vs Ms. Harrison has ended. Mr. Osgood, you're free to go. You, however, Ms. Harrison, stay put."

I sigh and feel someone take my hand as I close my eyes. When I open them, they meet the eyes of Ramon and his calm smile.

"Get over here," I whisper as I pull him closer and give him a harsh kiss.

"Welcome home my little lovebirds!" says my mother as we enter the kitchen. "Your faces are being printed on magazines as we speak," she states as she turns her phone to us.

It was a picture of us kissing at court. Below it was another one of us where Ramon was turned to me and holding my hand.

"If that isn't love, I don't know what is." my mom sighs as she looks back at the picture.

I look up at Ramon and he slides on arm around me and silently drags me out of the kitchen. When we're out of sight, he gently pins me to the wall without making a sound.

"Ready for round two?" he whispers in my ear.

I bite my bottom lip and nod as I slither my hands around his waist. He picks me up and I eagerly wrap my legs around him as he carries me up to our room.

"I want you naked. Like now. Take everything off so I can fuck you on every surface of this room." he groans.

"Oh, you want me naked? How badly do you want it, Ramon? Tell me, my love, I can fulfill all of your desires." I say as I get off him and dart across the room.

"What, we're playing tag now?"

"I'll let you play with my titties if you catch me." I laugh.

"You're not going to win this game."

"That's the plan," I reply as I move to the bed.

Chapter 25

He darts toward me and I jump down moving to where was originally was.

"Darling, if I catch you, I won't just play with your titties, you're playing a very dangerous game my love." he grins.

"Mm, but you still haven't caught me yet so you can eat my ass you sore loser." I smile as tease him by pulling up my dress. I pull the rest of it off and suddenly feel his arms grab me.

"Gotcha," he says as he whispers in my ear then moves down and gently bites at my neck. My knees buckle and he picks me up. He takes me out of the room and goes down to the end of the hall. He uses one hand to open the door and he closes it behind him when we're inside. He takes us to the edge of the bed in the middle of the room and placed me on it.

"I'm gonna punish you just for doing that." He says in my ear as he towers over me, wrapping his hands around my neck. He kisses me slowly then he trails a hand down from my neck to the top of my panties. His finger hooks in it and he plays with the band of it. He suddenly yanks it off, twists me around as he holds my arms behind my back, then slaps my ass with full force. I gasp at the sting. He rubs at the spot he struck then brings the pain once more as he bites down with his teeth.

"Now, look who's actually eating ass," he whispers and kisses the redness of my bottom.

"Shut up," I say as I turn my head to the side.

He darts his eyes up at me and he moves to press his body against my back. His hands go up to my neck and he turns my face, even more, to look at him.

"What did you say, darling?"

"You heard me. Shut up and fuck me already."

"Wow, look who's being bratty now. I could punish you for that you know."

"Do it then," I smirk. "Punish me in any way you want." I arch my back and push my ass against his bulging cock. "Why don't you fill my ass with your dick and rub my clit until it swells."

Ramon looked taken aback as I finished my sentence.

"I never knew you had such a foul mouth." he grins as he begins to kiss down my jawline to my neck. "So descriptive. Is that what you want me to do to you baby?" he whispers.

"Yes, and so much more." I moan.

He flips me over again and his mouth latches onto my right breast as he pinches the left. I gasp as his wet mouth turns the peak of my breasts as hard as diamonds. No, not diamonds. Rubies. They were now red and swollen from his teeth and I loved the sting it gave. Ramon moves down and begins to nibble at my skin, making small red marks all over my chest until he reaches my sex. He looks up at me and our eyes meet. He grins and then darts his tongue out and laps up in between my folds.

"Fuck..." I moan as I drop my head back onto the bed.

I could feel his breath against my pussy as he chuckles and he stands up to move to the drawers in the side of the room. I watch him as he brings out a few ropes, a chain, and a few other things that I couldn't see. When he turns around, only the ropes were in his hand.

"Go to the top of the bed and get on your knees for me."

"Yes sir." I quickly say, eager for anything. I just want him to touch me as much as possible.

He moves to one side of the bed and takes one of my arms. He takes the first rope and ties my hand to the post near it. He moves to the other side and does the same thing then he uses the last two to spread my legs apart and tie them to the bottom posts. When he finishes, he moves in between my legs and kisses my body up to my mouth.

"I'd love to do what you suggested but you've got punishments lined up for making me chase you."

He gets off of the bed then comes back with the chain and a blindfold. He takes the silk blindfold and wraps it gently around my eyes. I feel his hands graze my skin, slowly moving all over my body. For just a second I feel nothing. Suddenly something claps onto my nipples and I gasp, arching my back off of the bed as I pull at the ropes that bound my hands.

"You're fine my love, it's just clamps."

"They feel...different."

"I know princess. Do they hurt?"

"A little, just the good kind."

"Good," he says closely, I feel his breathing against my skin.

He kisses my chest a few times before I no longer feel him again. Another few seconds go by before I feel the bed dip in between my legs again.

"Lift up for me princess," he whispers and I obey. I feel his hand move under me and suddenly a foreign object is being pushed up my ass. I gasp again and squeeze without thinking.

"Relax baby,"

"I know, I just wasn't expecting th-"

I moan as the vibrator turns on.

"Oh my God."

He moves his hand from the vibrator and slides a finger in between the inner folds of my pussy. I shiver and shake a little as he slides his finger back down and then slips it in. He fingers me slowly and I can feel every push and pull. Then his mouth takes the place his fingers were and his tongue pushes inside of my entrance. He sucks on my clit, grazing his tongue over it every few seconds, and licks me all over. The way he laps up my juices, so desperate for more as if his mouth and tongue want to be interdigitated with my cunt. He finally stops and when I no longer feel his mouth on my I whimper and slightly pull at the ropes.

"I'm right here baby, I'm not going anywhere," he whispers. He was on my right side now. Unexpectedly, I feel a few strips glide over my bare stomach. Whatever it was, struck me lightly on my inner thigh which made my pussy wet even more. It was a whip. As the whip comes down on my inner thigh again, this time the right, I feel my wetness dripping out of me and glide down my legs.

"Damn my love," he says as he places a hand on my pussy. "You must really like this," he says as he takes the whip and slaps it, replacing where his hands were. I gasp and nod at the contact.

"M-more, Ramon I n-need m-more-."

Another strike comes down on my thigh again. Slightly harder than before.

"Celestia."

"Sir-" I quickly rush out. "I meant sir. I need more sir. Please." I breathe out.

"Good girl," he whispers and rewards me by sucking on my breast and whips me on the thigh once more.

"Are you wet enough for me?" he then says as he slips two fingers inside of me.

"Yes sir,"

"You think you're ready for me to fuck you?"

"Yes, please, yes!"

He pushes in deeper and curls his fingers and it grazes on my g-spot, making me moan loudly.

"Let's not have your mother wonder why you're moaning." he grins as he bends down to kiss me and I giggle a little.

"I wanna try something," he whispers in my ear. "Do you trust me?"

"Of course," I reply. I then feel the bed dip and rise as he gets off.

A few minutes passed.

"Ramon?"

"I'm right here baby," he replies from what I think is the other side of the room. The bed dips again and I feel his hands caress my cheek. I gasp when I feel a hot, thick liquid-like substance touch my skin. It felt oddly satisfying with the burn that disappears just as fast as it came. Like when hot glue from a glue gun touches your finger.

"What is that?"

"Take a guess," he whispers to me as I feel another section, lower than before, being touched with the hot liquid. It feels thick, but I don't feel it moving ever since he dropped it on my chest. I feel another part of me go hot, this time on my inner thigh. The liquid glides down but stops midway. I furrow my brow in confusion about how liquid could stop so fast. The same thing happens on my other thigh after a few seconds and I buck my hips at the heat spreading all over my body. A light bulb finally went off in my head.

"Wax?" I respond.

"Yep, a melting candle," he replies. He starts to peel the wax off of my skin and it awakens new sensations inside of me.

Ramon finally unties the blindfold from my face and I blink a few times to adjust my eyes.

"Hi baby." he smiles as he looks down at me.

"Hi," I grin back. He kisses me gently and then unties my wrist from the rope. He unties the rest and I'm finally free from the binds. I immediately hook my arms around his neck and pull him down to me.

"I still want you to fill my ass with your dick and rub my clit until it swells. Not that it already isn't." I smile.

"You're a very naughty woman you know that?" he grins back.

"All women are. You just have to coax it out of them."

He smiles and kisses my lips. "Fuck being a princess, you're now my queen," he replies and gives me more kisses. When he comes up, something flashes in my head and my pussy drips again with new juices. I take his head in my hand and bring my mouth to his ear.

"Since I'm now your queen, I think it's only proper for me to be queening you right now."

He pulls back and I can see the lust glowing in his eyes. I move to the side and turn him around so he replaces where I once was. I slowly bring my leg over him so that I was now straddling him in between my legs. I move up and spread my legs until I was right above his face. He stares at my cunt just as hungry as it was. I lower myself on him and he eagerly starts to lick my pussy and suck on my labia. His tongue pushes into my entrance and I start to grind my hips in a circular motion. He groans at the movement and more juices flow out of my pussy.

"Fuck! Faster Ramon!" I moan as he thrusts deep inside me. "I-I'm so close," I say as each word spills out of my mouth with every pushing motion of his hips. He picks up the pace and holds onto my waist dangerously tight with his right hand while his left is making circles on my swollen clitoris.

My orgasm hits me hard, and so does his. We both collapsed on the bed, both exhausted yet satisfied. I turn to nearly mold myself with his side and he wraps his arms around me to pull me closer. Today might have started on a low note, but it sure as hell ended on a great one.

Chapter 26

"Baby, I'll be fine. If anyone says anything, I got my friends to kick their asses." I reply as he kisses me on my forehead for the fifteenth time today.

"If anyone so much as looks at you the wrong way, call me."

"You're going to be at work thought, I don't wanna bother you," I argue.

"I don't care. You call me alright? I don't wanna hear what happens from someone else. I want to hear it from you, okay?" he argues back.

"Alright babe, but I promise you I won't need to call because nothing is gonna happen," I say as I lean in and kiss his lips before I get out of the car and walk towards the building.

Today was the last day of the semester and I honest to God couldn't wait to be done until the fall semester since I wasn't doing summer. As I walk to my last class and Stephanie, Luke, and Ethan wait for me at the end of the hall. I wave at them when I get closer and Stephanie makes a full sprint towards me.

"Ah! I missed you!"

I laugh. "You saw me a couple of days ago."

"Too many days ago for me." she smiles.

"What's up C!"

"Yeah, and how are you doing?"

"I'm fine," I say with a smile.

"No one should be fine after that. Just know that if you need someone to talk to, we're here for you," replies Ethan. Luke nods right after in agreement.

"I know, but I'm really fine. I just don't ever wanna go through that again."

"And we hope you don't. They'll have to go through your boyfriend, James, and us," says Luke.

"Thanks," I say. I then turn my face to see professor Finn walking down the hall. "We should head in."

They follow me inside of the classroom and we sit in our seats.

"Celestia. Wait. Do you have a minute?"

"Yeah, Professor Finn,"

"First off, I heard about um Mike, and then the whole court dispute over that woman. I just wanted you to know if you were okay and how you were dealing with it."

"I'm fine actually. It did scare me since many times I didn't know if I was gonna make it out alive or not but, I'm here so,"

"Good, good, that's good. Just know that I'm here for you okay, even though you might not have me as a professor. Anytime you need to talk, just text or call."

"Thanks."

"Before you go, I know this might seem out of the blue, but I swear that I mean no harm by it. I'm suspicious of Ramon's intentions with you."

"How come?" I squint my eyes at him.

"He isn't the loyal man you think he is. I saw pictures of him, with other women the day you were taken. Here." he replies as he digs in his bag. Once he finds the envelope, he hands it over to me.

I take it from him with shaky hands, afraid of looking inside. There was no way in hell Ramon would cheat. He wanted me first. He pestered me until I said yes to him. He made me feel happy. He said he loved me. And I love him.

"This is a lie."

"I wish it was Celestia. I'm sorry."

"R-Ramon would never do this to me," I say as I tear open the envelope.

I pull out the first picture and I swallow down the hurt forming in my throat. There was Ramon with a redhead. The next is a brunette he's kissing on the cheek. He looks happy as if he'd forgotten all about me. The award for the fakest person and best lie goes to Ramon. And the award for the most gullible person goes to me. I didn't wanna see anymore. I slip the photos back inside and before I knew it, a tear drops on top of the envelope, making it wet. Why would he go all the way to Tennessee to save me then? He should've just left me there.

"Hey, hey, don't cry. He doesn't deserve you. He's not worth your tears." he whispers as he takes his thumb and wipes my tears away.

"It's okay, here sit down," he says as he takes me gently by the shoulders and guides me to his chair behind his desk. When I sit down I put my head in my head and cry. I knew I wasn't good enough for him. I'm not good enough for anyone. This is why I don't want to fall in love. Because any little thing can break it all apart.

"Screw him. You'll find a better man. Someone who can take care of you and treat you like the queen you are...someone like me."

I jerk my face to stare at him.

"What is wrong with you?!"

"I'm just being honest here. You do like an honest man do you not? I'm simply saying just take me into consideration. You're a very beautiful and very bright young woman Celestia. I'll make you happy-"

"No."

"No?" he arches an eyebrow at me as he places his hands on both sides of the chair and leans in.

"Is it because he's a good fuck? Is that it Celestia? Because I can do what he can. And I can do it better. I know my way around whips and chains too sweetheart. I'm better at it than him." he smirks.

"No. Now move."

"Oh, but I need a yes."

"You're not gonna get it from me. Find someone else to play around with."

"You like it rough, don't you? I saw those pictures of you two, I'll bet you look very nice tied up to my bed-"

"FUCKING BITCH!" he screams after my fist connected with his face. "Listen here you little shit-" he says through his teeth as he takes his hand and tightens it around my jaw.

"She said no dickhead. Take a hint." It was Luke. he had grabbed him by his shirt. The look on his face even scared me.

"Let's go C. Steph got it on recording she's reporting this to the police as we speak." I hear Ethan at my side and he grabs my arm to pull me out of the chair and away from Luke and Finn. He holds onto me tightly, somehow, afraid that I might fall.

When Luke finally lets go of him he follows us out of the room and walks on the other side of me. I started to shake. I felt weak, and I never liked feeling weak.

"C? Are you okay?" Asks Ethan as he stops walking. Luke stops as well and looks down at me questionably. I could see his eyes darting to the envelope in my hand but he didn't ask about it.

"I-I'm fine. I j-just need to sit down." I say, but it comes out in a whisper.

"I'll get her some water," says Luke and he leaves. Ethan quickly looks around and then he brings me over to a chair in the hall. He sits me down slowly and rubs my back as my breathing begins to get heavier. Luke comes back with a water bottle in hand and opens the top, handing it over to me. I take a swig and I cough violently as it goes down the wrong pipe.

"I'm fine. I'm okay." I say through coughs. "I'm just having a panic attack. God, I haven't had one of those in years."

Ethan continues to rub my back until I'm able to stop shaking and coughing.

"Is she okay? What happened?"

I look up to see Stephanie with a police officer from the campus behind her.

"I'm all good. Panic attack, that's all."

"Oh, um-"

"Ma'am, can you confirm that it was you in the video?" interrupts the officer as he flips Stephanie's phone to me.

I look at the video. There wasn't much to see, from where it was being taken in between the cracks of the doors.

"Yes. And that's professor Finn." My mouth curls up slightly as his name comes out of my mouth. "In class 134D."

The officer nods and he heads down the hall to where the classroom was. I sigh and stand up.

"Steph, do you mind dropping me off somewhere?"

"Of course, but, didn't Ramon drop you off? Isn't he coming to get you?"

"He is, but I'm not going with him. I need some space right now."

"Alright then, where to?"

"Lucy's"

"Alright, what's the deal, I know you don't need space from Ramon. What happened?" asks Stephanie as she drives down the road.

"He cheated on me."

"What?! Are you actually serious? Like dead ass?"

"Yeah Steph, when Mike took me he was messing around with other women. That's why Professor Finn pulled me to the side and he showed me pictures, but I think he thought that after I knew, he could just slip his way in and look like a persona with good intentions."

"Are the pictures in that envelope? Damn now that's fucked up. Especially since he was the one who went all the way to Tennessee to find you and bring you back, it just doesn't make sense."

"That's what I thought!"

"But then again, he was a playboy before you both started talking. Hmph, damn now I don't wanna trust no man."

"You'll probably be fine Steph, I just have bad luck with men. Right now, I just don't wanna see him right now."

The tears start to spill all over again and I wipe at them furiously.

"Dammit, no. I'm not supposed to cry."

Steph parks the car in the front and pulls me in for a tight hug.

"It's okay, keeping it in isn't going to be good for you. Come on, I know seeing Lu will make you feel better."

"Y-you're right," I sniff as I wipe away at my tears again and open the door. Steph walks with me to the front of the apartments and heads inside with me and we take the elevator up to the fourth floor. When we step out, we go down the hall until we reach Lucinda's apartment. I knock on the door and wrap my arms against my chest. Lucy opens it after a few seconds and smiles but her smile turns into a frown with concerned eyes as she looks at me.

"What happened?"

"Long story short, professor Finn tried to feel her up, but not before telling her that Ramon cheated on her."

"He cheated on you?! That bastard."

"I'll text you later C okay?" She says as she gives me another hug. "I'll swing by tonight Lu, with food too cause we definitely need a girl's night."

"Say less. Text me what time. Come inside C."

We say bye to Steph as she goes back down the hall and Lucy closes the door behind her.

"Alright, come on let's get you in the bath with some wine to clear your head and vent to me.

Chapter 27

"This still doesn't make any sense to me, like we're talking about the same man who showed up banging my door at two in the morning frantically pacing about as I told him where you were. Yet he still cheated?"

"I know, usually I would want to hear it from him but. He had pictures Lu, and they were the type that had the time and date in the corner and it sure as hell looked recent too. There was no photoshop from what I saw either. Pass me the bottle please?"

She passes me the bottle next to her and the thick bubbles move closer to me as she hands it over.

"Now, I definitely have to see those pictures. If he did cheat, I personally want to fuck him up with my heels."

"I took them with me after the incident so they're on the counter," I say as I pour myself another glass. "Alright, last glass for me then I'll get out of this bath, I don't wanna look like a prune later." I smile.

"Ha, you're gonna look like a prune eventually when you turn into a grandma." she laughs as she flicks her hand against the water at me.

"Can't be a grandma if I don't have any kids," I state taking a large downfall of wine.

"No! I who am I gonna be an auntie to then!"

"I don't know," I shrug and laugh. "Go find a child and claim them as your niece or nephew."

"You're no fun," she playfully pouts.

"We should have someone look at these, I know a person who is good with pictures and stuff like that, she can find out if they were photoshopped or not," states Lucy as she grimaces at the pictures in her hand.

"Thanks, I really hope they aren't real-"

There was a knock at her door and I get up from the floor and walk to the door to open it. It was Steph struggling to carry a few bags.

"Girl, let me help you with that," I say as I take a bag from her.

"Damn Steph, did you bring your entire kitchen or something?" laughs Lucy as she gets up to help us.

"Lol, no, I just bought large chips and sodas."

"Nice," I reply from the kitchen. I take out the drinks and open the first bag of chips taking that and a case of ginger ale back to the living room. I sit on the floor again and start to grab a few of the Doritos to stuff in my mouth.

"I just saw the pictures, and damn Ramon sucks ass for that," says Stephanie as she opens a ginger ale for herself.

"Exactly, we should go to his house right now and start burning his clothes on his balcony like Taylor Swift."

"I fully agree, let's go crazy on the asshole."

" Y'all are a mess." I giggle. "But, I don't know what I'm gonna do yet like he just met my mom and they're vibing and everything. She's staying with us right now current-"

My phone rings from the couch and I pick it up.

"Speak of the devil," I mutter as I answer the phone.

"Hi, mom,"

"Sweetie, where are you? Ramon said you weren't picking up your phone and he's just about ready to send every police station looking for you."

"I'm fine mom, I'm with Steph and Lu, we're having a girl's night."

"That's great, but why didn't you tell Ramon hon? He's really worried about you. I thought you'd be home so I could tell you that I had to leave, but you weren't there."

"Oh, so you're not at the house then?"

"No, I'm headed back home. But anyway, just don't forget to tell Ramon where you are, I know you can be forgetful sometimes."

"Oh, I didn't forget. I just found out that he cheated on me."

"He what? Ramon? He wouldn't. Just a few days ago we were talking about how he was head over heels for you. What happened?"

"My professor had pictures of him with other women that were recent. I honestly don't think he would cheat but then again his rep with women before me was a little, well, not so good so, it's fine though, I'm staying at Lu's until I want to go back but I wanna find out if it's true or not."

"Mm, I get it. Stubborn as always, just like your father." she sighs. "I hope they aren't true, I want my grandbabies."

"Mom!"

"Alright, alright. Just make sure that you don't get hurt okay? If he hurts you, you tell me immediately and I'll personally come to drag him."

"Yeah mom, I will. I gotta go now, love you."

"I love you too baby, stay safe."

I hang up the phone, shut it down, and then toss it back on the couch.

"I'm honestly over today."

"As you should be, you know, you've really grown when it comes to relationships ending badly. Look at you not giving a shit. I don't know whether to be worried, scared, or both." Lucy laughs.

"I just think it hasn't registered to my brain yet, give it time." I laugh back, stuffing more chips into my mouth.

"Well, we'll worry about that later, right now you worry about you and your wellbeing." perks up Steph.

"But I mean," I sigh as I think. "It's not like I'd believe Professor Finn over Ramon ya know, it's just that I'm a little uncertain about all this, and as I said before, I just wanna know if the pictures are fake or not cause they could be photoshopped and they could be old pictures and he could've changed the date on them just to make it look real. But I know for sure that if I went back home to talk to him I'm scared that it'll end in a fight and I don't want to fight with Ramon because I fucking love him so much I can't bear the thought of us not being together. I was already terrified that I'd never see him when Mike took me, and when I thought they'd take him away from me in court."

I look up and both Stephanie and Lucy were looking at each other like I was speaking nonsense.

"Wait, wait, wait. Back up."

"Did you just say that you loved him?"

"Yeah?"

"When did this happen? Girl, we need the tea!"

"I totally forgot to tell you! How could I! Okay, okay, so there was a day where I came back from class and he got me gifts, and then we went to this BDSM place that he owns and we literally had the best sex ever. And then in the morning, we went to Virginia with his driver Wyatt to celebrate his birthday and spend some time there as well. It was amazing, I met Wyatt's family and his kids are just so cute and his wife is just gorgeous. But our fun ended when that dumb bitch started making claims that her baby was Ramon's so we had to come back and go to court and then my mom also showed up that day. It's been a good week up until today pretty much."

"Damn, your in the deep end of the relationship." nods Steph.

"Wait, did you say BDSM? As in whips, and ropes, and that dominating stuff?" asked Lucy.

"Yeah..."

"Oh is Ramon like into that kind of stuff?"

"Yeah, he was the one who introduced me to that type of lifestyle. I actually find it way better than plain vanilla sex." I state.

"Really? I mean it did sound really interesting when you presented it in class, now I know why you were able to spit out facts and add a little commentary here and there, it's cause you researched first hand. I've always wanted to try it but I was so scared and I didn't know who the right people were to talk about this stuff with." Stephanie grins

"Well, you can definitely ask Ethan or Luke, since you seem to be getting cozy with them, enough about my love life, what's up with you and Ethan? You know, when we first met them, I sensed you had the hots for him." I grin back, poking her side teasingly.

"Your right, Ethan is cute and I do kinda have a crush on him. I always saw him around with Luke in the halls last semester, they were so playful and close for a second I thought they were gay, turns out they aren't."

"Ooh! Are you talking about the two cuties I met at the club that one night?"

"Yeah, them. I don't know, I kinda wanna talk to Ethan and ask him out but I'm so stupid when it comes to boys."

"I'll definitely, give him hints for you." I smile.

We spent the rest of the night talking about boys, watching movies, doing our nails, all while filling ourselves with junk food and drinks. I don't know if the decision of coming here instead of going home to face my problems was a great idea, but it was fun just to forget about everything and have fun with the girls. I needed this. Tomorrow me can deal with all my problems.

Chapter 28

I take another painkiller for my headache. She wasn't answering her phone and her friends weren't answering my calls anymore after they chewed me out, which I was in fact very confused about. I miss her badly.

"Is something wrong Mrs. Madeline?" I say as I answer the phone.

"Well, yes and no."

"Why? God, did something happen to her?" I started to panic.

"No, no, she's fine. She's with Stephanie and Lucy."

"Why didn't she tell me anything? Is she upset? I couldn't have possibly done anything to make her upset."

"Something happened while she was at school, I also called her friend Lucy to get more info, I'm trying to help you out here Ramon, but you know how stubborn my daughter is. She likes to find out things on her own. She thinks you cheated on her."

"What? Why would I do that? I'm not the type of person to-I love her!"

"I know Ramon, but I got a call from the university, they wanted to notify me about her professor. He pulled her aside after class and he tried to touch her inappropriately."

My blood boiled as she told me this.

"I also heard that he showed her pictures that were recent of a redhead kissing your cheek and another brunette wrapping her arms around your waist as you looked down at her, but the problem is that she thinks those pictures are real."

"But why though, why would she willingly believe that I would hurt her like this?" I ask.

"In my opinion, I just think that she wants space. She wants to figure it out on her own. I don't think that she believes it, especially after everything you've done for her, but I think she's just playing detective right now. As her mother, I can tell she's scared. She's scared to confront you about it. This relationship she has with you is all new to her, because for once in her life, it isn't a toxic one. She's afraid that if she went about her day and came home, it'd be gnawing at her on the inside, thinking is it true every time she looked at you. She doesn't like others to deal with her issues, but she doesn't want to deal with them herself. Give her about a day or two and then talk to Lucy. If you reason with her then she can convince Celestia to come back."

"Thank you, Mrs. Madeline."

"No problem Ramon, I really like you two together and she's being stupid by messing it up and letting the littlest of things come between you both. But I get her, I was like that once, in the exact same situation with her dad when we were dating, we used to laugh about it all the time. Hah, like mother like daughter I guess. But look at me I married the man, and hell I'll be damned if she doesn't have a happy ending as I did."

"She will," I whispered.

I drive to her university first. When I get there, I go straight to the first officer I found.

"Mr. Osgood? Do you need any help, sir?"

"I do, in fact, I'm looking for Professor Finn."

"They escorted him out a few hours ago. Did you need him for something?"

"Not really, I just wanted to talk. You wouldn't happen to know about him touching someone after class would you?"

"Yes, I do, I'm not sure if it was her friend but someone came to me with a video and-"

"Do you have the video?"

"No sir, it's on the person's phone."

I close my eyes, pressing my teeth together.

"Thank you,"

"Y-you're welcome sir."

I walk away from him and go back to my car. I wasn't gonna get any answers from her friends so there's no point in asking them anything. The only way I was gonna get Celestia to talk to me is if I proved to her myself that the pictures were fake. I don't think she believed they were real. As her mother said, I agree with her. I think she's scared. She doesn't want to yell at me and argue with me but what she doesn't understand is that she could yell at me all day every day and I'd be fine just as long as at the end of the day she was with me and in my arms. If only she'd just come to me, I would've gotten rid of every doubt she has because if she thinks that I would do something so downright stupid to hurt her, then she's wrong. I picked up my phone from the holder and dialed Rose's number.

"Hey, Ramon, what's up?"

"Problem. Celestia thinks I cheated on her."

"Now, why would she think that?"

"Well today that son of a bitch Finn, an old friend of mine, showed her some pictures of me with a redhead and another with a brunette. Her mother claims that she doesn't believe it and it's fifty-fifty on how she feels, you know, considering that before I met her I technically played around with women. She said that she just needed some space, but I'm just trying to get her to talk to me Rose. She won't answer my calls or texts."

"Okay, we'll figure this out, she's probably just used to men treating her like shit, blame that on Mike. But, I'll text her, and I'll see if I can get her to talk to you. Where is she now?"

"She's at a friend's. Lucinda's her name."

"Okay, give me her number so I can call her first. I need to see those pictures for myself before I talk to Celestia."

"Thank you, Rose, I can't thank you enough."

"What're best friends for? Plus, I really like Celestia for you, she makes you actually show your feelings," she states as she laughs through the phone.

"Yeah, whatever," I reply smiling.

"See? You know it's true."

"I know, but I can't help it, I really love her ya know?"

"I know Ramon, okay send me Lucinda's number so I can call her, and then I'll call you back."

"Alright, talk to you later."

"Bye,"

I ended the call and sent Lucy's number to her. I really hope she can reach her. I want my Queen back home.

Chapter 29

I practically lunge at my phone when I get a call from Rose.

"Were you able to call her?"

"I was, took a long ass time though. Anyway, she sent me the pictures and I just sent them to your phone. I can see why it looks like you cheated."

I put the phone on speaker and look at the pictures she sent me.

"Wait is that us?"

"Exactly right."

"When was this?"

"The day that you came to me when we were trying to find her after Mike took her. I remember I kissed your cheek goodbye. If I was her and saw that, with no context, I'd think something of it too. Especially since the timing of that picture was really wrong and it looks like we just finished making out or something. But this other one, you definitely know who this is."

"That's my half-sister for fuck's sake! Where did Finn even find this picture?"

"Considering Celestia doesn't even know that you have a half-sister, I can also see why she'd think you cheated."

"Dammit, this picture was taken like years ago!"

"Yeah, but Finn edited it so well that it looks like he took the pictures himself. I mean look at them, he even got the dates and everything in the corner of it!"

"Now I wish he was bad at photography, this should've never happened."

"Oh also, when I talked to Celestia's friend, she said that they had gone to a friend of hers to find out if the photos were real or not. Celestia was starting to think that you actually might have cheated on her but I explained the pictures to her once I saw them so as we speak she's telling Celestia everything and convincing her to come back."

"Thank God, I was beginning to worry that the longer she didn't know the more it would eat at her and she'd end up believing it. I know how she is."

"Now, all we have to wait for is Celestia, the ball's in her park."

"She'll come back I know she will, I gave her the space that she wanted."

"And good for you for doing that, because most men would either chase after her, which in her case would probably only make her suspect even more."

"Yeah, I guess so. Thank you again, Rose, I owe you one."

"It's all good. I'm just glad this mess was all figured out."

"Mhm."

"So, are you gonna go to her?"

"I really want to, but the question is does she want me to come to her?"

"I don't know what she's thinking. But all I know is that she definitely loves you, Ramon. You two were meant for each other. You won't find love with anyone else like that. So I suggest you do whatever it takes to keep her. Women can be very oblivious to true love, most of us put ourselves down so much, that we've forgotten that we're freaking Goddesses and that there's someone who truly loves us for what they see instead of what we're trying to be."

I called Lucinda and she finally answered.

"Is it alright if I come over? I wanna see her."

"I don't think that's the best idea right now Ramon."

"Why not?"

"Well, she..."

I hear a bit of shuffling and movement for a moment.

"She's been chewing herself out for even believing in the slightest bit that those pictures were real. After I talked to Rose, I told Celestia how it was just a misunderstanding and how the pictures just looked bad with no context and she just began to tear up, and then her silent tears became cries, I honestly thought she might have been on her period or something cause that's a mood swing if I ever saw one. Anyway, seeing you right now is the last thing she needs. She's not mad or upset at you and she told me that she wants to apologize but right now she just needs time to herself and she needs a distraction from her thoughts, as her best friend I'm doing that. I'll take care of her."

"Thank you, Lucy," I sigh.

"It's no problem, Ramon, I'll get her back to you as soon as she gets a hold of herself, I promise. It'll only be a day or two more. She'll bounce back and laugh at all of this later."

"Ha, that's my girl for you," I say smiling. "If she needs anything, just call me. I got everything."

"Alright then, I'll text you with updates."

"Thanks, bye."

"You're welcome, bye."

I hang up and lay flat on the bed and close my eyes. What I wanted right now, so badly, was to hold her and tell her that its okay, that everything will be fine, that we were fine.

Chapter 30

Yesterday went by in a blur. I don't know how many times I cried, pigged out on leftover junk food from two nights ago, and then cried some more. I felt so shitty, but most of all, I felt stupid as fuck. I haven't gotten out of bed at all today, except to pee or eat. I had coffee this morning to try to keep myself awake but my body just rejected it. I was upset at myself and I didn't know how I was going to get out of this mindset.

"Alright, get up Celestia, you need to at least take a shower, you can't lay here all day."

"Why not, I have nothing better to do anyway." I groan as I flip onto my stomach and bury my face in the pillows.

"Okay, why don't we go out tonight, you, me, and Steph, we can all get super cute and wear lavish outfits and even rent a limo, just so we can go to Mcdonald's or some other fast-food restaurant.

"Okay, that actually sounds very tempting not going to lie." I lightly laugh.

"See? Come on Celestia, get up, you can't keep beating yourself up for the littlest things. You need a distraction that's what you need. I'll buy you all the food you want today if you get up."

"Mm, promise?" I grin.

"Yeah, yeah, I promise. Come on now, out of bed. You're body print is starting to form in it." she laughs.

I laugh at her joke and push myself up.

"God damn, I look like a fought a raccoon," I say as I look at myself in the mirror across from the bed.

"Exactly, so go take a shower, get yourself something to eat, and when I get back from work I don't wanna see you moping in bed again."

"Yes, mother ." I smile and roll out of the bed.

"I'll see you later bestie," she says as she leaves the room.

I don't physically move until I hear her leaving out of the apartment.

When I get in the shower, I take my time and wash my hair as well, as I comb my fingers through my hair, it calms me, just for a moment, until it reminds me of Ramon and I fight the urge to cry again. I was really going to be dehydrated at this rate if I didn't stop. I shake away the thought and continue with washing my hair.

After my shower, which took quite a while since I shaved as well, I patted myself dry, moisturized, and then walked back to the room to get my undergarments. I love that I can come over to Lucy anytime. We used to live together until I had enough for my own apartment, now she just leaves this room for guests, but she still has a few of my old things stored away for me. I grab a matching red lace set and slip them on. Then I take a pair of shorts and a crop top in black and put them on as well. As I brush out my hair and braid it into two large braids going back, I look at the mirror, but I'm not looking at myself. I'm looking at my phone on the nightstand. Something inside me is telling me to turn it on and call him. At least I can give him that. I at least owe him that for leaving in the first place without telling him anything. I place my brush down on the dresser and go to grab my phone off the nightstand. I turn it on and wait for the lock screen to load. When I put in my password. All the notifications come flooding my screen. There were many missed calls from Ramon and a few texts as well. I opened his last text. He texted that he missed me.

After our conversation, I felt better. I plug in my phone and place it back down on the nightstand. I get up and go into the kitchen to make myself something to eat. I take out two eggs and a ramen bowl, it was already one in the afternoon so there is no need to make any type of breakfast. As I cook the eggs my stomach growls at the sight of them sizzling in the pan. I add a few seasonings on top and turn away from them to make the ramen noodles. I pour hot water into the bowl, add the flavor packet, and close it back up, placing a small flat item on top to keep it covered. Then I'm back on the eggs. I look at my sunny-side-up eggs and deem them ready to eat. I turn off the oven, take the eggs, and put them right over my ramen after uncovering it. My stomach growls again. Damn. I was really hungry. I take my ramen and sit down at the counter.

It was only one twenty-five when I finished and I didn't know what to do. I go to the living room and look at the bookshelves, skimming for a book to read that I'd most likely finish until Lucy gets back. I ended up pulling out a small book in the bottom corner and looking at the front, it had cuff links in the front but what drew me in was the six words on the cover.

He possessed me and obsessed me...

Reminds me of Ramon, I thought. I take the book and lay on the couch opening it up to the first chapter.

"Ah, good. You're not back in bed," says Lucy as she closes the door behind her.

"No. I got myself together."

"Good, we're you reading?"

"Yeah, this is a really good book by the way."

"Yeah, I read that one way too many times to keep count. It's a series."

"Really? I should definitely get them for my library, I've been wanting to put one in my future house but I can't have books laying around my apartment."

"I can definitely recommend more of those kinds of books for you later. By the way, you still wanna do what I suggested this morning?"

"Oh, the fast-food thing? Sure why not, let's go crazy. Also, I talked to Ramon."

"What? When? What'd you say?"

"I just told him how I felt and that I missed him. He said that my mother explained everything to him after she called me."

"Ah, so are you gonna go back home tonight then?"

"I'll go in the morning, I still wanna hang."

"Alright, I'll call Steph, and then we'll get ready together."

I nod as I place the book back in its place on the shelf and then go back into the kitchen. I go to the fridge and pull out an egg salad along with some sliced bread.

"Can you make me one too? I only had a yogurt for breakfast."

"Sure," I say as I pull out four slices of bread and put them all in the toaster. Lucy calls Steph and tells me that she'll be there in about thirty minutes as I wait for the toaster to pop.

"Here ya go," I say to Lucy as I hand over her egg salad sandwich.

"Thank you," and she immediately stuffs her mouth with it.

"Damn, and I thought I was hungry." I giggle.

"Shut up, I was so swamped at the restaurant today, I couldn't even get a break to eat." she laughs.

"Don't choke now,"

"I should be telling you that." she smiles as she takes another bite.

I roll my eyes and smile. I take a bite of my own and sit down next to her on the couch. She turns on the TV and we watch random episodes of the office until we're finished with our sandwiches.

"The third stooge is here!" says Stephanie as I open the door for her.

"A mess I tell ya. Omg, that dress is gorgeous."

"Thanks, I literally wore this to prom just to make my ex jealous."

"Nice, as you should," I reply and take her makeup bag from her hand. She uses her legs to close the door behind her and I lock it. She then follows me to my room where Lu was taking a shower.

"What are you guys wearing?"

"I'm wearing a red dress, thank God I forgot to take it with me so it's been here with Lu for years, and Lu is wearing the yellow dress she wore to prom as well."

"She looks good in yellow. doesn't she."

"Hey Steph!" says Lucy as she comes out of the bathroom in her matching yellow underwear set.

Stephanie whistles and I laugh.

"Yep, yellow is definitely her color," I state.

"Awe, stop it, you make me blush." Lucy jokes as she unwraps her hair from the towel and plugs in a blow dryer to dry it off.

I take my phone and connect it to Lucy's Bluetooth speaker and play music before I unbraid my hair and let it fall into waves. I decide to do my makeup first and I play around with my eyeliner, making it a bold and bright red. I add a white eyeliner on top and choose lashes over mascara tonight. I do the rest of my face, lastly adding a red lipstick to my lips. When I was finished, Stephanie was already in her dress, hair up in a braided bun with two soft curls in the front, and she was helping Lucy zip up the back of her dress. Stephanie's dress stuck to all her curves and reached to the floor with a very small train at the back of it. In the front, the deep V gave all attention to her breasts. Lucy's dress was a bright yellow two-piece dress. The bottom was a high-low skirt and the top had one sleeve. There were tiny rhinestones on the bottom of the dress that trickled up and seemed to fade away the more it did and it circled the entire bottom of the dress. I walk to the closet and sift through the clothes until I find my red dress. I can't even remember the last time I wore this dress. Or if I even wore it ever. I pull it out of the plastic cover and hold it up and sigh. I take it out of the hanger and unzip the back then step into it.

"Can one of you zip me up please?"

"Sure," says Steph as she comes over to me.

She zips me up quickly and I turn around to look at myself in the full body mirror across from me that leaned against the wall. My dress was a bright red at the top and as you faintly looked down it seemed to get into a darker shade of red to the bottom. The dress had a slit on both sides that reached up to my thigh and the top had off-the-shoulder puff sleeves.

"Wow, I haven't looked this pretty in like forever." I exhale.

"Look at you! Ahh, so pretty I'm going to cry." sniffs Lucy.

I turn around and look at the bottom of the closet to find the shoes that I bought with the dress. There they were in the corner and still in the box. They were open-toe heels with strings to tie up to my mid-calf.

"Y'all we look hot," says Steph as she looks at herself in the mirror.

"I know, I'm so glad we did this. I haven't looked this cute in so long." sighs Lucy as she looks at herself as well and

"Okay, now that we're all glammed up, where are we going to eat?" I laugh as I slip on my shoes and tie them.

"McDonald's!"

"You seem a little too McHappy." laughs Lucy.

"That joke was so bad," Steph replies as she shakes her head at her.

"I know, I know, but I couldn't help it."

Suddenly Lucy's phone rings and she answers it.

"Yep, we'll be down in a few." she quickly hangs up and looks at us. "Alright, ladies our chariot awaits."

"You did not actually get a limo did you?"

"I did." she grins as she grabs her bag.

"Omg yes we're riding in style!" squeals Stephanie.

"We're going all out, I love it." I smile and grab my phone to slip it into my small purse.

We all leave the apartment and we bump into James who seemed to be on his way inside.

"Wow, Lucy. You look beautiful." he clears his throat and looks at the rest of us. "Y'all look absolutely amazing."

"Awe, thank you, James," says Lucy, and I could see her cheeks turning a light shade of red.

"Where are y'all headed?"

"McDonald's," Steph smirks.

"You're joking right?" replies James as he looks at us with playfully concerned eyes.

"Nope. We legit got ready just to go to McDonald's. We're bored, and I needed a distraction and a fun night out."

"Well, I won't ask any more questions then." he chuckles as he opens the door to his apartment.

"Wait, before you go can you take a picture of us please?"

"Sure," he says. "I can take it on my phone."

He pulls out his phone and takes a few pictures.

"Check your phone I just sent them to you."

Lucy checks and she shows us the pictures.

"You really know how to take pictures J, these are great."

"Thanks, I dabble in photography a little bit."

"I'm coming to you for my birthday pictures." smiles Lucy.

"Say less. I'm gonna head in now, have fun beautiful ladies." he smiles back.

"Thank you, see ya!" I say and we head to the elevator to the first floor. When we step out of the elevator the man in the front smiles at us and opens the door to let us out. We say thank you and turn to see the limo out in front. The driver opens the door and we file inside.

"This limo is so pretty it looks like a jeep," says Stephanie.

"I know, it's great isn't it?"

"It is, how in the world did you get a limo at this time?"

"You'll find out later." she grins at me.

I give her a questioning look and she just shrugs and continues to smile.

"Holy Fuck! Are you sure that's a McDonald's?" exclaims Stephanie as she steps out first.

"Yep, this is McMansion. Just wait until you see inside," replies Lu.

I'm the last to step out and I look up at the place in awe.

"Wow, it is pretty."

"By the way, Celestia, I think someone is waiting for you by the door." smiles Lucy.

I look at her and furrow my brows. "What? Who and why..."

I turn my face to the door and my mouth begins to slightly quiver.

"Ramon," I whisper. I pick up my dress so I don't trip on it and I run to him. He swoops me up and I crush him in between my arms. I look at him and smile then kiss him deeply.

"I'm so sorry," I whisper.

"Nothing to be sorry for, I just missed you an awful lot. Hey, don't cry."

"I'm fine, they're happy tears," I say as I blink the tears away and smile at him. God, I missed you. I've been moping around all day."

"I know, Lucinda called me to complain." he chuckled.

"Awe my fave couple back together and happy." gushes Steph.

As I look at her I see James, Ethan, and Luke all dressed in tuxedos with ties that matched our dresses coming up behind her.

"Oh my God, look who joined the party!" I say and Lucy and Steph both turn around.

"This is like prom all over again." gasps Lucy. "Well, well, well, if it isn't the one who made fun of us for dressing up to eat fast food."

"Hey, I had to make you believe I wasn't in this," replies James as he puts his hands up in defeat.

"We couldn't let you ladies have all the fun now," smiles Ethan as he casually puts his arm around Stephanie's shoulders. "Hey sweetheart," winks Luke as he comes closer.

"Omg, you guys are matching me!" she says excitedly as she looks at Luke also.

I turn back to Ramon and lay my head on his chest and smile. He looks down at me and kisses the top of my head. Something I missed dearly.

"Let's go inside,"

Everyone stops taking pictures and they follow us inside the restaurant. There were only a few customers and they looked super confused when we walked in and it only made us laugh to ourselves. We find an area to fit us all and we give our orders to the boys and they go to order. As we girls are sitting and taking silly pictures, I can't help but smile until my cheeks hurt. Lucy moves closer to me and links her arm with mine.

"Thank you for this, I needed it," I say to her.

"Oh, it's not me you should be thanking. This was all Ramon."

"You mean?"

"Yep, everything, except for the idea. This stupid but brilliant idea was mine." she laughs.

"Well, still thank you."

"Anytime bestie."

"We should go dancing!" says Stephanie as she stands up.

"Dancing? Are you crazy, I'm so stuffed I can't even turn in this dress." huffs Lucy as she pats her stomach and slouches further into the seat.

"Awe come on, it'll be fun, let's go slow dance under the moon, it's full!"

"We should come dance with me, Lu," asks James and he offers his hand to her.

"Ugh, fine," she smiles.

She takes his hands and he guides her outside to the back.

"Wanna?" asks Ramon. As the rest of them follow James and Lucy.

"Sure," I say and he takes my hand and we go out back as well. He spins me around and pulls me closer to him and as he slips his arms around my waist I lean in and place my head on his chest while we slowly sway.

"Thank you, Ramon."

"For what my Queen?" he says as he looks down at me.

"For not giving up on me, for staying by my side, for loving me, everything."

"I would never give up on you. Ever," he whispers as he kisses the crown of my head. "I refuse to let you go. I've been silently watching you from afar for years and you finally let me in."

"I'm just sorry that I left you alone this week, I should've just talked to you. The only love that I've received was from my parents and the very few friends I have that I can count on one hand, Ramon. When I saw those pictures, it only reminded me of Mike and that he isn't the only shitty person out there. You had a reputation with many women before we decided to spend that one week together and with my luck at love, I thought I'd end up broken hearted all over again and I don't think I was ready for that."

"I'm sorry for making you think that way, I don't want to remember my past with other women, no offense to them but they were just objects to me. I didn't care about them. The only person I've ever cared about in my life was you. It will always be you." he says as he takes my chin in his hands and leans down to kiss me fondly.

"By the way, why didn't you tell me that you had a half-sister?" I say looking up at him.

"I'm not sure, we both never really talked about our families except your mom when she came over. But my half-sister, we don't really talk much, I usually only saw her when my dad was alive and he made her go to events and shit, but after he died, she kind of just disappeared and did her thing, making a name for herself instead of simply being the daughter of Keelan Osgood."

"I understand."

"Yeah, anyway, the pictures that you saw, they weren't fake, but the one of me and her was taken years ago at an old lakehouse that her, me, and Finn used to go to. I didn't even know he still had those pictures."

"Mm okay," I say softly and let my head fall back on his chest.

We continue to sway to nothing but the beating of our hearts and I sigh as I look at Lucy with James smiling at one another, then I look at Steph, who is dancing with Luke but laughing as Ethan pokes at her sides and tickles her, making her giggle nonstop, trying to get his turn.

All of my friends are in one place. I couldn't have asked for a better group of people. And most importantly, I was in the arms of my lover and I was never going to leave him again. From now on, I will fight anything that comes between us. We both will.

Chapter 31

"I'm going to take a shower babe, I can't believe you let me sleep with my face caked like this, and now if I dare to look in the mirror, I know I'm going to look like a damn raccoon."

"A damn cute raccoon at that, you we're so tired, I didn't want to wake you up," Ramon grins as he kissed my forehead. "Care if I join?"

"You're welcome to." I smile as I peel off the undergarments I wore from yesterday and let them drop to the floor.

I look up and find Ramon smiling at me with his head tilted to the side.

"What?" I ask.

"Nothing, you're just so damn fucking hot."

This has me grinning myself. "Alright, you better hurry if you wanna join me," I reply as I turn around and walk to the bathroom. Ramon's hands are on my body in seconds and he turns me around, picking me up and wrapping my legs around his waist as he smashes his lips onto mine.

"What was that for?"

"Just cause."

"Well, do it again. Just cause." I smile.

He kisses me again, a little softer this time but deeper than the first and he moves us to the showerhead in the corner of the bathroom. He gently places me back down and turns on the water. I move to the side a little, just because I hate cold water. After a few seconds, Ramon puts his hands under the water and then slides them down my shoulder. Deeming it safe, I move under the water and let it fall directly on my face and hair. Ramon turns me around to face him where he was now holding a soapy washcloth in his hands. He then gently starts to wipe at my eyes and the rest of my face until all the makeup was completely gone. He smiles and kisses me again then places the cloth down. Picking up a loofah and adding more of my favorite shower gel to it, he turns me around again and begins to move it all over my shoulders and down to the rest of my body. He starts to caress my ass and I faintly arch back to him. I turn around and lean in to kiss him. As our kiss gets deeper I can feel his cock getting harder and rising in between my thighs. It's hard to ignore it now, and I dip a hand in between us and wrap it around him. I slowly start to move my hand around it back and forth in a twist-like motion which only makes him bulge in my hands. He takes his own hand and puts it between my legs and he starts to rub at my clit with his fingers. I spread my thighs apart a little more for him. He moves us so that my back is now against the wall and I take a leg and wrap it around his hips, allowing his cock to push closer to my sex. I can feel my own juices slipping out of me and I moan, pushing into him more. Without breaking our kiss he takes the tip of his cock and brings it right to my labia and swipes it across. I coil at the movement and then moan again as he slips himself inside of me. He starts to move in slow but powerful strokes and I look down to watch as it goes in and out. This awakens my need to be fucked more and I think he can tell as well because he picks up my other leg and gives me one good slam into my pussy. His tempo quickens and he and I lock eyes as he pounds into me harder. There's nothing but the sound of my moaning, his grunting, and the sound of bodies pushing against each other.

"Fuck, I missed this. I missed you." I moan as I bounce on him even more.

"Same here my love, I was desperate to plunge my cock back into that sweet, wet, cunt of yours." he groans as he buries his head into my shoulder.

I moan once more and my head tilts back with pleasure. I grip onto his shoulders tightly and my nails nearly dig into his back.

"Ahh, faster baby, make me come, make me come, make me come!"

Ramon groans in my ear and gives me one good thrust inside of me and I feel it so deep that it has my legs starting to shake violently as I get close to orgasm. He holds me up with one hand and then takes his other down to my clit and starts rubbing it slowly, driving me to the edge. My eyes begin to roll back and I gasp. He slips out of me and he bends down.

"I want you to come in my mouth." and he immediately put his lips onto my pussy. His hands entwine with mine as my legs quiver and he pushes me back towards the wall so I don't fall. He sucks on my clit and licks in between my inner labia. My orgasm releases out of me in a rush after he slips two fingers deep inside. He only spreads my legs further apart and pins me to the wall. His mouth doesn't stop moving over my now swollen cunt and I can already feel the next orgasm coming.

"You tastes so good, baby, I could eat you all day." he groans before he slides his tongue again in between my glistening slit.

He then moves up to pay attention to my breasts and he snags a nipple into his mouth. As he does so, he grabs a handful of my ass and squeezes.

"My ass needs attention too." I moan as I pull at his hair and bring him up to kiss him deeply. He grins and swiftly turns me around, bending me at the waist. He smacks my ass and I can already feel the fulfilling sting that it leaves behind. He takes his cock and pushes through my tightness and a gasp escapes my open lips. He starts to pound into me all over again and I brace myself by placing the palms of my hands against the shower wall. Ramon then picks me up and holds my thighs apart as he continues to fuck my ass. And he turns us around so I now have a full view of us in the bathroom mirror.

"You like the way I fuck you?"

"Y-yes, baby, very much." I moan loudly.

"Look at me while my cock drills into you," he whispers and I look up, our eyes locking with each other in the mirror. I moan his name and in response, he pushes into me deeper,

"Faster baby, I-I'm s-so close!"

I move a hand down to my swollen clit and rub in circles and he takes his hand and pushes a pair of fingers inside, curling it deep. A second orgasm hits me hard and I shake against him, wrapping a hand behind his neck. He turns my face to him and kisses me deeply as he comes inside of me after he gives me one last thrust.

"Yes, mom, I'm fine," I assure my mother for the fifth time.

"Just know, if you need me, call and I'll be there," she replies.

"I know, I promise I will. Bye,"

"Alright hon, I'll talk to you later, bye. I love you,"

"I love you too."

She hangs up and I place my phone down on the nightstand.

"You're mother again?" asks Ramon as he climbs into bed with me and nuzzles his head in my neck.

"Yep, she just wanted to check up on me."

"Ah. What are you reading?"

"An online book, by the way, you don't have a library here do you?"

"I don't, but I do have books lying in different places. Why? Do you want one?"

"If you have space, I've been wanting to buy a bookshelf so I can buy physical copies of books but my apartment had no space."

"I can get you an entire library with shelves going up many feet if that's what my Queen wants," he smiles and kisses the tip of my nose.

I softly smile and close my eyes.

"Thank you, my love," I whisper to him and give him a quick peck to his lips.

I curl myself into his chest and he wraps and arm around me. I continue with my book and he starts to nibble on my earlobe, my cheek, my neck.

"You're distracting me baby,"

"No, I'm not, I'm just simply showing my love," he mumbles.

He begins to suck on my neck and I close my phone and put it to the side. I move on top of him and straddle him with my legs.

"My queen,"

"My Casanova." I smile.

We were naked. Our bodies, entwined. We were simply comfortable around each other completely. I rub the sleep from my eyes and look at Ramon's soft sleeping face. I slowly smile to myself and move closer, careful not to wake him up. My smile easily turned into a frown. I most likely caused this man so much pain when I left which makes me upset at myself. Suddenly my stomach felt as if my organs were tied up in knots. I thought nothing about it but after a few seconds, it became worse. I quietly got out of bed and headed for the bathroom. I almost didn't make it to the toilet when I hurled my lunch from today in it. Ugh, maybe I ate way too much. And maybe it was probably a bad idea to have sex multiple times on a full stomach too. I get up after flushing and go to the sink to brush my teeth. I look at my breasts. Ramon was right, they seemed to have grown a few sizes bigger. Maybe it was the birth control pills. I stop mid-thought and my eyes go wide. I didn't even take one yesterday. Matter of fact when was the last time I did take one? My heart beats faster as I speed walk back into the room and dive for my phone. I open my Flo app and stare blankly at the big red circle telling me that I should be on the third day of my period.

Fuck.

Chapter 32

"Babe? Are you okay?"

"Yeah, yeah, I'm fine." She groans in the bathroom.

She turns to see me walk into the bathroom. I kneel next to her and pull her hair back.

"Have you been feeling sick all day my love?" I ask.

"No, it hit me just no-" She hurls into the toilet again.

"Do you want me to get you anything?"

"No, I'll be fine, I probably just have an upset stomach. Maybe I ate too much," she mumbles as she gets up to wash her mouth again.

"Are you sure?"

"Yeah, I'm sure baby,"

"If it continues, I'm bringing you to the emergency room."

"No, no, I'll be fine I promise," she argues and walks out, getting back in bed.

I sigh at her. She's been throwing up since last night and I don't think that she realized that I've been watching. I get under the covers beside her and pull her closer to me. Careful not to pull hard at her stomach so she doesn't throw up again. I didn't want to leave her but I had many missed meetings that I rescheduled for today. I kiss the top of her head before I get back up and she peeks at me from under the covers.

"Where are you going?"

"To the office, I have rescheduled meetings today."

"Oh, I forgot today was Monday, I'll be ready in a few," she says as she gets up.

"Nope, stay in bed and rest, you're sick."

"I am not sick Ramon,"

"Sick or not, you aren't feeling well so you're staying home."

"Fine."

"Thank you," I sigh and I kiss her again.

I open the covers to put her back into bed and pull it up to her chin.

"It'll only be a few hours, so I'll be home soon okay?"

"Alright, bring me Chipotle?"

"Okay baby, I'll bring you two bowls, does that sound good?"

She practically moans in delight. "God, you know me so well, how did I get so lucky?"

"I'm the lucky one," I reply as I finish fixing my tie and kiss her lips.

When I get into the office I pull out my phone and call Lucinda before my first meeting.

"Hey, are you busy right now?"

"No, I'm home all day today. Why?" she asks.

"Can you do me a favor?"

"Sure, what's up?"

"Celestia's at home right now, she's been throwing up since last night and I just want to make sure she has someone there in case something happens."

"I got her, are you gonna be out long?"

"No, I just have a hefty amount of meetings today but I'll be back before six."

"Alright then, I'll head over there now,"

"Thank you, Lucy,"

"Of course, no problem. You owe me food though," she laughs.

"Want some Chipotle? I was getting some for Celestia as well," I reply.

"Say less, just get me the same thing she has."

"Okay then, thank you again."

"Your welcome, I'll see you later."

I hang up, order their food for them, and head inside of my office.

Celestia

The door rings and I trudge my way over to it. I open it thinking it's my food but I find Lucy on the other side of it.

"You really do look like shit," she snorts and saunters inside.

"I definitely feel like shit," I lightly laugh as I close the door.

"Ramon told me you were throwing up since last night, are you sure you don't want to go to the emergency room?"

"No, I'll be fine. I'm not sick."

"If you aren't then why are you-OH, MY GOD!"

She gives me a wide grin and hugs me tightly.

"I'm gonna be an aunt finally!" she squeals. "Oh my goodness, you didn't tell Ramon. He is going to flip."

"Let's not get ahead of ourselves now, I could or could not be. I didn't take a test yet."

"You should! Like right now. Wait, I'll be right back I passed a pharmacy on my way here, I'll go get you a pregnancy test."

"Alright, hurry back. I don't think I can take this worrying any longer, it's starting to get to me."

She grabs her bag and keys and heads back out.

"It says you have to wait at least five minutes."

"Well, this is the longest five minutes I have ever endured. I'm scared Lu,"

"There's nothing to be scared of, you could possibly be a mom! This is exciting! Haven't you both ever talked about having kids before?"

"Not really, but I did think of it during the few days we were at the beach."

"See? It won't be so bad-"

The timer goes off and it rings in my ears. The five minutes were up and my heart raced. With shaky hands, I pick up the test.

"Ugh, I can't look, what does it say," I ask as I show the test to Lucy and squeeze my eyes shut.

"See for yourself mama," I open my eyes to see her full grin as she tilts the test back to me. I look down and see the two red lines and my heart skips a beat.

Ramon

I rushed home as fast as I could and when I got inside, I found both Celestia and Lucy on the couch. Lucy was flipping through Netflix shows and Celestia was reading her book from yesterday.

"I'm home babe,"

She turns her head and faintly smiles.

"Hi, baby,"

"Alright, it's time for me to go, don't forget to text me what happens," says Lu to Celestia as she leans down to hug her.

"I will, bye bestie."

"Bye!"

I nod at Lucinda as she grabs her bag and leaves.

"Thanks for the food Ramon,"

"Of course,"

She closes the door behind her and I lock it then go to Celestia.

"What were you up to today my love?"

"Nothing really, pretty much just read all day. Come. Sit. I wanna talk to you about something."

I tilt my head in question and move to the couch, sit next to her and pull her close. She smiles at me and then proceeds to lay her head on my thighs. She looks up at me and then stares past me to the ceiling. I could see her eyes become a little glassy and my heart skips a beat.

"Are you okay my queen?"

"Yeah, I'm fine. I just wanted to tell you something important."

"What is it, baby?"

"I'm-" she pauses and takes a deep breath. She looks at me and then closes her eyes.

"I'm scared."

"What are you scared of?"

She sighs and pulls out something from her sweatpants. It was a pregnancy test. My heart goes wild and I automatically grin at the word positive. Celestia was pregnant and she was having my baby.

"Baby, are you okay?" she asks me as she places a hand on my cheek, pulling me away from my thoughts.

"I'm more than okay my love, you're having my baby. I couldn't be happier." I whisper to her and lean down to kiss her lips.

"I don't know if I can do this. I do want the baby, I've been thinking about it, but I don't think that I'm cut out to be a mother."

"You'll be a great mother, no doubt about it."

"You think so?"

"Of course, you're good with kids, just look at Wyatt's. They all love you."

"I guess so. I'm excited, nervous, and terrified all at once. Oh my God. I have to tell my mother."

"Right. Are you going to call her now?"

"Yeah, I probably should. She is going to be so excited, she's been wanting to be a grandma since forever, I don't know why anyone would want to be a grandma willingly but okay I guess." she shrugs and lifts herself off of me.

"Slowly now,"

"I'm pregnant, not going through therapy," she laughs.

"I just want you to be careful baby," I reply as I kiss the top of her head.

She leans into me and lays her head on my shoulder as I lift her up and place her on my lap.

"Do you want a boy or a girl?" I ask her after a short moment of silence.

"A girl," she responds. "I've always told myself that I'd have a girl first, then a boy. How about you, what would you want it to be?"

"I didn't really think about it, but I think I'm just really happy that I'm gonna be a dad."

She smiles at me and then wraps her arms around my neck before she kisses me deeply.

"Can I take you somewhere tomorrow?"

"I'll go anywhere you want me to as long as you're there." she smiles.

I smile back and gently rub her cheek with my thumb.

"Alright. Don't worry about what you're wearing, I'm getting you something."

"Okay, may I ask where we're going? Or is it a surprise?"

"A surprise," I grin.

Chapter 33

Ramon brought everyone over and Steph, Lu, Rose, and I stayed in one room while Ethan, Luke, James, and Ramon stayed in another.

"I wonder why he's invited all of us as well," questions Steph as she zips up the rest of her dress.

"I definitely know, but I'm keeping my mouth shut." smiles Rose.

"What?" I say as I whip my head around to look at her. "He told you where he was taking us?"

"Yep, all I'm going to say is that it's far and we have to take his jet. But that's all I'm giving you. This is your surprise after all."

"Awe dammit, can't you at least tell me the place we're going? Y'all know I hate surprises. Hence why I was scared finding out that I'm growing an actual human being in my stomach." I reply as I point to my belly.

"Girl, you'll be fine, It's a cute surprise," she says.

"Yeah, it's gonna be so adorable!" perks up Lucy.

I gasp as she places the last pin in my hair.

"Don't tell me that you're in it too,"

"I am, I had to help him with something, you're not getting anything out of me," she says as she spins me around in my chair to give my hair and makeup a once over.

"Am I the only one here that doesn't know?" I pout.

"Yep, well besides Steph of course, but she'll find out later," replies Rose.

"Y'all are so cruel to me."

"It's for your own good," Lucy laughs as she glides the makeup brush across my cheek. "Alright, all done, go put on your dress."

I get up and go to the closet to pull out the white dress hanging in it. It was one of the whitest dresses I've probably ever worn. It has a slit on the right leg, both sides near the waist were open with a diamond-like pattern to show off my skin. There were no sleeves and the top of the dress almost looked like the ears of a cat. I take it off of the hanger and Rose helps me inside of it, zipping me up. I look at myself in the mirror and smile. Lucy comes next to me and lays her hands and head on my shoulder.

"You look absolutely breathtaking C,"

"Thank you, this dress does take my breath away," I sigh.

"You're so lucky, your man has taste in fashion." giggles Rose. "Step out with me Steph,"

I put on my silver earrings and bracelet and the new white-collar Ramon gave me this morning. It was a simple thin collar with a silver heart in the middle.

When Steph and Rose step back into the room, Stephanie had a smile on her face from ear to ear.

"Damn, not you too," I pout again.

"No pouting, you're gonna mess up your face," says Lucy as she uses her fingers to gently lift up my cheeks.

"Okay, okay, no more pouting."

We then hear a knock at the door.

"We're all dressed, come in," says Rose.

James opens the door and I catch him smiling at Lucy before he enters the room.

"You all look beautiful, Ramon wants to know if you all are ready to go."

"Yeah?" questions Rose as she looks back at us to confirm.

I nod my head as I slip on my flats and grab my purse in one hand and my heels in the other. We leave the room and follow James downstairs to the living room where the others were waiting.

Luke whistles in approval and Stephanie giggles. Ramon walks up to me slowly and smiles at me, kissing me fondly.

"Hi, Queen,"

"Hi King," I smile back.

"You ready?"

"Always,"

Seven or so hours can make you think quite a lot. I wondered about the baby that I now had growing inside of me. I wondered about how far Ramon and I came along. And I wondered about how proud my dad would be to see his little girl all grown up.

I look out and see the Eiffel Tower, gleaming with lights, as we fly by it.

"You brought us to Paris?" I whisper to Ramon, my head laying on his shoulder.

"I did, your mother told me that you've always wanted to come here."

"She did?" I reply, looking up at him.

"She did. And she told me every embarrassing thing that you've ever done. Including the time when you had your first period." he smiles.

"She. Did. Not." I say as my eyes go wide.

His grin gets wider and he just nods.

"Oh, God. Kill me now," I whine and turn away from him.

Ramon laughs and only pulls me closer to him.

"Why would she tell you that?" I shake my head.

"She got on the memory train and I couldn't stop her, plus being able to see your baby pictures was fun, you are so cute," he replies as he nuzzles his head in my neck.

"Better I wasn't there then, I would've been so embarrassed," I say, putting my face in my hands.

He chuckles a little then turns my face to face him. He lightly kisses me and smiles down at me.

"I love you," I whisper to him as I look him in the eye.

"And I love you," he replies kissing me again.

We were staying at another place of Ramon's. I'm convinced that he has a place in every country at this point. We went out to eat and now we were on our way to Versailles, France after an afternoon in Paris.

It was dark out now, but all the dim lights looked like little stars that had fallen from the sky.

"Are you going to tell me where you're taking me?" I ask Ramon as he takes my hand and helps me out of the car.

"Nope, you'll find out soon enough," he smiles.

I look to my left and Lucy gives me a small wink.

"I love how easily gullible you are," she says and giggles.

"Don't tell her that!" James says and he pulls her away from me.

Ramon wraps his arms around my waist and we walk for a few minutes in silence. As we walk, I notice that we were in a garden. A very large and spread out one at that. As the walkways came from different sides and connected in different places it looked like we were going through a maze.

"We're in the back of the Versailles Palace, my love," he whispers to me as he notices me looking at the huge architecture.

"It's so beautiful, I've only seen it in pictures-oh, what's this?" I ask as I see a string quartet playing in the middle of the garden right behind the large circle of water. My friends were already dancing together and I smile, remembering the first time we were like this.

"Another night of dancing," he replies and holds out his hands.

I smile, placing my hands in his, and he spins me into his arms.

"Can I ask you a question?" I ask mid-dance.

"Yes,"

"Is there a reason behind all this or did you just want a lovely night out with your girl and your friends?"

"Both," he grins.

"Awe, come on, you gotta give me something baby,"

"Nope, as I said before, you'll find out soon enough,"

I sigh and he pulls me closer and places my head on his shoulder as we move back and forth.

The song seemed to be coming to an end and I notice that James had vanished and come of them were sitting by the bushes.

"Remember that day when I brought you a few gifts before you went to the club?"

"Yeah?"

"Remember what you guessed it was?"

"Uhh," I look up as I think back to that day. "I don't remember."

"Well, you ask for something and today, I brought it for you." he smiles. "Turn around."

I turn and gasp at the small Maltipoo puppy in the arms of James.

"A puppy?"

"Not only a puppy," James says and gives me a wink.

He lets the dog go and it jumps from his arms and runs over to me. I scoop it up in my arms and gently pet its head as he licks my face. It was the cutest thing ever.

"I can't believe you actually got me a puppy. What in the world could be better than this precious pup-?" I question as I turn around.

Ramon was on one knee. With a ring box in his hand. With a beautiful ring inside of it. With a wide smile on his face. Tears start to form in my eyes and my lips start to quiver.

"Celestia, for years I have quietly watched you from afar and the biggest mistake I have ever made was not talking to you sooner. I am so glad to have met you and I am ready to spend the rest of my life with you. I can't wait to start a family with you. And I can't wait for you to be the first person I wake up to and go to sleep to. So, Celestia Hadleigh Crowe, will you marry me?"

"Yes, a million times yes!"

Chapter 34

I slip the ring on her finger and it fits perfectly. Our friends are behind us, celebrating and I pull her to me, kissing her deeply.

"I love you, I love you, I love you," she says in between our kisses.

She gently places the puppy down and I pick her up and spin her around in my arms.

"You don't know how happy I am, I've been holding onto that ring for days," I say smiling at her.

"Really?"

"Yes, really. I wanted to find the right time to ask you but I never got the chance to. And I wanted to make it special for you, because you are special, and you deserve the world."

I place her down and Lucy quickly grabs her in a tight hug as she squeals. I silently laugh at the moment and pick up the puppy who was grazing her paw on my shoe.

"Hey girl, couldn't wait to meet mommy, yeah?" I say as I rub her head.

"Congrats man," James says.

"Yeah congrats, you lucky man," grins Luke.

Ethan walks over with Stephanie and they congratulate me as well.

"Thank you," I nod.

We all turn towards the abrupt squeal to see Celestia with her phone in her hand. She must be talking to her mother. I go over to her and wrap my hands around her waist, placing my chin on her shoulder.

"Congrats Ramon, hon! You outdid yourself with that ring, it's gorgeous! And that puppy is absolutely a sweetheart!" says Madeline through the phone.

"Thank you, Madeline," I responded smiling.

"Alright mom, I'll talk to you later okay?"

"Alright my lovely, have fun in France!"

"Bye!"

Celestia hangs up and puts her phone away then turns to face me. She smiles at the pup in my hands and scratches her ear.

"Is it a girl?"

"Yeah, I didn't name her though. What would you like to call her?"

"Peach, she reminds me of a peach tree somehow,"

"Peach it is then," I smile.

"Thank you for tonight Ramon, you don't know how happy you've made me," says Celestia beside me in bed.

"You've made

me

the happiest man alive right now," I smile and kiss her forehead.

"Awe, look at you being cheesy,"

"It's not cheesy if it's the truth."

"Oh shut up, just admit that you're cheesy."

"Never," I grin.

I pepper her face with multiple kisses as I pull her in. My hands glide down to her waist and move around to her ass. Her hand moves down as well and her fingertips trace the front of my boxers. She dips her hand inside and drags it along my length down to my balls and brings it back up again. I groan before I kiss her deeply.

"Careful now, you wouldn't want to add another baby to that womb would you now?"

She lightly giggles but doesn't stop gripping onto me.

"That's definitely not how it works but I do like the sound of that." she grins.

I smile at her and use my hand to yank off the lace panties that she had on. I then move to her breasts while my fingers lightly play with her clit. I suck a nipple deep into my mouth and I smile as I hear her moans escaping from her mouth.

"Fuck, baby,"

She arches towards me and I move myself down to her legs. I spread them apart, licking my lips at the sight of her glistening wet cunt. I place myself in between her legs and I slide my tongue through her inner folds. I do this a few more times, going faster as each second goes by and her moans grow louder. I start to suck on her clit and I can feel her legs threatening to shut so I hold them apart.

"I-I'm going to come, faster baby, make me cum."

I swirl my tongue and lap up all her juices until her legs begin to shake. Her stomach coils as she comes into my mouth.

"That's it, baby," I whisper as I take her hands and entwine them with mine.

She then places herself up and gets on her knees, pulling off my boxers. She watches as my cock springs out into her hand and she licks her lips before she pushes me to lay flat and opens her mouth to swallow me whole.

"Fuck, Celestia."

Her head bobs as she sucks on me and she moves to slide her tongue up and down my length as she cups my balls and moves them in a rotating motion. I'm so close now and without warning, she moves on top of me and slips in right inside of her.

"Come inside of me my love," she moans as she starts to bounce on my cock. I hold her legs apart and begin to thrust into her ruthlessly until I did.

"Thank you for making my childhood dreams come true," she says to me as she caresses my cheek.

"And what childhood dream would that be?" I ask.

"To go to Paris. And to get proposed to. It's all my little self wanted."

"Anything for you my queen. I'm just glad my nagging finally got you to stay with me." I chuckle.

She laughs as well. "If I knew of all the amazing things to happen, I would've let you nag me all you want."

"Well, I still do that on a daily basis," I grin.

"Well, starting now, you have nine months not to."

"No promises," I wink. "But I will make sure that you are happy every step of the way."

"Good luck with that. When I start crying out of nowhere, you'll be so concerned, you'll start to wonder how awful I can get."

"Never. I can't wait to see when you're showing, it's going to be so cute."

"Yeah, definitely cute when I'm waddling like a penguin to the kitchen for the twentieth time to get food."

"Of course, why wouldn't it be?" I smile.

"Ugh, now that just reminded me that I won't be able to wear most of my clothes." she pouts.

"Don't you worry," I respond, kissing her forehead. "I'll take you shopping and everything. I'll even put in the library in one of the empty rooms downstairs for you so you can read all day to your heart's content."

"Every day I think to myself how in the world did I get so lucky?" she whispers as she tucks her head into my chest.

"I wonder the same," I say and look down at her. Her eyes were closed and she had fallen asleep. I sigh and comb my fingers through her hair. I am so damn lucky. The luckiest man in the entire universe.

Chapter 35

Celestia

Ramon moved my things into the empty bedroom downstairs for me and you'd think that I'd get used to seeing myself with a large belly, but it just feels so weird.

"We're going to be late my love," says Ramon as he wraps his arms under my stomach, gently lifting it, giving me relief.

"Thank you," I whisper as he kisses my cheek. "I'm ready, I was just thinking."

"What about?"

"How I'm still not used to this," I laugh as I place a hand on my stomach, staring into the mirror.

"You're almost there. Only one more month to go. You ready to find out the gender?"

"I've been ready. I tried so hard not to peak at the info." I laugh and turn to face Ramon.

He smiles and gives me a quick kiss. "You look beautiful by the way."

"Thank you, baby," I say.

He takes my hand and leads me out of the house. Wyatt was waiting for us with the car and when he spots me he opens the door.

"Thank you, Wyatt," I smile.

"No problem, Celestia. How are you holding up?"

"Eh, could be better. I'm just ready to go back to my jeans." I laugh.

"Soon enough you will," he laughs with me as well.

Ramon pulls me close once Wyatt closes the door and gets inside.

"My mother is going to be so thrilled to see me, well more so her unborn grandchild but close enough."

"It is her first grandchild after all," says Ramon.

"True, she really hopes it's a girl so she can spoil her like crazy, don't know if I should be worried or not," I laugh. "Considering you might not be opposed to that and help along the way."

"I can't promise that, you know I'm going to spoil him or her."

"Don't spoil them too much, you've already broken me, I don't even use my own money anymore," I grimace at him.

He just smiles and rubs the top of my hand with his thumb.

"Again, no promises. Isn't that right little one," he says as he bends down to kiss the top of my belly.

"Oh!" I exclaimed as I felt a kick in my lower right side. "Ramon they just kicked!"

"Where?"

"Here," I say as I take his hand and place it where it happened.

The baby kicked again a little rougher this time.

"Ow,"

"You running out of space in there?"

"They might be, hang in there baby, one more month," I say.

"We're here,"

"Oh, welp, let's get this party started."

Wyatt opens the door for us and Ramon gets out first, holding out his hand for me. I take his hand and push myself out of the car. He holds onto my waist as we walk inside. My mother was waiting for me in the hall. She was wearing a baby pink blouse with baby blue slacks. Her hair was down and wavy.

"Hi, mom!"

"Hi, sweetie! Ramon lovely to see you as always, hope she hasn't made you want to run yet," she laughs.

"Not at all Madeline. I've kept her busy with books and food." he laughs.

"Y'all act as if I'm not here," I say shaking my head. "I'm not that bad."

"Considering what you put me through before giving birth to you, I'm surprised this little one hasn't caused you trouble too," replies my mother as she rubs the top of my belly.

"Alright, the others are probably waiting for us."

"Oh right, right, I was sent out here to tell them when you got here, hold on."

My mother sends off a quick text to someone and then gestures for us to follow her to the elevator. After a few seconds, the doors opened and we were now at the top of the building. The scenery was beautiful with all the flowers and fairy lights scattered everywhere. Confetti is popped when we enter and my mom walks us over to a table.

"You ready mama?" grins Lucy as she hands me the huge black balloon.

"Definitely," I grin back as I take it from her.

I place the balloon in front of me and wait for them to finish counting down before I popped it.

The pink glitter explodes out, pink smoke surrounds us and everyone yells in excitement.

"Congrats my love, you got your girl," grins Ramon as he wraps his arm around me.

"I did, I really did. I can't believe that I'm having a girl," I smile, fondly staring down at my belly.

My mom pulled me for a side hug and I closed my eyes, smiling.

"I'm so happy for you baby," she whispers.

"Thank you mom," I reply as she lets go of me.

"Did you guys pick out names yet?" asks Stephanie after she comes up from her seat with Peach to congratulate me.

"No actually, we wanted to find out the gender first."

"Makes sense, by the way, Peach has been begging to see you," she laughs as Peach wiggles in her hand.

"Awe you missed mama Peach?" I smile and take the puppy from Steph. Peach licks my cheek and wags her tail in excitement when she sees Ramon coming over as well.

"Hey Peach," says Ramon as he rubs just below her ear.

I see a flash of a camera in my peripheral vision and I look up to see James taking another picture.

"You didn't think I wouldn't make an album of the both of you did you?" he smiles.

I lightly giggle at him and shake my head.

"By all means go ahead," I reply.

He continues to take pictures of us three and takes more pictures of us with our friends.

"Ah, there you are Peach, for a sec I thought that you disappeared on me." says my mom. Then she faces me with a huge smile on her face.

"I can't believe it's a girl, I get to spoil her rotten!"

"Not too much, I already told Ramon that y'all better not,"

"No promises," she winks and walks away.

I shake my head as Peach cocks her head at me.

"Only you listen to me Peach," I say, smiling at her.

"It's true, once that kid pops out of you it's going to cause you so many sleepless nights."

I look up and smile as I see Aurora with Evelyn in hand and Luna and Mateo at both of her sides.

"Aurora! When did you get here?"

"Hey! I just got here. I had to pick up the kids from school," she grins. "Congrats by the way! I'm so happy for you,"

"Thank you, hey Matty and Luna, hi Evelyn," I gush.

"Hi Princess CC!" replies Mateo as he looks up at me and Luna smiles and waves.

"Oh wow, I see you have a missing tooth Luna, did the tooth fairy give you anything?"

"She did! I got five dollars! I'm gonna get big girl teeth now!" she grins, even more, to show where the hole was.

"That's great!" I smile as I bend down and swipe at her chin.

"So, how are you holding up? Come, sit. You shouldn't be on your feet as much." asks Aurora.

We move to a table to continue our conversation.

"I'm hanging in there, it hasn't been as bad as I thought it would be, but then again it's different for everyone," I say.

"That's true. When I was pregnant with Matty, he caused me almost no pain and I barely had any contractions until it was time to give birth. I kept going to my doctor cause I thought that he wasn't moving and I had a miscarriage."

"Really?"

"Yep, But with Evelyn and Luna, they gave me hell." she laughs.

"Huh-Oh!"

I look down as Evelyn reaches over from her mother's lap and places both of her hands on the sides of my belly. I smile at her as she looks up at me with her pretty blue eyes.

"That could be your future best friend Evie," whispers her mother.

"I'm so happy I'm having a girl. I can dress her up and we can have matching clothes and everything." I say smiling as I think about it.

"I know, it's so much fun."

"Thank you for this ladies. I loved it."

"Of course C!" smiles Rose. "We've been wanting to plan this for ages ever since you got pregnant."

"Right," agrees Lucy.

Steph nods in agreement as well. "Yep, it was so much fun, even I'm now tempted to have one.

"Mmhm, with who?" smirks Rose.

"I know with who," smiles Lucy as she pokes Stephanie's side. "Ethan, I've been watching them flirt all day while they were setting stuff up."

"I have no idea what ya'll are talking about, we're just friends."

"Just friends huh? I don't think friends look at each other like they're ready to risk it all."

"Oh come on not you too, we weren't flirting, we were simply-"

"Simply what?" says Lucy with a look.

"Talking. Having a normal conversation. That's it."

"Well I didn't see anything, but I did wonder if you liked him before," I state.

"Really?"

"Yeah, when we first met him and Luke, she kept making goo-goo eyes at him."

"Are y'all some type of love detectives?"

"Well let's say that you weren't flirting. He's super cute. I say you should go for it."

"She's right," I say.

"Go worry about your husband-to-be," Steph says as she smiles and shakes her head at me.

"Maybe I will," I say, sticking my tongue out at her playfully.

As Lu and Rose convince her to talk to Ethan, I walk over to where Ramon was sitting. He sees me walk over and smiles at me. Motioning for me to come and sit on his lap.

"Am I not heavy? I'm carrying a whole human."

"Nope, did you have fun today?"

"I did," I smile and kiss him.

"That's good,"

"You got any more plans for us today?" I smile at him.

"Not really, but if you want to go somewhere, I'll take you anywhere you want my love."

"I don't think I can walk anymore," I laugh. "But I do want Ice cream."

"A night in with Ice cream and a movie?"

"That sounds nice,"

"Alright then, wanna disappear now?" he grins.

I nod and slowly get up from his lap, letting in and out a deep breath.

"Jesus, I don't think I can hold myself up anymore."

"One more month baby, you got this. If I could take even just half of what you're feeling I would," he replies as he comes behind me and gently lifts up my stomach again like this morning, blissfully relieving some of the pain.

"What's wrong? Is she okay?" asks my mom as she walks over with a concerned look on her face.

"I'm fine mom, I'm just in a little pain."

"How much pain from one to ten? Are you sure you're okay?"

"Yeah, I'm just gonna go home and lay down."

"Okay, call me if you need me."

"I will," I nod as she takes my hand in hers before she walks away.

"Ready to go?" asks Ramon.

"Yeah, let me just say bye to everyone."

He gently lets go and I walk to where the girls were.

"Hey, Ramon and I are gonna head out,"

"Okay, you've been here for hours, your feet must be killing you," says Lucy.

"Yep," I chuckle. "I'm gonna go home and pig out on Ice cream and watch a movie."

"Sounds cute, go rest and have fun," says Rose as she hugs me goodbye.

"Where's Steph?" I ask.

They smile widely and look at each other.

"What?"

"Well, we caught her and Ethan heading out the door a while ago. They looked very jumpy. I'm pretty sure that this very moment she's screaming his name at the top of her lungs." laughs Rose.

"Rose! Omg," I gasp.

"Tell me I'm not right," she laughs again. "They're definitely fucking."

"I agree with that, she really likes him. She just doesn't want to admit it," replies Lucy as she shrugs.

"Definitely text me if she comes out after I leave. I want all the deets." I grin as I wave them goodbye.

"What movie do you wanna watch?"

"I'm feeling romantic comedy,"

"Romantic comedy it is," says Ramon as he hands me over the tubs of mint chocolate chip and Vanilla Ice cream.

He turns on the Tv and finds a movie for us. We watched

Isn't It Romantic and 50 First Dates. The last thing I remember seeing before I fell asleep was Ramon kissing the top of my head and then all over my belly. Whispering sweet nothings to his future daughter.

Chapter 36

"Good morning my queen,"

"Good morning my king," she says as she kisses the small of my back as I cook. "The eggs smell great baby,"

"I made you omelets and sunny side up with hashbrowns," I state.

"God, I love you,"

I lightly laugh before turning off the stove and turning to face her.

"You're welcome my love," I say kissing her forehead. "Okay, go back to bed, I'll bring you your food in a few minutes."

"Alright," she smiles and gives me a quick kiss before she walks back to the room.

I take a plate from the cupboard, place the omelets, eggs, and hashbrowns on it and place it on the breakfast tray. I also add a glass of orange juice, and a bowl of fruit and then bring it to the downstairs bedroom where Celestia was.

"Come to mama," she smiles as I place the tray beside her and get in bed.

"What about me?" I grin.

"I'll get to you later, I need food in me first. And so does this little one," she states as she lunges for the first omelet and puts nearly half of it in her mouth. Peach climbs onto the bed and wags her tail as she stares at the plate of food in front of her.

"Never get in the way of a pregnant lady and her food." I laugh as I scratch behind Peach's ear.

"You got that right," she responds. She takes a piece of her egg and gives it to Peach who quickly eats it and then hops off the bed.

"Alright, baby names. What are we thinking?"

"I'm not sure, I do know I want a name with a good meaning behind it though," she replies, stuffing another egg into her mouth.

"That makes sense. I was thinking of Evangeline, Aurelia, or Calliope.

"Calliope is such an adorable name." she sighs, laying back against the pillows. Then she turns to face me with a smile.

"You've thought about this before haven't you," she says as her smile gets wider.

"Yeah, a little. Ever since you told me you were pregnant, my mind has gone crazy thinking about how to best take care of you and the baby."

"Another reason why I love you," she smiles.

I move the tray out of the way, placing it on the empty nightstand next to me, and pull her close.

"Ah, so there's a list of reasons?" I question, smiling back.

"Yep,"

"May I ask what the reasons are?"

"There's so many I don't think I can say them all, but I will tell you my favorites."

"I'm all ears," I state.

"Well, I love you because you love my flaws, I love you because you look at me as if I'm the only girl for you, I love you because you still give me butterflies when I wake up next to you, I love you because you have never given up on me, and I love you because you still loved me even if I didn't deserve to be loved."

I look at Celestia. Her face. Her eyes. Her lips. My future wife, the mother of my child. My queen. My world. My everything.

"I'm so damn lucky to have you," I say as I pull her even closer and kiss her lips slowly.

She kisses me back with the same momentum and her fingers brush up my face to my hair.

"I love you, I love you, I love you," she whispers to me in between our kisses.

"And I love you," I responded smiling. "Come on, let's get you in a bath."

"Oh, I almost forgot about that." she giggled as I kissed her forehead.

"I'll be right back," I say as I get up and take the breakfast tray with me back to the kitchen.

After I washed and placed everything back in its place, I went back into the room and gently moved the covers off of her, and offered my hand to help her up.

"I can't wait for the day when I can look down and see my feet again. But I will miss my built-in table though," she says as she pats her belly.

I lightly laugh as I take her hand and lead her to the second bathroom down the hall.

"Oh, however, will you live without a built-in table."

"Shut up, It was nice to be able to lay down and put a bowl of popcorn on myself with the only worry of a ticking time bomb kicking it off."

I laugh again. "Makes sense."

She looks at herself in the mirror and I stand behind her after letting the water run, wrapping my arms around her.

"Soon, we'll have a little girl in our arms. She's going to be just as beautiful as you, with the most gorgeous eyes, the prettiest smile, and the cutest little cheeks like yours." I say and kiss her cheek.

She smiles and her shoulders lift. I start to take off her dress from the bottom and as I do, I kiss up her legs, her thighs, her stomach, her arms, her shoulders, her neck, then her lips. She looks up at me and kisses me back a little longer before I move her into the bath.

"Look at this one Ramon, I think this one is cute," Celestia says as she turns the laptop to face me.

"That is adorable, she would love that," I respond.

"You know what I wanna do?"

"What?"

"I think I'm gonna paint her room. Like a Disney theme or something. But we should have an entire Disney marathon before, so we can see what she likes."

"That would be cute. Don't forget about Disneyworld. We can take her there when she's able to go on most rides though,"

"Oh my God yes! She would have so much fun."

"Yes, she would," I reply.

She goes back on the laptop and starts to search for baby clothes. As we both look, we find a few matching ones, and after a good hour, we ordered everything in our cart.

"Now, I wanna watch a Disney movie," she laughs after closing the laptop.

I laugh as well and grab the remote from the nightstand next to me.

"Which movie do you want?" I ask her once I open the TV.

"Umm, ooh, let's go with Tangled. It was one of my favorite movies as a kid."

"Alright, Tangled it is." I smile as I look for the movie and play it.

"Ramon. I think Peach heard the doorbell, someone must be at the door," says Celestia.

I see Peaches vanishing figure run out of the room and I hear her barking. I pause our movie and get up to see.

"Come on Peach, be nice," I say as I gently pick her up. When I opened the door I could only stare and blink. There, with suitcases in hand was none other than my mother and my half-sister.

"Hey bro, long time no see."

Chapter 37

I struggled out of bed and made my way down the hall to the door.

"Ramon? Is everything okay? I-oh."

I look at who is at the door and there are two women with suitcases in their hands. One of them I remember from the pictures. If she's his step-sister then the other lady must be his mother.

"Ah, another unexpected thing, when did you get a dog? And Oh! You must be Celestia. Such a beautiful daughter-in-law, my, my you're ready to pop!"

"Mother," Ramon whispers.

"Oh, quit being so sensitive, you haven't even called your mom in ages," she says as she steps in with her daughter in tow.

"I called you months ago when I was in Paris," he mutters.

"Still ages ago. Celestia dear, it's so lovely to finally meet you, it's upsetting how I heard about you at first from newspapers than from Ramon himself. Do you know the gender?" she asks after she hugs me.

"It's a girl," I say as I look down.

"Ah, wonderful! Come we have so much to talk about. First, come meet my daughter Lilly."

She gestures for Lilly to come our way and she smiles and waves as she walks over. Ramon comes around and places his chin on my right shoulder. Peach peaks over from his arms and then leaps out of them, going directly to sniff Lilly's shoes.

"Mother, how long do you plan on staying?" asks Ramon as his head nods to the suitcases.

"Not that long, about a week or two. I just wanted to see how you've been holding up. Lilly missed you too. Isn't that right Lilly?"

"Yeah, big bro, I really missed you," she responds mockingly.

"I really missed you," Ramon mocks back, and I laugh at their conversation.

"Don't mind them they've been like this since they were children." his mom dismisses.

She takes my hand and takes me away from Ramon, heading for the living room. It takes me a minute to fully sit down and she sits next to me.

"Oh! How rude of me, call me Clarissa or mom. Whichever you prefer."

"Alright," I smile.

I'm being shifted up as Ramon sits behind me, laying me back on his chest and placing his arms over mine as he rubs his thumbs against the top of my hands.

"I can tell that Ramon here is head over heels for you. I haven't seen him show this much affection since his first childhood teddy bear."

"Well the same goes for me," I say as I look up at him with a smile.

He looks down and gives me a quick kiss on my forehead before I look back up.

"Y'all are too cute, have you picked out names for the girl yet?" Clarissa asks.

"We've only started thinking about it today actually."

"What were you thinking of?"

"Well, so far we have Evangeline, Aurelia, Calliope, or Anaisa.

"Those names are so precious! I absolutely love them all."

"Thank you!" I say.

Clarissa and Lilly took me out shopping for baby clothes and they helped me buy things to put in my bag to bring to the hospital.

"Celestia look at this one!" says Lilly.

I turn to her to see her holding up a fluffy white polar bear onesie. My heart melted as I imagined my little girl in it.

"Oh that is so cute," I sigh. "Maybe I should buy it later though since it's about to be summer, we've got a long way till it gets cold."

"You're right," she replies as she puts it back. "Ooh, we need to find something for her to wear for when she's born."

"Yes, let's look for something pink and white, something pale probably."

"I'll go look over in that section," she says and rushes over to where she pointed.

Clarissa comes up next to me and sighs.

"You know, she's so excited for this baby just as Ramon is. Lilly can't have children."

"Really?" I say looking back at her.

"Yeah, she loves kids, always babysitting and going anywhere they would be just to play with them. It's sad that she can't have her own."

"Does she want to adopt?"

"Yes, she plans on it. Though she isn't sure whether she wants to get married first before she adopts or be a single mother. But she's only twenty-three so she has time.

"Oh, she's the same age as I am."

"Yeah, I did notice that you're so young, you're practically finished with college, getting married, and have a baby on the way. You have your life together. Not many people have that." she smiles.

"I never thought that I'd even be like this so quickly. After my first boyfriend, I simply planned on getting my degree and moving on with my life. I told myself that love would come later. And I guess it's true. Love comes when you least expect it. And it definitely works in annoying ways." I lightly laugh.

"How so?"

"I remember when Ramon first made advances on me. He followed me everywhere and nearly went down on his knees just to spend time with me. I was too focused on the rest of my life. When I told him yes-" I blush as I remember the first week we had together.

When I told him yes, I quickly realized that he was serious and I took a chance. And I'm glad I did."

"Mhm, I see," she responds with her eyebrows lifted.

"I found something!" says Lilly as she comes back with two onesies. One was pink, grey, and white. The other was pink and white.

"I really like this one!" I state, taking the first one from her.

"That one's nice," Clarissa replies. "It's simple but really cute."

"I'll take the other one as well, a girl can never have enough clothes," I laugh.

"True that," Lilly chuckles. "Alright, we should probably head out before we buy the entire store," she says, nodding her head towards the full shopping cart.

I shrug, smiling, but push the cart towards the register at the front.

When I finished paying, we went to order Chinese food to go. Once we got our food we grabbed my bags, walked back to the car, and went home.

Ramon holds me close as we continued to watch the interrupted movie. It was currently eleven forty-two pm.

"It's getting late, you should go to sleep baby," whispers Ramon after I yawn for the third time.

"No, the movie's almost over, I wanna see the wedding," I say, stifling through another yawn.

"Haven't you seen this many times before?" he chuckles.

"Yes, but I still love to see it,"

"I can't wait to see ours,"

I smile, closing my eyes. "Mmm yes, I cannot wait to be called your wife," I mutter.

"Go to sleep my love, you can barely keep your eyes open."

"Do I have to?"

"Yes, if you do, I promise we'll look at wedding stuff tomorrow, does that sound good?"

"That sounds great. Promise you won't get bored? I know some men don't like to plan these kinds of stuff."

"How could I ever be bored? Planning our wedding sounds like the best idea on earth, I can't wait to see what dress you wear when you walk down that aisle, surrounded by thousands of your favorite flowers."

"Mmm red roses,"

"Yes, red roses. Goodnight my Queen, I love you."

"I love you more my King."

Ramon

As she drifted off to sleep, I pull the covers over her and kiss the crown of her head. Love me more? All the love for her inside of me for this woman is indescribable and infinite. Everything I have ever wanted is in her. It is her. And only her. To see her smile, to hear her laugh, to wake up to that beautiful woman every morning is the reason why my heart beats.

"I can't wait to spend the rest of my life with you, Celestia."

Chapter 38

My eyes flutter open from a well-rested sleep. It feels like I haven't slept this great in ages with this baby. Ramon was still sleeping softly next to me with his back turned. I quickly kiss in between his shoulder blades and then shuffle out of bed. I paddle to the bathroom and look at myself in the mirror. Ugh, I looked awful and for some odd reason, I felt like looking nice today. I brushed my teeth, took a shower, and even managed the brush out the knots in my hair. I put my hair in a messy bun and then wrap the large towel around my body before I walk out into the room. I go to the closet and look through all of my maternity dresses. I skimmed back and forth through the clothing before I settle on one. It was a lovely cerulean robe-like dress that was sheer in the stomach area. It showed off my baby bump while the rest of the dress flowed loosely around my legs. The tule going to the bottom made me feel like Cinderella. I then sit at the mirror and stare at the makeup in front of me. Why the hell not. I pick up my brow brush, brush them out, and then add a tiny bit of mascara to my eyelashes. Lastly, I take my lip gloss and add a layer to my lips. I look a little more alive I thought to myself as I place the tube down. I get up and slip on my slippers before going to the kitchen to make myself breakfast.

Ramon kisses my forehead as he greets me in the library.

"You look beautiful my darling, what's the occasion?" he asks.

"Good morning, just cause, I felt yucky this morning."

"Mmm, alright. What're you reading?"

"The Crown by Kiera Cass, love the plot twist at the end. You know, I was very surprised to see you pick this series out for me."

"That's because I've read this one, and the eight before it. I bought them all for you because one, I thought you would like them as much as I did, and two, you remind me of America."

"How so?"

"Her red hair reminds me of your fiery personality. And she took a chance on Maxon even if she didn't want to at first, just like you did with me in the beginning." he smiles.

"I didn't even think about it like that, you're so sweet,"

"I'm simply stating facts here," he replies as he steals another kiss. "Did you eat yet lovely?"

"Yes, I did."

"Alright then, I'll go make some food for my mom and Lilly then I'll come back with the laptop and we can talk about wedding plans."

"Oh right! Yay, my twelve-year-old self is internally screaming right now," I grin.

He chuckles and heads for the door.

"Don't tell me you were one of those kids that played wedding day."

"Oh yes, I went the whole mile. My mom even has a VHS tape of me trying to walk down our hallway in her heels and veil that she wore when she got married."

"Now, I'm definitely calling your mom. I have to see that."

"Even better, I'll let her play it at our reception."

"Definitely. I'll see you in a bit." he winks and heads for the kitchen.

I place the bookmark inside of the book and lift myself up from the loveseat, making my way to the kitchen. Clarissa and Lilly were nearly finished with their breakfasts as came up to the counter.

"Good morning you two."

"Morning my future daughter-in-law," she smiles.

I smile back. I always smile when she mentions it.

"Morning Celestia! How's baby doing?"

"She's doing good, quieter than usual," I state.

"How so?" she replies as Ramon takes the plate from her and she gets up from the stool.

"She actually let me sleep well last night," I say looking down at my belly.

"I don't know how you all do it. I value my sleep way too much."

"Well, I got many more days of no sleep for me when she's born. I have a feeling that she's going to keep me up all night,"

"Oh she definitely is," says Clarissa as she enters the conversation. "This one here," she says pointing to Ramon. "Never let me sleep for a few months. I had to hire a caretaker just to get some sleep. All he wanted was to stay up. Half of the time it was to simply stare at the decoration hanging from the crib."

"Ha, guess who's the favorite kid now?" taunts Lilly as she sticks her tongue out towards Ramon's back as he washes the last of the dishes.

"Still me," he grins and splashes a few droplets of water towards her.

"Stop it you two, anyway, Ramon tells me you are looking at wedding plans today?"

"I am, would you two like to help?"

"Oh, that would be wonderful!"

"I should call my mom as well, I know she'll want to comment on things here and there."

"No need my love, she'll be here in twelve minutes," says Ramon as he comes up from behind.

"Huh? What do you mean?"

"I had her come over. Since my mom was here, I thought she'd want a friend and they could finally meet as well."

"You're right! Thank you for doing that. It was very sweet of you,"

"Sweet is my middle name," he says as he kisses my neck.

"Ugh, ew, gag. That has to be one of the cheesiest lines ever. Your middle name is Dace stupid."

"Dace? That is such a pretty name. I just realized that I never knew your middle name," I say turning to face him.

Ramon chuckles. "That's because most people don't know."

"Yeah, it was his great grandfather's name." replies his mother.

Before she can continue, the doorbell rings. Ramon goes to open the door and soon leads my mom into the kitchen.

"Hi, mom,"

"My little girl! Well not so little now, look at you! Ready to burst!" she says as she squeezes me in a side hug.

"And you must be Clarissa! Hi!"

"Hi! I am, and this is my daughter Lilly,"

"Hello!" Lilly waves.

"Hi, Lilly,"

My mom makes conversation with Clarissa and Lilly, mostly talking about children and Ramon and I getting married. I look to Ramon who gets the hint and he joins me as I walk myself back to the library. He goes to our room and comes back with the laptop in his hands.

"They'll be in there for hours I feel," he laughs as he sits next to me.

"Right, I'm sure Lilly won't be in there for long though," I smile.

"True, alright. Before we get into anything, what colors are we looking for?"

I giggle at myself and take the computer from him.

"What's so funny?" Ramon asks.

"Nothing, just laughing at myself, you're going to think I was either really bored or crazy."

"Why?"

"You'll see," I say as I log into my Pinterest.

I scroll down to the four private boards at the bottom and hand the computer back over to him. He looks at the computer screen and then at me.

"There's no way-"

"Yep, blame my twelve-year-old self."

He opens up the summer board and scrolls through, clicking on a few pictures as he goes.

"You really thought this through,"

"I did," I grin. "Although, most of those things are probably not my taste anymore."

"Makes sense, you did make this about eleven years ago."

"Well, at least we won't need to stress much about what we want. I've always wanted a spring or summer wedding in a mansion-looking venue, with a big backyard where we can dance under the stars."

"You've had the same dream since you were a child. Never change. And stop growing up so fast." says my mom as she enters the room and kisses the top of my head with a smile. She plops herself down on my other side and takes one of my hands in hers.

"Are you still planning that Disney-themed wedding?"

"Ha, no. I might sneak in some elements here and there but no."

She laughs just as Clarissa walks in with Lilly in tow.

"There you all are, how's the search going?"

"We didn't even need to do much, she's got everything on Pinterest." Ramon smiles.

"Ah, a woman after my own heart. We're going to be best friends." squeals Lilly as she sits in front of me on the floor after grabbing the laptop from Ramon.

"Oh my gosh, this summer board is so pretty. I love the colors!"

"Thanks, I was going for a light and flowy look," I state.

"Well, you definitely got that. I just realized that you don't have a dress board."

"I don't really know what I want to wear actually."

"Really? Then we should go dress shopping!"

"That would be nice, but, I'm currently ready to give birth at any day, so I think we should wait until after."

"Makes sense. Alright then. But when we go he can't come." she grins.

"What why not?"

"Because I'm not going to pass up the chance to see you cry for the first time in my life as she walks down that aisle and if you see the dress she picks then it won't work."

Ramon rolls his eyes at her but smiles as I lightly laugh and lay my head on his shoulder.

"We're gonna take her away from you for forty-eight hours before the day you get married as well."

"No. That's not gonna happen."

"Come on, you're no fun! We'll have a girl's night out, I can literally plan everything. I promise to keep your precious wife safe at all costs." she says as she draws an x over her heart.

"Fine. But don't tire her out."

"No promises on that." Lilly grins then turns to me. "So, who else are we bringing to this party?"

"My best friends of course." I smile.

Lilly made me look at a few dress styles just to find a range of styles I seemed interested in while Ramon talked to my mom about my embarrassing wedding moments from the fake ones in our backyard to the real ones I participated in. It made me smile to see Ramon and my mother so close. And his mother got along real well with mine as well.

"If only our fathers were here," I say as I interrupt my thoughts.

Ramon looks at me with a slightly questioning face that was ever so faint.

"I meant that it would be nice if they were here and bonding as our mothers did," I say.

"That would be nice, but unfortunately my father doesn't bond with anyone. And it's how he raised me to be. But my mom was there to twist his ways and make me the person I am today."

"Well, I'm glad she was there."

"Yeah, me too," he replies smiling.

His phone vibrates on the nightstand on my side and he lifts his head gently to see.

"Can you look at that for me?" he asks.

I pick up his phone and look at the notification.

"It's from James," I say. But then I look at his lock screen. It looks like me. From this morning.

"When did you take this picture?" I ask.

"This morning," he smiles.

"You were awake?"

"I was,"

"And you watched me the entire time."

"Yes, it was lovely to watch I might add. Very cute. The second you dropped that towel to the floor I was ready to pounce, but sadly I must wait."

I narrow my eyes at him but a smile plays across my lips.

"You're very naughty Mr. Osgood."

"I could say the same for you when you slipped on that matching baby blue set underneath. Mrs. Osgood ," he responds as he glides a hand under my dress and pulls at the fabric of my underwear.

"Don't start something you can't finish," I warn him.

He simply smiles and kisses my forehead, pulling me closer. Then he whispers in my ear.

"Just because you're pregnant doesn't mean I won't stop pleasing you, I am still perfectly capable of eating out that pretty little pussy of yours."

I shiver under his voice and bite my bottom lip.

"Well in that case," I whisper as I part my legs slightly.

"Do as you please. Sir."

Chapter 39

The weeks went by quickly and I stayed at Celestia's side like a thorn on a rose. She got very irritable at every little thing and I tried to soothe her pain and frustration as best as I could. My poor baby. If I could take the pain away I would. At this very moment, I curse Adam and Eve.

"Ramon, I'm hungry again. Why am I so damn hungry? I'm gonna gain weight- and why the hell is my feet so big? No one told me that I was gonna go up an entire shoe size. I don't want to do this anymore I can't-"

"Hey, hey, you're fine. You're doing fine. Just a few more days. Here, come sit down and I'll make you some food. Whatever you want." I whisper as I hold her tightly.

She looks up at me and sighs.

"Eggs. All I want is eggs. It's the only thing I can eat right now that won't make me throw up."

"I'll make you a plate of scrambled eggs, does that sound good?"

"Yes, it does, and thank you. No one asked you to put up with my moods."

"I'm not putting up with anything darling. Your ready to give birth any day now, I don't blame you."

I kiss her forehead and take her to the library to have her lay on the couch. Then I go back to the kitchen to start her eggs.

When I finish her eggs, I bring the plate over to her with a fork and she immediately digs into it.

I chuckle slightly and make my way back to clean up.

"Are you finished, my love?" I ask as I walk back into the library.

"Yeah, I am. I feel a little better." she smiles.

I nod and take the plate from her to go and wash it. Mid washing, I hear a piercing scream of agony from Celestia and I drop everything, rushing to her in seconds.

"What's wrong?"

"C-Contrac-Shit!" She yells out as she tries to get up from the couch.

"Sit, honey," I say trying to soothe her as I look at my watch, mentally counting the seconds.

After a minute had passed, I looked down at Celestia. Her eyes were closed, and she was breathing hard.

"That shit hurt like a bitch." she groans. "Now my back hurts."

"Darling," I softly say as I move a few hair strands out of her face. "We could possibly be having our little girl today." I smile.

She looks up at me and smiles back before she shuts her eyes close again.

"God, how nice would that be." she sighs. "I'm not one to tolerate pain much these days. I don't know how long I can take this anymore."

"You're doing great, my love. I wish I could transfer the pain from you to me."

"I know, I know, I'm just saying that cause I'm exhausted."

"I know this is hard for you. I can't imagine doing all this." I sigh as I sit next to her. I twist her so that her back faces me and I start to rub at the tenseness in her back with my thumbs.

"Mm, that feels good." she happily groans as she lays onto me. "I'm so tired I just want to sleep but for some reason, I can't."

"Well how about laying on me. Try to see if you can sleep. I'll be right here." I say soothingly combing my hand through her hair.

"I'll try but I know I won't be able to."

"Just try," I whisper and tilt her back to my chest. She closes her eyes and I pull her hair back from her face. The sound of her breathing is calming but it doesn't last. She jerks up and moans in pain again.

"Another one?" says Madeline as she enters the room with my mother and Lilly in tow.

"Y-ye-Ahh! H-how long h-has it been s-since the f-first?"

I check my watch. "Four minutes. We need to get you to the hospital."

"It hasn't been an hour yet."

"Your contractions are four minutes apart. I want to make sure that you and our little girl are safe, well, and in good hands. We have to go, my love," I say as I take her hand.

The second I place her hands in mine, I can feel her shaking.

"You're shaking, Darling are you okay?"

She looks up at me and I see the slight quiver in her lips and her eyes turn glassy.

"Hey, what's wrong? Baby talk to me." I say, pulling her in close.

"I'm s-scared. I'm not ready. I can't do this Ramon."

"Listen, you are one of the strongest women I know. You're giving life to a human being. I'd be scared too if I was in your shoes. But I'm gonna be there with you every second, and we're gonna have a beautiful baby girl, and she's gonna look like you, and we can go on our trips to Disney, and we'll spoil our princess rotten." I whisper to her. She smiles and places her head on my chest and sighs.

"You got this Celestia, be that powerful bad bitch I know you are!" replies Lilly as she hugs her from the side.

"Alright, someone please grab my hospital bag; and let's have this baby."

"Yes, we're in the hospital right now, she's about 5 centimeters dilated. About to get an epidural. I need you to make sure no one knows which hospital we're in. I'm not dealing with the paparazzi today. My number one priority is my fiancé and my baby. Yes. Thank you, James."

I walk back inside of the room and I see them placing the plastic on her back and then putting the needle up her back. I move to face her and take her hands in mine as she slightly winces.

"You're doing great my Queen," I whisper to her.

She nods, eyes still closed, and squeezes my hand tighter.

"Hey sweetie, how are you doing?" her mother asks after placing herself next to me.

Celestia opens her eyes and slightly smiles.

"I'm just ready for this numbing medicine to kick in and this baby to come out."

Her mom chuckles. "I hear ya," she replies before she sits on the seat in the corner. Entwining her fingers and placing them on her crossed knees.

"Babe?"

"Yes, my queen?"

"If I yell at you, I'm sorry."

"If that's what it takes to make you feel any better then yell at me all you want." I smile as I kiss her forehead.

"Alright, mama push, a few more. She's almost out."

Celestia squeezes her eyes as her grip on my hand tightened to the point where I couldn't feel my fingers. She groans and grunts as she pushes and she moves herself to lean onto me, propping herself up more so that it caused her to be under less pressure.

Soon the cries of our little girl rings around the room.

"You did it darling, she's here."

"F-finally. May I hold her?" she breathes out in a rush.

The doctor nods and a nurse hands her over to Celestia.

"Hi, hello, aren't you just adorable,"

"She is, isn't she, I told you she was gonna look like you," I say.

"Yeah, but look. She has your eyes, and n-nose..."

Celestia clutches her chest tightly.

The monitor next to her starts beeping.

The baby is being taken from her by a nurse.

The doctor rushes to her side to feel her pulse.

"What is going on?!" I ask as I look at the doctor.

"She seems to be having a stroke."

"What? H-how?"

"Sir, we need you to leave the room." says a nurse beside me.

"No. There's no way in hell I'm leaving her side."

"But sir were-"

"No. I don't want to hear it." I say a little too harshly. "Stay with me baby please, I can't lose you."

Chapter 40

I have never felt fear, not when my father threatened me, not when his business crumbled down the first year it became mine, not for anything. But for the first time in my life. I felt fear. I thought I was going to lose her. I couldn't handle that. I shook with fear, so much that the nurses became worried about me. But I told them to put all their focus on her because if she wasn't okay, I was sure that I wouldn't be either. Celestia was my ride or die. My she moves, I move. My magnet.

"Is she going to be okay now?"

"Yes, she'll be perfectly fine. It was just a blood clot that had formed in her arm. We took it out as quickly as possible. It's best to let her rest and stay here for at least a day or two, just to see how she feels.

I sigh deeply and finally fall back into the seat I had moved next to her bed. I kiss the top of her hand that I had been holding for hours and lean against the bed. I feel a hand on my shoulder and I slightly turn my face to see who it was.

"How is she?" asks my mother.

"They said that she'll be fine. She's just going to stay here for a few days just to make sure nothing else happens."

"Alright, I don't even need to ask if you're going to stay by her side cause I know that you are. If you're hungry or anything just call me and either I or Lilly will bring something over for you."

"Thanks, mom."

"Of course hon," she replies as she walks out of the room. Leaving me alone with Celestia again.

It took her a few hours before she woke up after the doctor took out the clot.

"My Queen, you scared the living shit out of me," I whisper to her as I smooth her hair.

"What happened? Wait. Where's our child?"

"Shh, don't worry, she's fine my love, I was just worried about you. You held her for about a minute before you-"

I swallow the lump in my throat and closed my eyes for a second before I open them again to look at her.

"You had a blood clot that formed in your arm. I was scared that I was going to lose you."

She looks at me fondly and smiles as she brings her hand to my cheek.

"You could never lose me. I'll always be here. Literally, till death do us part."

I smile back and kiss her forehead.

"I love you,"

"I love you more," she smiles.

"I love you most. Don't try to say anything after." I smile back. "I'll go ask for our little girl," I state, then leave the room before she can get a chance to say anything else.

When the nurse comes back with our baby, I watch as Celestia's eyes light up with happiness and it warms my heart. The nurse places her on Celestia's chest and her arms fold around the baby's body. The nurse also checks on how Celestia was doing as she fiddles with the monitor.

"Hi there, she's so precious and so tiny." Celestia grins.

"Mr. Osgood, are you and you're wife ready to name her?"

Celestia looks at me, then back at the baby.

"Aurelia suits her. What do you think?"

"It does suit her indeed, My little golden one," Celestia smiles as she rocks her back and forth.

"Alright, I'll get the paperwork, and Mrs. Osgood, you're all good to go and you're free to leave when you want. I'll get the release form as well." says the nurse before leaving the room.

"Mrs. Osgood huh?" she smiles giving me a look.

I laugh lightly. "I couldn't help myself. The opportunity was right there on the form and I took it."

"Now what if you get caught?"

"Don't worry my love, I won't." I smile.

"Speaking of names? What about a middle name for her?"

"I wanted to have her middle name be after you and Clarissa." Celestia states. "But I haven't found a name."

"Why don't you make one then," I suggest.

"Really? I don't want it to look weird you know, I'd figure I just pick a name that already exists. Or we can just take one of the other names we had for her and make it her middle name."

"Well, I like the idea of combing them," I say.

"Combining what?" her mom interrupts as she walks inside the room.

"We were thinking of combining your name with my mother's name as Aurelia's middle name," I reply. "We could do Marissa or Madesa," I say to answer Celestia's question.

"Madesa sounds unique. You don't hear that name every day. It has a nice ring to it." she says.

"I like that- oh, looks like little Aurelia wants to be back with mommy," replies Madeline.

She hands the baby over to Celestia and kisses the top of both their heads.

"Alright, I'm gonna go back to Clarissa and Lil and say bye before I go to my meeting. I'll see you later my sweet."

"Meeting?" Celestia questions.

"Oh, I did forget to tell you! Ramon, I thought you would've told her by now. I'll be moving here to New York so I can be closer. It's time that I start moving on from our old house. There's no use sitting there with all those rooms."

"Really? That's great mom! I can't wait to see your new place!"

"Yep, I'll be sure to send you the address once I move in. Who knows, maybe I'll find a job to keep me occupied as well."

"Just don't stress yourself out ma,"

"I won't I promise, I might be fifty and have some gray hairs but I'm still young and moving, I'll see you later my sweet. Congrats again." Madeline laughs before she leaves the room.

"Our mothers have been keeping an eye on her for hours while you were asleep." I laugh, smiling at Aurelia's little hand wrapping around my finger.

"I feel like if they could have another child they would."

"You're right," I chuckle.

"I'm so happy she's here."

"Me too, she looks just like you,"

She smiles in agreement as continues to rock Aurelia.

"Hi sweetheart, how are you doing?"

"Hey Clarissa," Celestia grins as she looks up. "I'm okay," she replies.

"Just okay? Do you need me to call a nurse for you?"

"No, I'm fine. I'm ready to go home with Aurelia. Being in the hospital for so long is starting to get to me.

"Tell me about it," my mother rolls her eyes smiling. "I wanted to leave the hospital bed and just run, especially after spending 14 hours on it."

"Fourteen?!" she gasps.

"Yep, Ramon was a breeze but Lilly near refused to leave, anyway, may I hold her? I've been dying to hold her since I could only see her through the glass."

"Of course!" Celestia replies as my mom comes over to the other side of the bed and she gently hands Aurelia over.

"Hello, Aurelia, such a pretty name for a pretty girl. Does she have a middle name?" she asks.

"Yeah, it's a mix of yours and my mother's. Madesa."

"Awe you two are so sweet. My, I haven't heard the name Madesa in ages."

"You knew a Madesa before?"

"Years ago, I think around high school. She was such a sweet girl though I only remember her because of her name."

"Mom, I got you the soda you asked for-awe look at her!" says Lilly as she enters the room with a can of sprite in hand.

She moves to the side of Clarissa and smiles at Aurelia as my mom holds her.

"By the way, your friends are here, they're on their way up."

"Ahh! I can't wait for them to see Aurelia." Celestia grins.

Celestia asks for help to get up from the bed and I follow her to the bathroom and close the door behind us. I brush her hair out while she brushes her teeth, then I help her back in bed just as Stephanie and Lucy enter the room.

"Congrats bestie! Oh my god look at her she's so cute and tiny!" says Lucy.

"Thanks," Celestia grins.

"Can I hold her?"

"Sure,"

"Hi, baby! Your godmother has arrived and she's gonna spoil you with so many clothes. Yes, she is."

As Lucy and Stephanie gush over Aurelia, I look back down at Celestia and smile at her. She looks up and smiles as well.

"What?" she asks in a faint voice.

"Nothing, Just looking at my wife."

"Soon to be,"

"Same difference, I considered you as my wife since the day I first said I love you."

Her smile grew and her eyes looked deeply into mine.

"God, you make me so happy. I love you."

"I love you more."
"I love you most-ha I win."
"For now," I grin.

Chapter 41

Giving birth to Aurelia four months ago was one of the most painful things I have ever done and even though I've had almost no sleep whatsoever for the past one hundred and twenty days, for her, I'd do it all over again. She and Ramon made me complete. We loved watching her grow, and how she learned to sit up on her own, to move around more, to laugh. I rock her little body back and forth in my arms as I try to get her to fall asleep. She loved when I hummed Disney lullabies to her. I could see it in her bright smile.

"Here, I'll take her. You need some rest baby," says Ramon as he gently scoops Aurelia out of my arms.

"Thank you," I sigh. I rub at my temples and climb into bed, going under the covers. "I have never wanted to sleep this much ever." I smile before I yawn and curl deeper under the blanket.

Ramon chuckles. "Well I watched my mother go through this, I know it's hard. She didn't have my father to be there with her to take over when she needed so I'm helping in any way I can to make this easier for you."

"What on earth did I do to deserve you?" I smile.

"I could say the same for you my love," he smiles back as he gently puts a now sleeping Aurelia into her bassinet. He then gets under the covers beside me and pulls me close.

"Now that Aurelia's here, we can focus on making you my wife in the eyes of the law."

"Mm, right because without the law I already am."

"Correct," he states and kisses the crown of my head. "Now go to sleep, you know she'll probably wake up in a few hours."

I nod in agreement, letting my tired eyes close.

"Thank you for finally letting me get some sleep, my little princess," I say beaming at Aurelia.

She coos and smiles as she reaches up to me. I sit down next to Ramon on the couch and stare at the laptop on his lap.

"Alright, I'm ready now," I say. "What do we have so far?"

"Well, I called the caterers and the florists, and ordered the invites," Ramon replies as he opens up my Pinterest board. "And don't worry, I got everything in the way the list was. Including the acrylic blush wedding invitations you wanted."

"Ah! Really? Where on earth did you find someone to make invitations like those?"

"I have my ways." he smiles. "Here let me show you the prototype."

"Ugh, they're perfect." I grin and then smile at Aurelia as she squeals and reaches for the screen. "Looks like she loves them too."

"Good, now I have the approval of both of my beautiful ladies. Speaking of beautiful, Lilly, Lucy, Rose, and Steph are coming over to take you dress shopping."

"Yeah, I heard. They texted me about an hour ago, I still haven't gotten ready." I laugh.

"Go get ready then, come to daddy Auri," says Ramon as he takes her from me and places her on his lap in front of the computer.

"I'll be quick," I say as I stand up and kiss the top of both their heads before I walk back into our room.

When I get back, Ramon and Aurelia were still on the couch but this time Ramon was on his back while Aurelia lay on his stomach. They were laughing as she aggressively patted her hands on his chest.

"You two seem to be having fun," I smile.

"Yeah, she's found that my chest and a drum make the same sound apparently."

I laugh and scoop her up from his stomach. She started to fuss.

"Oh, okay then," I say as I place her back. She giggles again and continues to pat her hands on Ramon. "Welp, since she wants to keep beating you like a drum, you'll have to change her. Don't forget okay Ramon?"

"I won't my queen, don't worry, go and have fun dress shopping, we'll be good here."

"Alright, but promise me you'll call me if you need me."

"I will, I will look you're already fussing. That's where she got her fussing from." he grins after getting up with Aurelia on his hip. "Tell mommy that we'll be fine cutie," he says turning to Aurelia. As if she knew what he meant she laughs and wraps her arms around him.

The doorbell rings just then and I give them both a look.

"Alright, I'm going," I say and kiss them both.

I open the front door and head out with the girls.

"Okay, we have to go shop for your bachelorette party first, then we can look around for wedding dresses and maybe even try on a few," says Lucy as we drive out of the driveway.

"What colors were you thinking C?"

"Well, I wanted to have multiple nights out with different colors."

"Ooh yes, definitely," says Stephanie.

"So, I was thinking the first night we wear gray and pink," I say.

"That's cute," replies Rose.

"Yeah, and the third day I know I want to wear the colors of the wedding so I would wear white and you all could wear the colors your bridesmaid's dresses will be. But I don't know about the second night so the colors can be up to you four." I smile.

"By the way, I talked with Ramon and I have a list of places that we can spend each night in. There's more than three so we have plenty to choose from," says Rose.

Stephanie takes the paper from Rose and her jaw opens at the words on the paper.

"Rome?! As in, Italy?! Like plane and tickets?"

"Yep, we're going all out for this." Rose grins.

"Don't tell me Ramon's planning on paying for all this?"

"Yep," she replies smiling even wider.

"I specifically told him not to take a part in any of this cause I knew he'd most likely be flying us all over Europe or something," I say shaking my head. "Now there he goes, spending his money."

"Well, he's spending the money that he's well-earned on the love of his life and her friends."

I smile and slightly chuckle. "He does like spending an unnecessarily large amount on me just to make me happy."

"Exactly!" she laughs.

It took us a few hours before we could find the perfect dresses for our three nights out bachelorette party. For the first day, we decided that we were going out to eat, lavishly, of course, thanks to Rose and Ramon. In La Pergola in Rome, Italy. I'll be wearing a dusty pink dress that reached the floor with long and loose off-the-shoulder sleeves, with a neckline that reminded me of Aurora's dress from

Sleeping Beauty

. The girls are wearing dresses in pebble gray in all types of styles. On the second night, we were going to a dance club in Papaya, Novalja, Croatia. Since it was on a beach we wore beach-like outfits. I wore a bright yellow two-piece bathing suit with a matching coverup with the words Bride-to-be on the back while the girls wore cerulean blue bathing suits with the words Bridesmaids on their coverups besides Lucy since she was my maid of honor. On our third night, I got myself a white suit dress with a row of four buttons to close it up. It had a one-shoulder neckline and the elasticity of it clung to my body in a flattering way. The girls wore similar suit dresses but they were in the colors burgundy, navy blue, and dark green. We were going out to lunch on the top of Point A restaurant in Athens, Greece which has such a beautiful view of the Acropolis Museum, and then a photoshoot after shopping.

"Oh my God, look, Celestia, you should totally try that dress on!" says Lucy as she points to a bridal dress on display.

"You think so? I do love the lace," I reply as I look at the dress.

"Let's go inside and try it on! You might find something else you like," says Stephanie as she and Lilly take my arm and usher me inside the store.

"Hi ladies! Welcome! May I help you with anything today?"

"She's looking for a wedding dress," Rose replies to the lady.

"But I'm not sure what I'm looking for yet," I say.

"Well that's totally fine, I can send you to a dressing room with a dress in each type of bottom, and then we can see which you prefer and we can go from there to narrow it down. Does that sound okay?"

"Actually, yeah that does. Thank you," I smile.

"Alright great, follow me this way, and to the rest of you ladies, feel free to grab some champagne and sit on those couches over there in front of that mirror.

"Don't mind if I do," grins Rose and the rest of them follow suit.

The lady takes me back to the dressing rooms the size of the ones celebrities might have and she hands me a robe.

"Change into this, and in the meantime, I'll be back with a few dresses for you."

"Thank you,"

"Of course," she smiles and leaves, closing the door behind her.

She brings back five dresses, each very different. She helps me put on the ballgown one first and then brings me back to the front where the girls were.

"Omg!" says Lucy, practically screaming.

I smile as I get on top of the platform and turn to face them.

"What do y'all think?"

"Love the top of the dress, but the bottom doesn't really seem you,"

"I see that too, it gives too much of a princess-like dress to me. You have to look regal. This is your big day."

I turn to look at myself in the large mirror.

"Yeah, I see it. There's too much organza fabric."

"Okay, let's try a different one shall we?" says the lady beside me.

"Alright,"

By the time we head home, I must've tried on at least twenty-seven dresses. But at least now I knew what type of dress I was looking for. But I was stuck between a slim-fitting dress, one that flared out, or a cathedral A-Line dress.

"Well, why can't you have both?" asks Ramon.

"Both? I mean I can have one to walk down the aisle and one for the reception like my mother did. But I still don't know which to choose for which."

"Since the cathedral on is bigger why don't you do that one for the aisle and the slimmer one for the reception."

"I might switch them." I grin. "Why am I even telling you this. You aren't supposed to know anything about my dress until the day of."

"Alright, alright, I won't ask any more questions," he chuckles.

"Mmhm, by the way, have you figured out what you're doing for your bachelor party yet?"

"Yeah, James, Ethan, Luke, and I are going skydiving in Rome and then have a couple of drinks in a bar later that night."

"Skydiving sounds super fun, so you'll be in the same place we'll be in."

"Yep, not too far," he smiles.

"I guess I'll just look up if I wanna find you,"

"Yep, I'll send you my love and kisses from the sky,"

"Okay, I'll be waiting," I say as I bury myself at his side.

Chapter 42

"Do you think that she'll stay with you mom?"

"She'll be fine honey, it's a good thing she isn't clingy like you were as a child otherwise you leaving for the next three days was going to be nearly impossible." replies my mother as she bounces Aurelia.

"Alright, I just don't want her getting upset."

"She's good here. Isn't that right cutie, Grandma's gonna take good care of you." she smiles. Auri pats her hands on Madeline's cheeks and laughs.

"I'll see you in three days princess," I whisper to her before I kiss her cheek goodbye. "Don't buy her too many things mom, I know you."

"What? I will do no such thing," she grins. "Go, the girls are waiting for you, bye!"

I shake my head and laugh before I leave. When I get in the passenger's seat, Rose drives off and we're on our way to the airport.

"Did you arrive yet my queen?"

"Yes, I just got off of the jet and we're about to head to the hotel right now, we have time to kill before dinner so we're going to a spa," I reply to Ramon on the phone.

"Alright have fun,"

"I will, I love you,"

"Love you more and most."

"Damn," I say grinning.

"I win,"

"Yeah yeah, I'll see you," I say before I end the call.

"Celestia, you coming?"

"Yeah, I am, I was just on the phone with Ramon."

"Nope, nope you are not allowed to talk to him for the next three days," Lucy shakes her head.

"Alright, I won't," I smile as I follow behind her.

We check in at the front desk and go up to the suite to put our things down before we go back down to the first floor where the spa was located.

"Where are you going C?"

"Oh, I'm just going to ask the front desk for something, I'll be right back," I say and quickly close the door behind me before they have a chance to question anything.

I walk back down to the front desk and as her for a favor for later.

"Welcome beautiful ladies! How may we assist you today?" smiles the lady at the front desk.

"We're all getting the ultimate spa package, thank you," says Rose.

"Alright, that will be a total of two hundred and ten dollars."

Rose takes out her card and hands it over to the woman.

"Thank you," says the woman after she hands Rose her card back. "Have a lovely stay ladies!"

"Thank you!" we all say as another woman comes up and escorts us to different rooms. We all change into robes and then go into rooms where we were to get our massages. After our massages, we were taken to another large room for manicures and pedicures.

"This hotel is so beautiful, I could stay here forever," says Lucy.

"I know right!" agrees Lilly as she lays down on the lounge chair. "What colors are you getting C?"

"White and gold. You?" I ask Steph.

"I'm going for a bold blue," she replies as she picks up a nail color.

"Nice," I nod in approval.

Five women then show up and they sit in the seats next to each of us. They first ask us to lay flat on the loungers and after, they put face masks on our faces. Then they begin doing our nails.

"Stay still C, I'm almost done," says Lucy as she curls the last few strands of my hair and then begins to pin them back and away from my face.

"Sorry, I'm just moving my hand too much," I reply, placing the makeup brush in my hand down on the dresser. Lucy pins a few more curls up as I move onto my eyeliner and mascara.

"There, all done!" she then says as she places both her hands on my shoulders.

"It's beautiful, as always, thank you, Lu,"

"Of course," she says and starts to take out the hair rollers from her hair.

After I finish the rest of my makeup, I get up and grab my heels to slip them on. I only had to wait a few minutes before they were finished and grabbed their bags and heels as well. We took the elevator up to the top floor where La Pergola was. It was breathtaking and we look around in awe as the hostess ushers us to the large seating area with what I thought of as the best view. We sit down, and as another woman comes up, we order drinks, then look through our menus after we thank her as she walks away.

"I have a surprise for you all," I state after I swallow the last bit of my shrimp.

"A surprise?" questions Rose.

"Yep, just a little something as a thank you, I don't know what I'd do without you girls. Lu, you picked me up when I was at my lowest. Steph, you made my college experience way more interesting than it ever will be and brought me out of my shell. Rose, you have done so much for me and stuck by me no matter what, even though you didn't really know me at first. And Lilly, you're gonna be my sister-in-law! And even though we've only met this year, you've embraced me with nothing but kindness. So thank you guys, for being there for me then and now."

"Awe, you're gonna make me cry, I can't ruin my mascara we have to take pictures later," sniffs Lucy.

I turn to face her and laugh a little as I give her a side hug.

"Alright, alright, no more sappy speeches. I'll be right back," I say and get up from the table, squeezing by her. I go to the hostess and ask her for the boxes I had the concierge bring up earlier. She pulls them from behind the podium and hands them over to me. I thank her and then make my way back to the table. Once I sit back down in my place, I hand each of them their boxes with their names on it. They raise their brows in confusion.

"Open them," I say nodding towards the boxes.

Lilly starts to open up hers first and the rest follow.

"Omg! This is so cute!" she exclaims.

"I never formally asked you all but I think you knew this was coming."

"Awe thanks C!" grins Lucy as she holds up her maid of honor glass.

Each of their boxes had a glass, a candle, another robe with their roles and names on the back that included a matching eye mask, and a necklace.

"You really know how to propose C. Maybe I should take you from Ramon myself," laughs Rose.

"As if he'd even let you try," grins Steph.

"Thank you Celestia. This means so much to me to be your bridesmaid." says Lilly as she clutches her box.

"You're welcome! And of course! You're not only my friend, you're family!" I smile.

"Alright, I know we said you weren't allowed to talk to Ramon for the these three days but he's just so childish and cute and totally in love with you, I have to let this one slip." says Rose and she hands me over her phone. I take it from her and put it to my ear.

"Ramon?"

"Hey, baby."

"What's up? Are you okay?"

"I'm having the time of my life right now, but, I wanted you too see something from where you were."

"See what?" I ask.

"Look out the window and look at the sky," he said.

I did as I was told and gasp. I could not hold in my wide grin as I saw the smoke writing in the sky.

"Sending you my love and kisses as promised."

Chapter 43

The three days came and went so quickly but I honestly couldn't wait to have Celestia in my arms again. The second the car pulls up, she jumps out of it and runs to me. I pick her up with my free hand that wasn't holding Aurelia.

"Hi baby," I grin and say after I slowly kiss her.

"Hi King, hello my little princess." she smiles as she places her hand on Aurelia's cheek.

"Ugh, I'd kill to be in your position right now C," groans Lucy as she comes up with Celestia's bag.

"Not that it's any of my business, but I think James has a thing for you," I say.

"Huh? There's no possible way, we might flirt a little, yeah, but he's like family to me, I think we've gone way too deep to be in a relationship now. Anyway, how were your three days?" she asks.

"It was good, but I'm just glad to have these lovelies back," I smile as I look at both of them.

"Good, cause now you're going to deal with Celestia's and friends every beck and call before this wedding." Lucy grins.

"I'm already a step ahead of all of you," I reply. "And you're updated Pinterest board only made things way easier for me."

"So what else is there to do then?" Celestia asks.

"You still haven't found you're wedding dress."

"Right. And they don't have their bridesmaid's dresses either. And I just realized that we don't have someone to bring the rings or flower girls, I don't know any little girls, and damn I also don't even know what the reception food will look like. There's so much to do."

"I've got everything settled. Let's get inside and I'll let you look through all of them okay, don't worry." I say and kiss between her furrowed brows.

"You know, I'm usually the one who's supposed to do everything." she softly smiles.

"You did, All I did was call people and schedule things." I smile back.

"Alright, come on Lu, let's go look at the stuff and then search for dresses."

"Ahh, yes, yes, yes! What are we waiting for? Let's go!" she grins and scoots past us into the house.

I follow behind her with Aurelia and Celestia still in my hands. I place Celestia down on the couch when we get to the library room and then place Auri on her lap before I grab the computer.

"So, these are the flowers that will be all over the place but this is what the reception will look like, however, there will be more flowers on the tables and lining up here and here," I say as I point.

"Okay, and for the ceremony?" she asks. after she passes Aurelia to Lucy after realizing that she wanted to hold her.

"This is the rough draft that they sent me, so it most likely will have the seating like this and the decoration where they are now unless you want something to be changed."

"No, this is perfect Ramon, everything you've shown me is perfect," she smiles at me.

"Okay, good, I wanted to make sure that everything was to your liking."

"This is everything I could ever ask for and more, thank you."

"For you, I'd do anything," I say and lean in for a kiss which was immediately stopped by a small hand and light giggles.

I turn to face Aurelia and laugh.

"Well then, I see how it is," I say.

Auri simply continues to laugh as I pick her up and she then starts to blow raspberries at me.

"That isn't very nice princess. Let's leave mommy and her friend alone and let's go watch a movie."

I place her on the bed in between me so that she can sit straight against me and I lay her baby bottle in front of her. As I click play on the TV she coos and claps her hands together as she sees the Walt Disney castle and fireworks.

"You like it, princess? Both you and mommy do," I smile and kiss the top of her head gently. As soon she sees the glowing golden flower she squeals with happiness and it just makes me smile even more. I love watching Aurelia and how she reacts to everything as she watches. She's even learned how to make awful faces at Mother Gothel. Which I find very hilarious.

The boat scene was her favorite. With all the lights shining in the dark, she tries to move closer to the TV so I help her.

"Someday, someone will look at you the same way Eugene looks at Rapunzel, my princess," I whisper to her, noticing that her eyes were starting to close shut. I waited until she was fully asleep to turn off the TV and then place her in her bassinet. I kiss the top of her head and turned off the lights before I left the room.

I went back into the library where Celestia and Lucy were.

"Can I come in or are y'all going to throw books at me for peeking?"

"You're in the clear Ramon, we've finished searching a while ago," states Lucy, her head lifting from the book in her hand.

"Did you find a dress?"

"Well, no. I'm having it made."

"Interesting, now I definitely cannot wait to see you in it." I smile, twirling her around after scooping her up from the couch.

"And that's my cue to be leaving you two love birds," grins Lucy as she gets up as well.

"Goodnight bestie, and thank you for today," smiles Celestia.

"Of course, night you two, say goodnight to mini you for me," she replies as she closes the door behind her after grabbing her purse and keys from the side table by the door.

"See I told you she was a miniature version of you," I grin as I lock up the door and look at Celestia.

"She can't be. The firstborn daughter is always the female version of her father. Aka, you."

"Well, I'm one hundred percent sure of what I said. Not only does she look like you, but she also acts like you. Case closed."

"Well then, since she's one hundred percent me, why don't we make another that's one hundred percent you," she whispers. My heart skips a beat, and my dick bulges in my pants in excitement.

"I definitely like the sound of that."

"Room?"

"Which on are we talking?"

"You should know exactly which one I'm talking about."

Chapter 44

He brings me up to the room with the unique door and then gently places me back on my feet. He leans in for a kiss but I quickly put a hand up.

"Go inside and wait for me." I simply smile.

"You're in no position to be directing orders at me, honey."

"Just give me two minutes. That's all."

"Alright, but don't make me come get you or that pretty little ass of yours is becoming red."

"Not that I would complain," I whisper under my breath.

"What did you say? I couldn't hear you very well."

"Nothing baby! I'll be back." I quickly say before I rush to our bedroom. I immediately head for my closet and look through the box in the corner. I fish through until I find what I was looking for and smile when I have it in my hands. I take off the jeans, tank top, and undergarments I was wearing and toss them in the hamper and replace them with the red thong and top. Taking a quick peek at myself in the mirror as I place my collar around my neck, I silently laugh before I walk out of the room.

I open the door quietly and I find Ramon with his back facing me. I move my hand behind me to lock the door and then I tiptoe closer to him. My hands slowly glide down his back and then slide around his waist.

"Told you I'd only take two minutes."

"Five more seconds and you wouldn't have-Fuck." he mutters under his breath after he turns around.

"What?" I ask innocently.

"I-I just wasn't expecting this," he replies as his finger hook at one of the straps of the thong. He pulls at it and then lets it go, letting the snapping sound echo the room.

"You remember this?"

"How could I forget this little get up. You were wearing that the day I saw you at the club when you did that very seductive dance of yours."

"Ha, yeah," I smile fondly at the memories.

"Do you miss it?" he asks as he puts his hands around my waist and pulls me closer.

"I do, but I also don't."

"Well, I did miss your dancing, when you were in that room, it felt like you were dancing only for me and my eyes only."

"That's because I was. I wanted to intimidate you. I wanted you to know that I was in charge."

"Oh how quickly that changed," he whispers into my neck which made my cheeks go red.

"Don't get all cocky now sir,"

He comes up from the crook of my neck and hooks a finger through my velvet collar. His lips glide up against my neck until his teeth bite at my earlobe.

"Tell me what to do one more time and I'm spanking that pretty ass of yours."

God, I felt very rebellious.

"You've said that before I got here. You're all talk." I grin.

He tugs at the collar and his hand strikes my behind. It sends a shiver of need down my spine. And I can feel my thong getting damp.

"Last warning,"

"Oh, I'm scared-"

He picks me up and pins me down on the bed behind us. I smile as he towers over my body.

"Don't you even dare. You really must not want to be fucked. But I know you're craving for it deeply right now," he says as his hand glides down my abdomen and cups my wet pussy. "See you're soaking wet already. I could simply leave you here right now. Without giving you anything."

I kept my mouth shut. There's no way I was going to let this night go by without a good fuck. I haven't had one in ages. It'll feel like the first time with him all over again.

"If you leave I'll just get myself off."

"That might help I'll admit, but you'd still be craving me." he smiles.

"Fuck me then."

"No."

"Please Ramon," I nearly moan out.

"Tell me how bad you really want it."

"I want it real bad," I whisper breathlessly.

"How far do you wanna take it?"

"All the way. I want all of it."

He smiles before he leans in and his mouth captures mine in a deep kiss. My hands are moved above my head, his left hand pinning them down against the mattress as he continues to kiss me while his right hand fondles my breasts and nipples, making them hard. I slightly arch my back to him so he could undo the top with his right hand and he then pulls it off. His mouth immediately moves to my breast and I gasp. His now free hand moves down and slips in between my now slick thighs and he quickly dives two fingers into my pussy, curving it just enough to graze my g-spot. I moan out loud, my pussy clenches at his fingers, and my back arches even more.

"M-more Ramon more!"

"In due time my queen. Patience."

Fuck patience. My heart was ready to leap out of my chest. I felt as if I was going to come just by that one thrust with his fingers. And his slowness was driving me crazy. As if he knew what I was thinking, he picks up the speed and his finger thrusts get harder, quicker, deeper. I moan again. With his hand, he quickly snatches off the thong and throws it across the room.

"Fuck, Ramon. I need you to-"

His mouth swiftly moves from my breasts right to my throbbing clit. His tongue moves up and down in between my folds and he now has both hands spreading my legs apart.

"You need me to what baby,"

"Fuck me. I need you to fuck me now."

"So demanding. You can wait my love. I promise it'll be worth it."

More moans escape my mouth as he moves on to pushing his tongue inside of me. My legs start to shake which causes him to only push them further apart. I could feel my orgasm rising inside and I don't think I'd be able to keep it in.

"Ramon I'm going to come." I breathlessly rush out.

"Come, baby. Come into my mouth." he groans as his tongue moves faster.

Finally, I could hold it in no longer and I let go.

My body was on fire. I left like a flame that burned for more. Burning for him. He wasn't kidding when he said the wait would be worth it.

"Fuck Ramon, faster."

He was more than happy to pick up the speed. Going deeper inside of my cunt, reaching my cervix and quickly pulling out almost fully, then ramming it back inside.

"O-Oh fuck! I can't ever get enough!"

"Good, because I'm nowhere near being done with you tonight."

It takes very little for me to be turned on by Ramon so coming at least three times or more tonight wouldn't be a problem. My drenched pussy clams around his length for the second time and I come all over his cock again. He doesn't stop with his thrusts, instead, he pushes his entire length into me as I began to shake. He finally unties my hands and my nails dig at his back and he groans as my back arches my body closer to his. The tips of my breasts are grazing his chest with only makes him groan more.

"Y-yes! Yes!"

He finally could no longer hold in his own and he came inside of me after one last deep stroke. We lay there, chest to chest, breathing heavily and staring into the eyes of the other.

"I love you."

"I love you more and most, my queen," he replies as he pushes my hair out of my face.

"You're never going to let me win are you,"

"Never," he smiles before he kisses my body as he moves down in between my legs.

He gives me a wink before his tongue invades my entrance all over again and I moan in delight.

Chapter 45

"Here. Have a glass. It might help," Lucy states as she hands me half a glass of White Zinfandel.

"Thank you, I'm such a nervous wreck right now," I sigh before I take a sip.

Lucy laughs as she finishes drying my hair and then starts to comb through it.

"Ramon's probably feeling the same way right now girlie, you're fine!"

"Awe, he has nothing to be nervous about, I'm the one walking down a long walkway with everyone's eyes on me. Including him." I say as she starts to layer my hair with a few extensions and then begins to curl my hair.

In the middle of curling a strand, there was a knock at the door which Stephanie rushes to open.

"May I take some pictures of the bride?" The man says as Stephanie lets him enter.

Lucy gives me a look to confirm and I nod.

"Alright, thank you. Hi," The man says as he holds out his hand which I shake. "I'm Nathan. Just keep doing as you were. I'd like to take pictures of details first, like your dress and jewelry then I'd like to take some pictures of you getting ready." he smiles.

"Okay, Hi Nathan," I grin. "The dress is hung up in that closet right over there, and the jewelry is right here beside me," I respond as I point towards the half-open closet, then to the earrings and necklace next to me on the dresser.

He nods and then comes over to the jewelry first.

Lucy took an hour for my hair, just to make sure that every strand of hair was in place and where she wanted it to be. The large waves of my hair frame my face neatly and I smile so hard when I see my reflection in the mirror.

"I have such a talented best friend. Ugh, this is just gorgeous Lu." I grin cheekily.

"Only the best for the best." she smiles back and squeezes me in a tight hug. "Now, your makeup. I'm gonna turn you so you can't see until I'm finished."

My makeup took a good forty-five minutes and Nathan took a few pictures during the near end of it just as he did while Lucy was doing my hair.

"Alright ladies, what do we think?" she states as she steps aside for the others to look.

"Omg, it's so beautiful and the simple look to it is just amazing," sighs Lilly.

Rose and Steph nod in approval and I nearly bounce off of my seat.

"Can I turn around now, I wanna see it too,"

"Okay, okay chill child." Rose laughs as Lucy turns my chair around.

I gasp as I look at myself. Is that actually me? Nathan takes a few pictures of the special moments from the corner where he was. I wasn't used to wearing natural colors much but this was so beautiful. I start to blink back tears of joy and Lucy quickly hands me a tissue.

"Don't ruin the perfection now."

"Sorry, sorry, I won't," I say, dabbing the tissue directly under my eye.

"Okay, my favorite part is here!" squeals Steph as she pulls out the dress from the closet.

"I'll step out, please tell me when you're finished, I'd like to take pictures of you in the dress," says Nathan before he leaves.

The girls help me get into my custom-made dress. When I was looking for the right dress. I wanted to wear something big and cathedral-like. But I also wanted to wear something slim. So why not wear both we thought. They helped me talk to a designer to design and make the dress for me. The back of the dress was low and stopped around my lower back near the lining of my hips. The train of the dress was to the floor and spread out. It had gems in places all over from where the zipper started. The front had an off-the-shoulder neckline that crossed over one another and the sleeves fanned out into a cape-veil behind me. The second part of the dress what was under the bottom half which I could pull off to reveal the mermaid dress under.

"Now this.

This

is a dress." sighs Lucy before she fans out my cape again after helping me up from putting on my shoes.

"Right! One of a kind." agrees Steph.

"Ramon literally has to faint when he sees you in this," says Rose.

"Let's not have him faint before the vows." I laugh. "Alright, someone please tell Nathan to come in."

Lilly goes to the door and asks him to come inside. The second he steps in his eyes drop to the dress and his mouth parts open slightly. We laugh at his facial expression.

"Well at least we know that's a good sign." chuckles Lilly.

Nathan asks me to pose for a few photos in different places around the room. Then they all help me move from the room to the garden outside.

"Wait, before she even steps a foot out of this room, we need to make sure that no one sees her," says Lu.

"She's right, I'll text Ethan to keep Ramon away from his windows," says Steph.

"Lil and I will make sure that the guests that are here are far away as well," she says as she takes Lilly's hand.

When everyone was in order, Nathan quickly takes pictures of me out by the flowers and the lake near the swans. We finally make it back to my room with about thirty minutes to spare. My heart races a little faster at the thought of me being a little bit closer to having Ramon as my husband.

"Here have some water, sit down, and scroll through your phone for a bit," says Lucy as she hands me a bottle of water and my phone.

"Thanks, I'm good, It's just the nerves coming back again. I can't tell if I'm excited or about to throw up. Could be both." I laugh.

"You're just excited. And you look absolutely breathtaking. I hope you enjoy today Congratulations." Nathan smiles as he leaves the room.

I thank him for his time and then go back to my phone. Fighting the urge to send off a quick text to Ramon.

I take a deep breath once more before the double doors open.

"This is it," I whisper to myself as I begin to walk down the aisle to the song.

I only saw Ramon at the end. Him and his drop-dead expression. As he wipes at his face and smiles at me the closer I get. As he fidgets with his cuffs and his hands. And as he swallows the lump in his throat as I finally get across from him.

Finally, I was here. He was here.

I know that for better or for worse. Through thick and thin. This man right in front of me. Ramon Dace Osgood, and what we have, is forever.

Chapter 46

"Here. Have a glass. It might help," James states as he hands me half a glass of White Zinfandel.

"Thanks, although, it won't do shit for me," I mutter as I lift the glass to my lips.

James only chuckles and pats my back before he goes to fix his tie.

"God, I can only hope that I'm this fucked up in love."

"You'll get there. Eventually. She's right there and all you have to do is reach for her." I say, giving him a smile at his reflection in the mirror.

He rolls his eyes but grins as he knows who I meant in this situation.

"You know it won't be that easy, we've known each other too long. I doubt she sees me as anything more than a brother or something."

"We both know that's not true and you're simply telling yourself that."

"Yeah, yeah, don't you have to get yourself in your tux? You seem to forget that you're the one getting married today."

"Oh, I didn't forget, as you can see I can barely keep still."

"Well, the sooner you get your suit on and get to that altar, the sooner you get to see your bride."

"Alright, alright, I'm getting up now," I state. I place my empty glass down and start to button up the dress shirt before I grab my navy blue suit to put on top. I check the time on my watch again and let out a shaky breath. About thirty minutes more. When I look up, Ethan is in front of me and is handing me my burgundy tie while Luke has settled himself in the seat across from me. I put on my tie as slowly as possible, messing around with it, hoping that time would magically go by faster. No luck. I put on my socks and shoes, mess with my hair a few times in the mirror and then sit back in the chair I was in before.

There was a knock at the door and my heart skips a beat. No, I needed to calm down. It couldn't be her. Her friends wouldn't let her see me until she walked down the aisle.

"I'll get it," says James as he walks to answer the door.

"Hi, I just wanted to get shots of the groom? Is he ready?"

"You ready Ramon? He's ready," he replies without waiting for my answer. He moves aside for the photographer to enter and the man walks up to me. He introduces himself and then asks to take a few pictures of me in the chair and a few with the others.

"I'd like to take some of you outside on the balcony and in the garden. Is that okay?"

"Yes, that's fine," I reply and hook my finger on the suit I had taken off for a few pictures. The photographer and I both walk out of the room and I feel a few snaps from the camera as I walk down the stairs of the mansion.

"Wait right there, let me take some here first."

I pause where I am and he rushes ahead of me to take more pictures. After those, we continue to walk until we make it to the balcony in the front. He tells me to stay up there while he goes outside to take a few pictures from below. He tells me how to position myself after every few clicks and then finally tells me to meet him in the garden. He finishes taking the rest of the pictures and I thank him as he leaves. I decide to stay out here for some air and I place my suit down on the bench near a rose bush before I remove my cufflinks, place them in my pocket and roll up my sleeves. I look out into the large and open lake and stare at the beautiful white swans with their cygnets.

"They're beautiful aren't they?"

I know that voice anywhere.

"I want to know who the fuck let you in and what the hell are you doing here Finn."

"Woah, don't get your panties in a twist now, can't I just come by to say congratulations?"

"You've just said it. Now leave before I take you out myself." I say through gritted teeth.

"Tsk. Still the harsh Ramon I know."

Something snapped inside of me and I pull him off the ground by his collar and I look at him dead in the eye.

"Listen and listen very closely. You might have been a really dear friend of mine but I never forget things. So I never forgot what you did to my wife. You're a fucked up man Finn. I do not have time to deal with a son of a bitch like you. You're just as bad as Mike and the rest of the shitty men in this world. Now, my patience is running really thin with you right now, and I know you have no fucking reason to be here other than to ruin a perfectly good day. So I'm going to need you to leave and I want you far away from this entire property. Test me and I will have your ass in jail faster than you can say your own name. Got it?"

"You can't do shit Ray," he grins.

"You think I'm bluffing?"

"I know you are."

"You motherfuc-" I say getting ready to swing at him.

"Ramon! What the fuck man- Woah what's this dickhead doing here?" James grimaces.

"Why don't you ask him, James? Before I beat the shit out of him."

"Put him down Ramon, he's not worth it. Don't let him ruin your day."

I forcefully drop him down and he stumbles a little before he stands upright.

"Thank you for sparing me, friend. James is it?"

"First of all who asked you to speak? Second, I'm not your friend. Not even an acquaintance. And third, I didn't spare you. I might not let Ramon fuck you up because he has somewhere else to be, but I'm not someone to fuck around with either. This is your last warning to leave before you get hurt."

"I get it." he starts to laugh. "Ramon doesn't want anything messing up his clean record so he has you to deal with his mess. Pretty nice duo if I say so myself. What are you his bodyg-"

James takes a full swing at Finn's face which causes him to land on the floor.

"You Bitch!" Finn yells out, holding his hands up to his now bloody and broken nose.

"I warned you. You didn't leave," he replies curtly as he pulls out a napkin and wipes his knuckles on it. He also pulls out his phone and calls someone.

Within a minute, the security from inside rush over.

"Get him out of here," I tell them. They nod and both of them grab Finn from the floor and pull him up, dragging him away.

"Thanks, you didn't need to do that."

"It was nothing. And I did. He hurt one of my best friends. I couldn't let him get away like that. Plus if I left you beat the shit out of him you'd come back all bloody and he'd probably end up with more than just a broken nose." James chuckles.

"Ha,"

I take a deep breath once more before the double doors open.

"This is it," I whisper to myself as I watch her begin to walk down the aisle to the song.

I only saw Celestia at the end. She, in her gorgeous jaw-dropping dress she hid from me for weeks. As she stares at me like no one else was in the room as she gets closer. As she smiles at me and a few tears spill from my eyes in her sight. And as she looks like a goddess to me as she finally stands across from me.

Finally, she was here. I was here.

I know that for better or for worse. Through thick and thin. This woman right in front of me. Celestia Hadleigh Crowe, and what we have, is forever.

Epilogue

"What have I created," I sigh to myself. "I've created a mini Ramon."

"You mean a mini Celestia, she's got your stubbornness." Ramon smiles, wrapping his arms around me from behind.

"You're just as stubborn as me pretty boy," I smile back.

"Who are you calling pretty boy?" he whispers in my ear right before he gently bites down on my collar bone.

"Ramon..."

"Shh," he whispers again, this time gliding the tip of his tongue across where he bit.

"Daddy?"

Ramon and I both freeze in place and stare at our five-year-old daughter that has come into the kitchen.

"Why are you licking mommy? Is she a popsicle?"

"Hi princess, um," he replies as he clears his throat. "Mommy just had a little booboo and I was just kissing it better."

"That's not a kiss," she fusses.

Ramon picks her up and grins.

"Well is this how you do it?" he asks as he kisses her cheek, then plants more light kisses on her other cheek and her forehead.

Aurelia giggles and as starts to add tickles to it and I laugh at the scene.

"Come on Ramon, you're gonna wrinkle her dress, and if you do I will personally see to it that you get the short end of the stick when my mother asks how."

"Alright my queen," he grins. "Down you go, princess."

"Daddy, how did mommy get to be a queen? I want to be one too!"

"Well, when you're all grown up like mommy and you find you're King, you can be one too. But for now, you will be my little golden princess always."

www.ingramcontent.com/pod-product-compliance
Lightning Source LLC
Chambersburg PA
CBHW070435170726
48291CB00002B/513

* 9 7 8 1 9 3 0 1 1 2 2 8 5 *